MYSTERY CATS

Felonious Felines from *Ellery Queen's Mystery Magazine* and *Alfred Hitchcock's Mystery Magazine*

A SIGNET BOOK

SIGNET
Published by the Penguin Group
Penguin Books USA Inc., 375 Hudson Street,
New York, New York 10014, U.S.A.
Penguin Books Ltd, 27 Wrights Lane,
London W8 5TZ, England
Penguin Books Australia Ltd, Ringwood,
Victoria, Australia
Penguin Books Canada Ltd, 10 Alcorn Avenue,
Toronto, Ontario, Canada M4V 3B2
Penguin Books (N.Z.) Ltd, 182–190 Wairau Road,
Auckland 10, New Zealand

Penguin Books Ltd, Registered Offices:
Harmondsworth, Middlesex, England

First published by Signet,
an imprint of Dutton Signet,
a division of Penguin Books USA Inc.

First Printing, December, 1991
10 9 8 7 6 5

FINICKY ABOUT YOUR MYSTERY FICTION? HERE'S THE WHOLE KIT AND CABOODLE...

"ARNOLD" by Fred Hamlin

Plump, ever-hungry Arnold gets nasty when anything comes between him and his dinner, but the escaped convict holding a .44 to his master's head is a dangerous opponent—even for a hero cat.

"THE FAITHFUL CAT" by Patricia Moyes

All that stands between a fortune-hunter and his wife's money is a Siamese named Pakdee, but, in a murderous game of cat-and-mouse, the cat has the advantage . . . and nine lives.

"HARDROCK" by Gary Erickson

There may be more than one way to skin a cat, but killing a tough old Tom can be a grave matter . . . or it can be a lesson a divorced father may never forget.

"THE LADY WORE BLACK"
by Hugh B. Cave

Guilt has been the undoing of many a murderer, but the haunting aftermath of one young punk's callous killing of an old lady has more to do with a cat than with his conscience.

AND A DOZEN MORE "TAILS" OF MURDER AND MAYHEM

MYSTERY CATS

REGISTERED TRADEMARK—MARCA REGISTRADA

PRINTED IN THE UNITED STATES OF AMERICA

PUBLISHER'S NOTE

These stories are works of fiction. Names, characters, places, and incidents either are the product of the authors' imaginations or are used fictitiously, and any resemblance to actual persons, living or dead, events, or locales is entirely coincidental.

BOOKS ARE AVAILABLE AT QUANTITY DISCOUNTS WHEN USED TO PROMOTE PRODUCTS OR SERVICES. FOR INFORMATION PLEASE WRITE TO PREMIUM MARKETING DIVISION, PENGUIN BOOKS USA INC., 375 HUDSON STREET, NEW YORK, NEW YORK 10014.

Contents

Introduction

There is an on-going love affair between mystery writers and cats. As any cat-lover knows, cats are featured in many mystery short stories and novels. The reasons seem clear: cats have distinctive and idiosyncratic personality traits that make them interesting and amusing characters in mystery fiction. And cats provide quiet companionship for many writers, whose profession is often a lonely one. It is perhaps the opportunity to observe cats at close range that inspires authors to feature their feline friends in their work.

In this collection, sixteen top mystery writers present a wide variety of cats in starring roles. We find cats that are clues in solving a crime, cats that protect their owners from harm, and even cats that take action to capture a killer. In this cast of cat celebrities you will meet Lilian Jackson Braun's SuSu, Theodore Sturgeon's Fluffy, Edward D. Hoch's Sparkle, Lillian de la Torre's Powder Puff, Ruth Rendell's Griselda, Patricia Highsmith's Ming, and, of course, Edgar Allan Poe's notorious Black Cat. Add to this list your own cat, who may want to curl up nearby to enjoy these stories with you.

—Cynthia Manson
March, 1991

SUSU AND THE 8:30 GHOST

Lilian Jackson Braun

When my sister and I returned from our vacation and learned that our eccentric neighbor in the wheel chair had been removed to a mental hospital, we were sorry but hardly surprised. He was a strange man, not easy to like, and no one in our apartment building seemed to be concerned about his departure—except our Siamese cat. The friendship between SuSu and Mr. Van was so close it was alarming.

If it had not been for SuSu, we would never have made the man's acquaintance, for we were not too friendly with our neighbors. Our apartment house was very large and full of odd characters who, we thought, were best ignored. On the other hand, the old building had advantages: large rooms, moderate rents, a thrilling view of the river, and a small waterfront park at the foot of the street. It was there that we first noticed Mr. Van.

One Sunday afternoon my sister Gertrude and I were walking SuSu in the park, which was barely more than a strip of grass alongside an old wharf. Barges and tugs sometimes docked there, and SuSu—wary of these monsters—preferred to stay away from the water's edge. It was one of the last nice days in November. Soon the river would freeze over, icy winds would blow, and the park would be deserted for the winter.

SuSu loved to chew grass, and she was chewing industriously when something diverted her attention and drew her toward the river. Tugging at her leash, she insisted on moving across the grass to the boardwalk, where a middle-aged man sat in a most unusual wheel chair.

It was made almost entirely of cast iron, like the base of an old-fashioned sewing machine, and it was upholstered in worn plush. With its high back and elaborate ironwork, it looked like a mobile throne, and the man who occupied this regal wheel chair presided with the imperious air of a monarch. It conflicted absurdly with his shabby clothing.

To our surprise this was the attraction that lured SuSu. She chirped at the man, and the man leaned over and stroked her fur.

"She recognizes me," he explained to us, speaking with a haughty accent that sounded vaguely Teutonic. "I was-s-s a cat myself in a former existence."

I rolled my eyes at Gertrude, but she accepted the man's statement without blinking.

He was far from attractive, having a sharply pointed chin, ears set too high on his head, and eyes that were merely slits, and when he smiled he was even less appealing. Nevertheless, SuSu found him irresistible. She rubbed his ankles, and he scratched her in the right places. They made a most unlikely pair—SuSu with her luxurious blonde fur, looking fastidious and expensive, and the man in the wheel chair with his rusty coat and moth-eaten laprobe.

In the course of a fragmentary conversation with Mr. Van we learned that he and the companion who manipulated his wheel chair had just moved into a large apartment on our floor, and I wondered why the two of them needed so many rooms. As for the companion, it was hard to decide whether he was a mute or just unsociable. He was a short thick man with a round knob of a head screwed tight to his shoulders and a flicker of something unpleasant in his eyes, and he stood behind the wheel chair in sullen silence.

On the way back to the apartment Gertrude said, "How do you like our new neighbor?"

"I prefer cats before they're reincarnated as people," I said.

"But he's rather interesting," said my sister in the gentle way she had.

A few evenings later we were having coffee after dinner, and SuSu—having finished her own meal—was washing up in the down-glow of a lamp. As we watched her graceful movements, we saw her hesitate with one paw in mid-air. She held it there and listened. Then a new and different sound came from her throat, like a melodic gurgling. A minute later she was trotting to the front door with intense purpose. There she sat, watching and waiting and listening, although we ourselves could hear nothing.

It was a full two minutes before our doorbell rang. I went to open the door and was somewhat unhappy to see Mr. Van sitting there in his lordly wheel chair.

SuSu leaped into his lap—an unprecedented overture for her to make—and after he had kneaded her ears and scratched her chin, he smiled a thin-lipped, slit-eyed smile at me and said, "*Goeden avond.* I was-s-s unpacking some crates, and I found something I would like to give to you."

With a courtly flourish he handed me a small framed picture, whereupon I was more or less obliged to invite him in. He wheeled his ponderous chair into the apartment with some difficulty, the rubber tires making deep gouges in the pile of the carpet.

"How do you manage that heavy chair alone?" I asked. "It must weigh a ton."

"But it is-s-s a work of art," said Mr. Van, rubbing appreciative hands over the plush upholstery and the lacy ironwork of the wheels.

Gertrude had jumped up and poured him a cup of coffee, and he said, "I wish you would teach that man of mine to make coffee. He makes the worst *zootje* I have ever tasted. In Holland we like our coffee *sterk* with a little chicory. But that fellow, he is-s-s a *smeerlap*. I would not put up with him for two minutes if I could get around by myself."

SuSu was rubbing her head on the Dutchman's vest buttons, and he smiled with pleasure, showing small square teeth.

"Do you have this magnetic attraction for cats?" I asked with a slight edge to my voice. SuSu was now in raptures because he was twisting the scruff of her neck.

"It is-s-s only natural," he said. "I can read their thoughts, and they read mine of course. Do you know that cats are mind readers? You walk to the icebox to get a beer, and the cat she will not budge, but walk to the icebox to get out her dinner, and she will come bouncing into the kitchen from any place she happens to be. Your thought waves have reached her, even though she seems to be asleep."

Gertrude agreed it was probably true.

"Of course it is-s-s true," said Mr. Van, sitting tall. "Everything I say is-s-s true. Cats know more than you suspect. They can not only read your mind, they can plant ideas in your head. And they can sense something that is-s-s about to happen."

My sister said, "You must be right. SuSu knew you

were coming here tonight, long before you rang the bell."

"Of course I am right. I am always right," said Mr. Van. "My grandmother in Vlissingen had a tomcat called Zwartje that she was-s-s very fond of, and after she died my grandmother came back every night to pet the cat. Every night Zwartje stood in front of *Grootmoeder*'s chair and stretched and purred, although there was-s-s no one there. Every night at half-past eight."

After that visit with Mr. Van, I referred to him as Grandmother's Ghost, for he too made a habit of appearing at 8:30 several times a week. He would say, "I was-s-s feeling lonesome for my little sweetheart," and SuSu would make an extravagant fuss over the man. I was pleased that he never stayed long, although Gertrude usually encouraged him to linger.

The little framed picture he had given us was not exactly to my taste. It was a silhouette of three figures—a man in top hat and frock coat, a woman in hoop skirt and sunbonnet, and a cat carrying his tail like a lance. To satisfy my sister, however, I hung it over the kitchen sink.

One evening Gertrude, who is a librarian, came home from work in great excitement. "There's a signature on that silhouette," she said, "and I looked it up at the library. Auguste Edouart was a famous artist, and our silhouette is over a hundred years old. It might be valuable."

"I doubt it," I said. "We used to cut silhouettes like that in the third grade."

Eventually, at my sister's urging, I took the object to an antique shop, and the dealer said it was a good one, probably worth $150.

When Gertrude heard this, she said, "If the dealer quoted $150, it's worth $250. I think we should give it back to Mr. Van. The poor man doesn't know what he's giving away."

"Yes," I agreed, "maybe he could sell it and buy himself a decent wheel chair."

At 8:30 that evening SuSu began to gurgle and prance.

"Here comes Grandmother's Ghost," I said, and shortly afterward the doorbell rang.

"Mr. Van," I said, as soon as Gertrude had poured his coffee, "remember that silhouette you gave us? We've found out it's very valuable, and you must take it back."

"Of course it is-s-s valuable," he said. "Would I give it to you if it was-s-s nothing but *rommel*?"

"Do you know something about antiques?"

"My dear *Mevrouw*, I have a million dollars' worth of antiques in my apartment. Tomorrow evening you ladies must come and see my treasures. I will get rid of that *smeerlap*, and the three of us will enjoy a cup of coffee."

"By the way, what is a *smeerlap*?" I asked.

"It is not very nice," said Mr. Van. "If somebody called me a *smeerlap*, I would punch him in the nose . . . Bring my little sweetheart when you come, ladies. She will find some fascinating objects to explore."

Our cat seemed to know what he was saying.

"SuSu will enjoy it," said Gertrude. "She's locked up in this apartment all winter."

"Knit her a sweater and take her to the park in cold weather," the Dutchman said in the commanding tone that always irritated me. "I often bundle up in a blanket and go to the park in the evening. It is-s-s good for insomnia."

"SuSu is not troubled with insomnia," I informed him. "She sleeps twenty hours a day."

Mr. Van looked at me with scorn. "You are wrong.

Cats never sleep. You think they are sleeping, but cats are the most wakeful creatures on earth. That is-s-s one of their secrets."

After he had gone, I said to Gertrude, "He must be off his rocker."

"He's just a little eccentric," she said.

"If he has a million dollars' worth of antiques, which I doubt, why is he living in this run-down building? And why doesn't he buy a wheel chair that's easier to operate?"

"Because he's a Dutchman, I suppose."

"And how about all those ridiculous things he says about cats?"

"I'm beginning to think they're true," said Gertrude.

"And who is this fellow that lives with him? Is he a servant, or a nurse, or a keeper, or what? I see him coming and going on the elevator, but he never speaks—not one word. He doesn't even seem to have a name, and Mr. Van treats him like a slave. I'm not sure we should go tomorrow night. The whole situation is too strange."

Nevertheless, we went. The Dutchman's apartment, we found, was jammed with furniture and bric-a-brac, and Mr. Van shouted at his companion, "Move that *rommel* so the ladies can sit down."

Sullenly the fellow removed some paintings and tapestries from the seat of a carved sofa.

"Now get out of here," Mr. Van shouted at him. "Get yourself a beer," and he threw the man a crumpled dollar bill with less grace than one would throw a bone to a dog.

We sat on the sofa to drink our coffee, while SuSu explored the premises, and then Mr. Van showed us his treasures, propelling his wheel chair through a maze of furniture. He pointed out Chippendale-this and Affleck-that and Newport-something-else. Perhaps they were treasures to him, but to me they were musty relics of a dead past.

"I am in the antique business," Mr. Van explained. "Before I was-s-s chained to this stupid wheel chair, I had a shop and exhibited at all the major shows. Then . . . I was-s-s in a bad auto accident, and now I sell from the apartment. By appointment only."

"Can you do that successfully?" Gertrude asked.

"And why not? The museum people know me, and collectors come here from all over the country. I buy. I sell. And my man Frank does the legwork. He is-s-s the perfect assistant for an antique dealer—strong in the back, weak in the head."

"Where did you find him?"

"On a junk heap. I have taught him enough to be useful to me, but not enough to be useful to himself. A smart arrangement, eh?" Mr. Van winked. "He is-s-s a *smeerlap*, but I am helpless without him . . . Hoo! Look at my little sweetheart! She has-s-s made a discovery."

SuSu was sniffing at a silver bowl with two handles.

Mr. Van nodded approvingly. "It is-s-s a caudle cup made by Jeremiah Dummer of Boston in the late 17th century—for a certain lady in Salem. They said she was-s-s a witch. Look at my little sweetheart! She knows!"

I coughed and said, "Yes, indeed, you're lucky to have Frank."

"You think I do not know it?" said Mr. Van. "That is-s-s why I keep him poor. If I gave him wages, he would get ideas."

"How long ago was your accident?"

"Five years, and it was-s-s that idiot's fault! He did it! He did this to me!" The Dutchman's voice rose to a shout, and his face turned red as he pounded the arms of his wheel chair with his fists. Then SuSu rubbed against his ankles, and he stroked her and began to calm down. "Yes, five years ago," he said. "Five years in this miserable chair. We were driving to an antique show in the station wagon. That *smeerlap* went through a red light—fifty miles an hour—and hit a truck. A gravel truck!"

"How terrible!" Gertrude said, putting both hands to her face.

"I still remember packing the wagon for that trip. I was-s-s complaining all the time about sore arches. Hah! What I would give for some sore arches today yet!"

"Wasn't Frank hurt?"

Mr. Van made an impatient gesture. "His-s-s head only. They picked Waterford crystal out of his-s-s cranium for six hours. He has-s-s been *gek* ever since." The Dutchman tapped his temple.

"Where did you find your unusual wheel chair?" I asked.

"My dear *Mevrouw*, never ask a dealer where he found something," said Mr. Van. "This chair is-s-s unique. It was-s-s made for a railroad millionaire in 1872. It has-s-s the original plush. If you must spend your life in a wheel chair, have one that gives some pleasure. And now we come to the purpose of tonight's visit. Ladies, I want you to do something for me."

He wheeled himself to a desk, and Gertrude and I exchanged anxious glances.

"Here in this desk is-s-s a new will I have written, and I need witnesses. I am leaving a few choice items to museums, then everything else is-s-s to be sold and the proceeds used to establish a Foundation."

"What about Frank?" asked Gertrude, who is always genuinely concerned about others.

"Bah! Nothing for that *smeerlap*! . . . But before

you ladies sign the paper, there is-s-s one thing I must write down. What is-s-s my little sweetheart's full name?"

Gertrude and I both hesitated, and I finally said, "SuSu's registered name is Superior Suda of Siam."

"Good! I will call it the Superior Suda Foundation. That gives me pleasure. Making a will is-s-s a dismal business, like a wheel chair, so give yourself some pleasure."

"What—ah—will be the purpose of the Foundation?" I asked.

Mr. Van blessed us with a benevolent smile. "It will sponsor research," he said. "I want the universities to study the highly developed mental perception of the domestic feline and apply this knowledge to the improvement of the human mind. Ladies, there is-s-s nothing better I could do with my fortune. Man is-s-s eons behind the smallest fireside grimalkin." He gave us a canny look, and his pupils seemed to narrow. "I am in a position to know," he added.

We signed the papers. What else could we do? A few days later we left on our vacation and never saw Mr. Van again.

Gertrude and I always went south for three weeks in winter, taking SuSu with us, and when we returned, the sorry news about our eccentric neighbor was thrown at us without ceremony.

We met Frank on the elevator, and for the first time he spoke! That in itself was a shock.

He said, "They took him away."

"What's that? What did you say?" We both clamored at once.

"They took him away." It was surprising to find that the voice of this chunky man was high-pitched and rasping.

"What happened to Mr. Van?" my sister demanded.

"He cracked up. His folks come from Pennsylvania and took him back home to a nut hospital."

I saw Gertrude wince, and she saïd, "Is it serious?"

Frank shrugged.

"What will happen to all his antiques?"

"His folks told me to dump the junk."

"But they're valuable things, aren't they?"

"Nah. Junk. He give everybody that guff about museums and all." Frank shrugged again and tapped his head. "He was *gek*!"

Wonderingly my sister and I returned to our apartment, and I could hardly wait to say it: "I told you the Dutchman was unbalanced."

"It's such a pity," she said.

"What do you think of the sudden change in Frank? He acts like a free man. It must have been terrible living with that old Scrooge."

"I'll miss Mr. Van," Gertrude said. "He was very interesting. SuSu will miss him, too."

But SuSu, we observed later that evening, was not willing to relinquish her friend in the wheel chair as easily as we had done.

We were unpacking the vacation luggage after dinner when SuSu staged her demonstration. She started to gurgle and prance, exactly as she had done all winter whenever Mr. Van was approaching our door. Gertrude and I stood there watching her, waiting for the bell to ring. When SuSu trotted expectantly to the front door, we followed. She was behaving in an extraordinary manner. She craned her neck, made weaving motions with her head, rolled over on her back and stretched luxuriously, all the while purring her heart out; but the doorbell never rang.

Looking at my watch, I said, "It's eight thirty. SuSu remembers."

"It's quite touching, isn't it?" said Gertrude.

That was not the end of SuSu's demonstrations. Almost every night at half-past eight she performed the same ritual.

"Cats hate to give up a habit," I remarked, recalling how SuSu had continued to sleep in the guest room long after we had moved her bed to another place. "But she'll forget after a while."

SuSu did not forget. A few weeks passed. Then we had a foretaste of spring and a sudden thaw. People went without coats prematurely, convertibles cruised with their tops down, and a few hopeful fishermen appeared down on the wharf at the foot of our street, although the river was still patched with ice.

On one of these warm evenings we walked SuSu down to the park for her first spring outing, expecting her to go after last year's dried weeds with snapping jaws. But the weeds did not tempt her. Instead, she tugged at her leash, pulling toward the boardwalk. Out of curiosity we let her go, and there on the edge of the wharf she staged her weird performance once more—gurgling, arching her back, craning her neck with joy.

"She's doing it again," I said. "I wonder what the reason could be."

Gertrude said softly, "Remember what Mr. Van said about cats and ghosts?"

"Look at that animal! You'd swear she was rubbing someone's ankles. I wish she'd stop."

"I wonder," said my sister very slowly, "if Mr. Van is really in a mental hospital."

"What do you mean?"

"Or is he—down there?" Gertrude pointed uncertainly over the edge of the wharf. "I think Mr. Van is dead, and SuSu knows."

"That's too fantastic," I said. "How could that happen?"

"I think Frank pushed the poor man off the wharf, wheel chair and all—perhaps one dark night when Mr. Van couldn't sleep and insisted on being wheeled to the park."

"Really, Gertrude—"

"Can't you see it? . . . A cold night. The riverfront deserted. Mr. Van trussed in his wheel chair with a blanket. Why, that chair would sink like lead! What a terrible thing! That icy water. That poor helpless man."

"I just can't—"

"Now Frank is free, and he has all those antiques, and nobody cares enough to ask questions. He can sell them and be set up for life. Do you know what a Newport blockfront chest is worth? I've been looking it up in the library. A chest like the one we saw in Mr. Van's apartment was sold for $40,000 at some auction in the east."

"But what about the relatives in Pennsylvania?"

"I'm sure Mr. Van had no relatives—in Pennsylvania or anywhere else."

"Well, what do you propose we should do?" I said in exasperation. "Report it to the manager of the building? Notify the police? Tell them we think the man has been murdered because our cat sees his ghost every night at eight thirty? We'd look like a couple of middle-aged ladies who are getting a little *gek*."

As a matter of fact, I was beginning to worry about Gertrude—that is, until the morning paper arrived.

I skimmed through it at the breakfast table, and there—at the bottom of page seven—one small item leaped off the paper at me. Could I believe my eyes?

"Listen to this!" I said to Gertrude. "The body of an unidentified man has been washed up on a down-river island. Police say the body apparently has been held underwater for several weeks by the ice . . .

About fifty-five years old and crippled . . . No one fitting that description has been reported to the Missing Persons Bureau."

For a moment my sister sat staring at the coffee pot. Then she rose from her chair and went to the telephone.

"Now all the police have to do," she said with a slight quiver in her voice, "is to look for an antique wheel chair in the river at the foot of the street. Cast iron. With the original plush." She blinked at the phone. "Will you dial?" she asked me. "The numbers are blurred."

MISS PAISLEY'S CAT

Roy Vickers

There are those who have a special affection for cats, and there are those who hold them in physical and even moral abhorrence. The belief lingers that cats have been known to influence a human being—generally an old maid, and generally for evil. It is true that Miss Paisley's cat was the immediate cause of that emotionally emaciated old maid reaching a level of perverted greatness—or stark infamy, according to one's point of view. But this can be explained without resort to mysticism. The cat's behavior was catlike throughout.

Miss Paisley's cat leaped into her life when she was 54 and the cat itself was probably about two. Miss Paisley was physically healthy and active—an inoffensive, neatly dressed, self-contained spinster. The daughter of a prosperous businessman—her mother had died while the child was a toddler—she had passed her early years in the golden age of the middle classes, when every detached suburban villa had many of the attributes of a baronial hall: if there was no tenantry there was always a handful of traditionally obsequious tradesmen—to say nothing of a resident domestic staff.

She was eighteen, at a "finishing school" in Paris, when her father contracted pneumonia and died while in the course of reorganizing his business. Miss Paisley herited the furniture of the house, a couple of hundred in cash, and an annuity of £120.

Her relations, in different parts of the country, rose to the occasion. Without expert advice they pronounced her unfit for further education or training and decided that, among them, they must marry her off—which ought not to be difficult. Miss Paisley was never the belle of a ball of any size, but she was a good-looking girl, with the usual graces and accomplishments.

In the first round of visits she accepted the warm assurances of welcome at their face value—yet she was not an unduly conceited girl. It was her father who had given her the belief that her company was a boon in itself. The technique of the finishing school, too, had been based on a similar assumption.

During the second round of visits—in units of some six months—she made the discovery that her company was tolerated rather than desired—a harsh truth from which she sought immediate escape.

There followed an era of nursery governessing and the companioning of old ladies. The children were hard work and the old ladies were very disappointing.

Penuriousness and old ladies were turning her into a humble creature, thankful for the crumbs of life. In her early twenties she obtained permanent employment as a "female clerk" in a government office. She made her home in Rumbold Chambers, Marpleton, about fifteen miles out of London, and about a mile from the house that had once been her father's. The Chambers—in this sense a genteel, Edwardian word meaning flatlets—had already seen better days, and were to see worse.

The rent would absorb nearly half her annuity; but the Chambers, she believed, had tone. The available flatlet looked over the old cemetery to the Seventeenth-Century bridge across the river. She signed a life lease. Thus, she was in that flatlet when the cat came, 32 years later.

She had taken out of the warehouse as much furniture as would go into the flatlet. The walls were adorned with six enlarged photographs, somewhat pompously framed, of the house and garden that had been her father's.

The radio came into general use; the talkies appeared and civil aviation was getting into its stride—events which touched her life not at all. Light industry invaded Marpleton and district. Every three months or so she would walk past her old home, until it was demolished to make room for a factory.

If she made no enemies, she certainly made no friends. The finishing school had effectively crippled her natural sociability. At the end of her working day she would step back 30-odd years into her past.

When the cat appeared, Miss Paisley was talking vivaciously to herself, as is the habit of the solitary.

"I sometimes think father made a mistake in keeping it as a croquet lawn. Croquet is so old-fashioned . . . *Oh!* How on earth did you get here!"

The cat had apparently strolled on to the window-sill—a whole story plus some four feet above ground level. "Animals aren't allowed in the Chambers, so you must go . . . Go, please. *Whoooosh*!"

The cat blinked and descended, somewhat awkwardly, into the room.

"What an ugly cat! I shall never forget Aunt Lisa's Persian. It looked beautiful, and everybody made an absurd fuss of it. I don't suppose anybody ever wants to stroke *you.* People tolerate you, rather wishing you didn't exist, poor thing!" The cat was sitting on its haunches, staring at Miss Paisley. "Oh, well, I suppose you can stay to tea. I've no fish, but there's some bloater paste I forgot to throw away—and some milk left over from yesterday."

Miss Paisley set about preparing tea for herself. It was Saturday afternoon. Chocolate biscuits and two cream eclairs for today, and chocolate biscuits and two meringues for Sunday. When the kettle had boiled and she had made the tea, she scraped out a nearly empty tin of bloater paste, spreading it on a thin slice of dry bread. She laid a newspaper on the floor—the carpet had been cut out of the drawing-room carpet of 34 years ago. The cat, watching these preparations, purred its approval.

"Poor thing! It's pathetically grateful," said Miss Paisley, placing the bloater paste and a saucer of yesterday's milk on the newspaper.

The cat lowered its head, sniffed the bloater paste, but did not touch it. It tried the milk, lapped once, then again sat back on its haunches and stared at Miss Paisley.

The stare of Miss Paisley's cat was not pleasing to humanity. It was, of course, a normal cat's stare from eyes that were also normal, though they appeared not to be, owing to a streak of white fur that ran from one eyelid to the opposite ear, then splashed over the spine. A wound from an airgun made one cheek slightly shorter than the other, revealing a glimpse of teeth and giving the face the suggestion of a human sneer. Add that it had a stiff left foreleg, which made its walk ungainly, and you have a very ugly cat—a standing challenge to juvenile marksmanship.

"You're a stupid cat, too," said Miss Paisley. "You don't seem to make the most of your opportunities."

Miss Paisley sat down to tea. The cat leaped onto the table, seized one of the eclairs, descended cautiously, and devoured the eclair on the carpet, several inches from the newspaper.

This time it was Miss Paisley who stared at the cat.

"That is most extraordinary behavior!" she exclaimed. "You thrust yourself upon me when I don't want you. I treat you with every kindness—"

The cat had finished the eclair. Miss Paisley continued to stare. Then her gaze shifted to her own hand which seemed to her to be moving independently of her will. She watched herself pick up the second eclair and lower it to the cat, who tugged it from her fingers.

She removed the saucer under her still empty tea cup, poured today's milk into it, and placed the saucer on the floor. She listened, fascinated, while the cat lapped it all. Her pulse was thudding with the excitement of a profound discovery.

Then, for the first time in 30-odd years, Miss Paisley burst into tears.

"Go away!" she sobbed. "I don't want you. It's too late—*I'm 54*!"

By the time her breath was coming easily again, the cat had curled up on the Chesterfield that was really Miss Paisley's bed.

It was a month or more before Miss Paisley knew for certain that she hoped the cat would make its home with her. Her attitude was free from the kind of sentimentality which one associates with an old maid and a cat. She respected its cathood, attributed to it no human qualities. The relationship was too subtle to have need of pretense. Admittedly, she talked to it a great deal. But she talked as if to a room-mate, who might or might not be attending. In this respect, the cat's role could be compared with that of a paid companion.

"Excuse me, madam!" Jenkins, the watchdog and rent-collector, who had replaced the porter of palmier days, had stopped her in the narrow hall. "Would that cat with the black-and-white muzzle be yours by any chance?"

A month ago, Miss Paisley would have dithered with apology for breaking the rules and would have promised instant compliance.

"It is my cat, Jenkins. And I would be very glad to pay you half a crown a week for any trouble it may be to you."

"That's very kind of you, madam, and thank you. What I was goin' to say was that I saw it jump out o' Mr. Rinditch's window with a bit o' fish in its mouth what Mr. Rinditch had left from his breakfast." He glanced down the passage to make sure that Mr. Rinditch's door was shut. "You know what Mr. Rinditch is!"

Miss Paisley knew that he was a street bookmaker, with a number of runners who took the actual bets, and that Jenkins stood in awe of him as the only tenant of any financial substance. Mr. Rinditch was a stocky, thickset man with a large sullen face and a very large neck. Miss Paisley thought he looked vulgar, which was a matter of character, whereas the other tenants only looked common, which they couldn't help.

"I'll give it proper cat's-meat, then it won't steal."

"Thank you, madam."

The "madam" cost Miss Paisley about £4 a year. None of the other women were "madam," and none of the men were "sir"—not even Mr. Rinditch. Two pounds at Christmas and odd half crowns for small, mainly superfluous services. For Miss Paisley it was a sound investment. In her dream life she was an emigrée awaiting recall to a style of living which, did she but know it, had virtually ceased to exist in England. It was as if the 30-odd years of unskilled clerical labor were a merely temporary expedient.

Through the cat she was acquiring a new philosophy, but the dream was untouched.

"I have to cut your meat," she explained that evening, "and I'm rather dreading it. You see, I've never actually handled raw meat before. It was *not* considered a necessary item in my education. Though I remember once—we were on a river picnic—two of the servants with the hamper were being driven over . . ."

She had to ask Jenkins's advice. He lent her a knife—a formidable object with a black handle and a blade tapering to a point. A French knife, he told her, and she could buy one like it at any ironmonger's—which she did on the following day. There remained the shuddery business of handling the meat. She sacrificed a memento—a pair of leather driving gloves, which she had worn for horse-riding during her holidays from school.

On the third day of the fourth month the cat failed to appear at its meal-time. Miss Paisley was disturbed. She went to bed an hour later than usual, to lie awake until dawn, struggling against the now inescapable fact that the cat had become necessary to her, though she was unable to guess why this should be true. She tried to prove it was not true. She knew how some old maids doted upon a particular cat, perpetually fondling it and talking baby-talk to it. For her cat she felt nothing at all of that kind of emotion. She knew that her cat was rather dirty, and she never really liked touching it. Indeed, she did not like cats, as such. But there was something about this particular cat . . .

The cat came through the open window shortly after dawn. Miss Paisley got out of bed and uncovered the meat. The cat yawned, stretched, and ignored it, then jumped onto the foot of her bed, circled, and settled down, asleep before Miss Paisley's own head returned to her pillow. Miss Paisley was now cat-wise enough to know that it must have fed elsewhere, from which she drew the alarming inference that a cat which had strayed once might stray again.

The next day she bought a collar, had it engraved with her name and address and, in brackets, *£1 Reward for Return.* She could contemplate expenditure of this kind without unease because, in the 30-odd years, she had saved more than £500.

That evening she fastened the collar in position. The cat pulled it off. Miss Paisley unfastened the special safety buckle and tried again—tried five times before postponing further effort.

"Actually, you yourself have taught me how to handle this situation," she said the following evening. "You refused the bloater paste and the not very fresh milk. You were right! Now, it will be a great pity if we have to quarrel and see no more of each other, but—no collar—no meat!"

After small initial misunderstandings the cat accepted the collar for the duration of the meal. On the third evening the cat forgot to scratch it off after the meal. In a week, painstaking observation revealed that the cat had become unconscious of the collar. Even when it scratched the collar in the course of scratching itself, it made no effort to remove the collar. It wore the collar for the rest of its life.

After the collar incident, their relationship was established on a firmer footing. She bought herself new clothes—including a hat that was too young for her and a lumber jacket in suede as green as a cat's eyes. There followed a month of tranquillity, shadowed only by a warning from Jenkins that the cat had failed to shake off its habit of visiting Mr. Rinditch's room. She noticed something smarmy in the way Jenkins told her about it—as if he enjoyed telling her. For the first time, there came to her the suspicion that the "madam" was ironic and a source of amusement to Jenkins.

On the following Saturday came evidence that, in this matter at least, Jenkins had spoken truly. She would reach home shortly after 1 on Saturdays. While she was on her way across the hall to the staircase, the door of Mr. Rinditch's room opened. Mr. Rinditch's foot was visible, as was Miss Paisley's cat. The cat was projected some four feet across the corridor. As it struck the paneling of the staircase, Miss Paisley felt a violent pain in her own ribs. She rushed forward, tried to pick up her cat. The cat spat at her and hobbled away. For a moment she stared after it, surprised and hurt by its behavior. Then, suddenly, she brightened.

"You won't accept pity!" she murmured. She tossed her head, and her eyes sparkled with a kind of happiness that was new to her. She knocked on Mr. Rinditch's door. When the large, sullen face appeared, she met it with a catlike stare.

"You kicked my cat!"

"Your cat, is it! Then I'll thank you to keep it out o' my room."

"I regret the trespass—"

"So do I. If I catch 'im in 'ere again, he'll swing for it, and it's me tellin' yer." Mr. Rinditch slammed his door.

Miss Paisley, who affected an ignorance of cockney idiom, asked herself what the words meant. As they would bear an interpretation which she would not allow her imagination to accept, she assured herself they meant nothing. She began to wonder at her own audacity in bearding a coarse, tough man like Mr. Rinditch, who might well have started a brawl.

In the meantime, the cat had gone up the stairs and was waiting for her at the door of her apartment. It still did not wish to be touched. But when Miss Paisley rested in her easy chair before preparing her lunch, the cat, for the first time, jumped onto her lap. It growled and changed its position, steadying itself with its claws, which penetrated Miss Paisley's dress and pricked her. Then it settled down, purred a little, and went to sleep. The one-time dining-room clock chimed 2 o'clock: Miss Paisley discovered that she was not hungry.

On Sunday the cat resumed its routine, and seemed none the worse. It tackled its meat ration with avidity, and wound up with Miss Paisley's other meringue. But that did not excuse the gross brutality of Mr. Rinditch. On Monday morning Miss Paisley stopped Jenkins on the first-floor landing and asked for Mr. Rinditch's full name, explaining that she intended to apply for a summons for cruelty to animals.

"If you'll excuse me putting in a word, madam, you won't get your own back on *him* by gettin' him fined ten bob. Why, he pays something like £50 a month in fines for 'is runners—thinks no more of it than you think o' your train fare."

Miss Paisley was somewhat dashed. Jenkins enlarged.

"You'd be surprised, madam, at the cash that comes his way. The night before a big race, he'll be home at 6 with more'n a couple o' hundred pound in that bag o' his; then he'll go out at a quarter to 8, do his round of the pubs, and be back at 10:30 with as much cash again."

The amount of the fine, Miss Paisley told herself, was irrelevant. This was a matter of principle. The lawyer, whom she consulted during her lunch hour, failed to perceive the principle. He told her that she could not prove her statements: that, as the cat admittedly bore no sign of the attack, the case would be "laughed out of court."

She had never heard that phrase before, and she resented it, the resentment being tinged with fear.

When she reached home, she found the cat crouching on the far side of the escritoire. It took no notice of her, but she could wait no longer to unburden herself.

"We should be laughed out of court," she said. "In other words, Mr. Rinditch can kick us, and the Law will laugh at us for being kicked. I expect we look very funny when we are in pain!"

In the whole of Miss Paisley's life that was the unluckiest moment for that particular remark. If her eyes had not been turned inward, she could have interpreted the behavior of the cat, could not have failed to recognize that its position by the escritoire was strategic. She was still talking about her interview with the lawyer when the cat pounced, then turned in her direction, a live mouse kicking in its jaws.

"Oh, dear!" She accepted the situation with a sigh. She was without the physiological fear of mice—thought them pretty little things and would have encouraged them but for their unsanitary habits.

Now, Miss Paisley knew—certainly from the cliche, if not from experience—the way of a cat with a mouse. Yet it took her by surprise, creating an unmanageable conflict.

"Don't—oh, *don't*! Stop! Can't you see? . . . We're no better than Mr. Rinditch! Oh, God, please make him stop! I can't endure it. I *mustn't* endure it! Isn't it any use praying? Are You laughing, too?"

Physical movement was not at Miss Paisley's command, just then. The feeling of cold in her spine turned to heat, and spread outwards over her body, tingling as it spread. In her ears was the sound of crackling, like the burning of dried weeds.

Her breathing ceased to be painful. The immemorial ritual claimed first her attention, then her interest.

After some minutes, Miss Paisley tittered. Then she giggled. The cat, which can create in humanity so many illusions about itself, seemed to be playing its mouse to a gallery, and playing hard for a laugh.

Miss Paisley laughed.

There were periods of normality, of uneventful months in which one day was indistinguishable from another, and Miss Paisley thought of herself as an elderly lady who happened to keep a cat.

She deduced that the cat wandered a good deal, and sometimes begged or stole food from unknown persons. She had almost persuaded herself that it had abandoned its perilous habit of visiting Mr. Rinditch's flatlet. One evening in early summer, about a fortnight before the end came, this hope was dashed.

At about half-past 8 the cat had gone out, after its evening meal. Miss Paisley was looking out of her window, idly awaiting its return. Presently she saw it on top of the wall that divided the yard from the old burial ground. She waved to it; it stared at her, then proceeded to wash itself, making a ten-minute job of it. Then it slithered down via the tool shed, but instead of making straight for the drainpipe that led past Miss Paisley's windowsill, it changed direction. By leaning out of the window, she could obtain an oblique view of Mr. Rinditch's rear window.

She hurried downstairs along the corridor, past Mr. Rinditch's door to the door that gave onto the yard, skirted a group of six ashcans, and came to Mr. Rinditch's window, which was open about eighteen inches at the bottom. She could see the cat on Mr. Rinditch's bed. She knew she could not tempt it with food so soon after its main meal. She called coaxingly, then desperately.

"We are in great danger," she whispered. "Don't you care?"

The cat stared at her, then closed its eyes. Miss Paisley took stock of the room. It was sparsely but not inexpensively furnished. The paneling was disfigured with calendars and metal coat-hooks.

The sill was more than four feet from the ground. She put her shoulders in the gap, and insinuated herself. She grasped the cat by its scruff, with one finger under its collar, and retained her hold while she scrambled to the safety of the yard, neglecting to lower the window to its usual position. They both reached her apartment without meeting anyone.

During that last fortnight which remained to them, Miss Paisley received—as she would have expressed it—a final lesson from the cat. She was returning from work on a warm evening. When some 50 yards from the chambers, she saw the cat sunning itself on the pavement. From the opposite direction came a man with a Labrador dog on a leash. Suddenly the dog bounded, snatching the leash from the man's hand.

"*Danger*! Run a-way!" screamed Miss Paisley.

The cat saw its enemy a second too late. Moreover, its stiff leg put flight out of the question. While Miss Paisley ran forward, feeling the dog's hot breath on the back of her neck, she nerved herself for the breaking of her bones. And then, as it seemed to her, the incredible happened. The dog sprang away from the cat, ran round in a circle, yelping with pain, while the cat clambered to the top of a nearby gatepost.

The man had recovered the leash and was soothing the dog. Again Miss Paisley extemporized a prayer, this time of thankfulness. Then the habit of years asserted itself over the teaching she believed she had received from the cat.

"I am afraid, sir, my cat has injured your dog. I am very sorry. If there is anything I can do—"

"That's all right, miss," a genial cockney voice answered. "He asked for it, an' he got it." The dog was bleeding under the throat, and there were two long weals on its chest. "That's the way cats ought to fight—get in under and strike *UP*, I say!"

"I have some iodine in my flat—"

"Cor, he don't want none o' that! Maybe your cat has saved 'im from losing an eye to the next one. Don't you give it another thought, miss!"

Miss Paisley bowed, sadly confused in her social values, which were also her moral values. The man's cockney accent was as inescapable as the excellence of his manners. Miss Paisley's world was changing too fast for her.

She enjoyed another six days and nights of the cat's company, which included four and a half days at the office. But these can be counted in, because the attention she gave to her work had become automatic and did not disturb her inner awareness of the relationship. She never defined that relationship, had not even observed the oddity that she had given the cat no name . . .

It was a Tuesday evening. The cat was not at home when she arrived.

"You've started being late for meals again," she grumbled. "Tonight, as it so happens, you can have ten minutes' grace." Her subscription to an illustrated social weekly was overdue. She filled up the renewal form, went out to buy a money order.

In the hall, Mr. Rinditch's voice reached her through the closed door of his apartment—apparently swearing to himself. There followed a muffled, whistling sound, as of cord being drawn sharply over metal. Then she heard a queer kind of growling cough and a scratching on woodwork—the kind of scratching sound that could be made by a cat's claws on a wooden panel, if the cat's body were suspended above the floor.

She stood, holding her breath, paralyzed by a sense of urgency which her imagination refused to define. She seemed to be imprisoned within herself, unable to desire escape. The sound of scratching grew thinner until it was so thin that she could doubt whether she heard it at all.

"You are imagining things!" she said to herself.

She smiled and went on her way to the post office. The smile became fixed. One must, she told herself, be circumspect in all things. If she were to start brawling with her neighbors every time she fancied—well, this-that-and-the-other—and without a shred of evidence—people would soon be saying she was an eccentric old maid. She wished she could stop smiling.

She bought the money order, posted it, and returned to her apartment, assuring herself that nothing at all had happened. That being agreed, everything could proceed as usual.

"Not home yet! Very well, I sha'n't wait for you. I shall cut up your meat now, and if it gets dry you've only yourself to blame." She put on the gloves with which she had held reins 37 years ago. "Just over a year! I must have used them to cut up your meat more than 300 times, and they're none the worse for wear. You couldn't buy gloves like this nowadays. I don't fancy tinned salmon. I think I'll make myself an omelette. I remember Cook was always a little uncertain with her omelettes."

She made the omelette carefully, but ate it quickly.

When she had finished her coffee, she went to the bookcase above the escritoire. She had not opened the glass doors for more than ten years. She took out *Ivanhoe*, which her father had given to her mother before they were married.

At a quarter past ten, she closed the book.

"You know I've never waited up for you! And I'm not going to begin now."

The routine was to leave the curtains parted a little—about the width of a cat. Tonight she closed them. When she got into bed, she could soon see moonlight through the chinks by the rings . . . and then the daylight.

In the morning, she took some trouble to avoid meeting Jenkins. As if he had lain in wait for her, he popped out from the service cupboard under the staircase.

"Good morning, madam. I haven't seen your pussy cat this morning."

Pussy cat! What a nauseating way to speak of her cat!

"I'm not worrying, Jenkins. He often goes off on his own for a couple of days. I'm a little late this morning."

She was not late—she caught her usual train to London with the usual margin. At the office, her colleagues seemed more animated than usual. A fragment of their chatter penetrated. "If *Lone Lass* doesn't win tomorrow, I shall be going to London for my summer holiday." A racehorse, of course. One of the so-called classic races tomorrow, but she could not remember which. It reminded her of Mr. Rinditch. A very low, coarse man! Her thought shifted to that very nice man who owned the dog. One of nature's gentlemen! *"Get in under and strike UP!"*

She did not go out at lunch hour, so did not buy any cat's-meat.

That evening, at a few minutes to 8, she heard Jenkins's footstep on the landing. He knocked at her door.

"Good evening, madam. I hope I'm not disturbing you. There's something I'd like to show you, if you can spare a couple o' minutes."

On the way downstairs there broke upon Miss Paisley the full truth about herself and Jenkins. Madam! She could hear now the contempt in his voice, could even hear the innumerable guffaws that had greeted his anecdotes of the female clerk who gave herself the airs of a lady in temporarily distressed circumstances. But her dignity had now passed into her own keeping.

He led her along the corridor, through the door giving onto the yard, to the six ashcans. He lifted a lid. On top of the garbage was the carcass of her cat. Attached to the neck was a length of green blind cord.

"Well, Jenkins?" Her fixed smile was unnerving him.

"He was in Mr. Rinditch's room again, soon after you came 'ome last night. You can't really complain, knowin' what he said he'd do. And hangin' an animal isn't torture if it's done properly, like this was. I don't suppose your poor little pussy cat felt any pain. Just pulled the string over the top of the coat-hook, and it was all over."

"That is immaterial." She knew that her cold indifference was robbing this jackal of the sadistic treat he had promised himself. "How do we know that Mr. Rinditch is responsible? It might have been anybody in the building, Jenkins."

"I tell you, it was him! Last night, when my missus went in with his evenin' meal, same as usual, she saw a length o' that blind cord stickin' out from under his bed. And there was a bit o' green fluff on the coat-hook, where the cord had frayed. The missus did a bit more nosing while she was clearing away, an' she spotted the cat's collar in the wastepaper basket. You couldn't hang a cat properly with that collar on, 'cause o' the metal. She said the strap part had been cut—like as it might be with a razor."

Miss Paisley gazed a second time into the ashcan. The collar had certainly been removed. Jenkins, watching her, thought she was still unwilling to believe him. Like most habitual liars, he was always excessively anxious to prove his word when he happened to be telling the truth.

"Come to think of it, the collar will still be in that basket," he said, mainly to himself. "Listen! He keeps it near enough to the front window. Come round to the front and maybe you'll be able to see it for yourself."

The basket was of plaited wicker. Through the interstices Miss Paisley could see enough of the collar to banish all doubt.

She could listen to herself talking to Jenkins, just as she had been able to see herself standing at the ashcan, knowing what was under the lid before Jenkins removed it. How easy it was to be calm when you had made up your mind!

When she returned to her room it was only five minutes past 8. Never mind. The calm would last as long as she needed it. In two hours and twenty-five minutes, Mr. Rinditch would come home. She was shivering. She put on the green suede lumber jacket, then she sat in her armchair, erect, her outstretched fingers in the folds of the upholstery.

"Before Mr. Rinditch comes back, I want you to know that I heard you scratching on his wall. You were alive then. We have already faced the fact that if I had hammered on the door and—brawled—you would be alive now. We won't argue about it. There's a lot to be said on both sides, so we will not indulge in recriminations."

Miss Paisley was silent until twenty-five minutes past 10, when she got up and put on the riding gloves, as if she were about to cut meat for her cat. The knife lay on the shelf in its usual place. Her hand snatched at the handle, as if someone were trying to take it away from her.

" *'Get in under and strike UP!'* " she whispered—and then Miss Paisley's physical movements again became unmanageable. She was gripping the handle of the knife, but she could not raise it from the shelf. She had the illusion of exerting her muscles, of pulling with all the strength of her arm against an impossibly heavy weight. Dimly she could hear Mr. Rinditch come home and slam his door.

"I've let myself become excited! I must get back my calm."

Still wearing the gloves and the lumber jacket, she went back to her chair.

"At my age I can't alter the habits of a lifetime—and when I try, I am pulled two ways at once. I told you in the first place that you had come too late. You oughtn't to have gone into Mr. Rinditch's room. He killed you in malice, and I betrayed you—oh, yes, I did!—and now I can't even pray."

Miss Paisley's thoughts propounded riddles and postulated nightmares with which her genteel education was unable to cope. When she came to full consciousness of her surroundings it was a quarter to 3 in the morning. The electric light was burning and she was wearing neither the gloves nor the green suede jacket.

"I don't remember turning on the light—I'm too tired to remember anything." She would sleep on in the morning, take a day off. She undressed and got into bed. For the first time for more than a year, she fell asleep without thought of the cat.

She was awakened shortly after 7 by a number of unusual sounds—of a clatter in the hall and voices raised, of a coming and going on the stairs. She sat up and listened. On the ground floor Mrs. Jenkins was shouting while she cried—a working-class habit which Miss Paisley deplored. A voice she recognized as that of the boilermaker who lived on the top floor shouted up the stairs to his wife.

"Oh, Emma! They've taken 'im away. Hangcuffs an' all! Cor!"

Miss Paisley put on her long winter coat, pulled the collar up to her chin, and opened her door.

"What is all the noise about?" she asked the boilermaker.

"That bookie on the ground floor, miss. Someone cut 'is throat for 'im in the night. The pleece've pinched Jenkins." He added: "Hangcuffs an' all!"

"Oh!" said Miss Paisley. "I see!"

Miss Paisley shut the door. She dressed and prinked with more care than usual. She remembered trying to pick up the knife, remembered sitting down in an ecstasy of self-contempt, then groping in a mental fog that enveloped time and place. But there were beacons in the fog. *"Get in under and strike UP!"* was one beacon, the slogan accompanied by a feeling of intense pride. And wasn't there another beacon? A vague memory of slinking, like a cat, in the shadows—to the river. Why the river? Of rinsing her hands in cold water. Of returning to her chair. Return. *£1 Reward for Return.* Her head spinning. Anyhow, "someone cut 'is throat for 'im in the night."

So far from feeling crushed, Miss Paisley found that she had recovered the power to pray.

"I have committed murder, so I quite see that it's absurd to ask for anything. But I really must keep calm for the next few hours. If I may be helped to keep calm, please, I can manage the rest myself."

At the local police station Miss Paisley gave an able summary of events leading to the destruction of her cat, and her own subsequent actions, "while in a state of trance."

The desk sergeant stifled a yawn. He produced a form and asked her a number of questions concerning her identity and occupation, but no questions at all about the murder. When he had finished writing down the answers, he read them aloud.

"And your statement is, Miss Paisley, that it was you who killed William Rinditch, in—in a state of trance you said, didn't you?"

Miss Paisley assented, and signed her statement.

"Just at present the inspector is very busy," explained the sergeant, "so I must ask you to take a seat in the waiting room."

Miss Paisley, who had expected the interview to end with "hangcuffs," clung to her calm and sat in the waiting room, insultingly unguarded, for more than an hour. Then she was grudgingly invited to enter a police car, which took her to county headquarters.

Chief Inspector Green, who had served his apprenticeship at Scotland Yard, had dealt with a score or more of self-accusing hysterics. He knew that about one in four would claim to have committed the murder while in a trance—knew, too, that this kind could be the most troublesome if they fancied they were treated frivolously.

"Then you believe Rinditch killed your cat, Miss Paisley, because Jenkins told you so?"

"By no means!" She described the cat's collar and

the method of killing, which necessitated the removal of the collar. She added details about the wastepaper basket.

"Then the collar is still in that basket, if Jenkins was telling the truth?"

But investigation on the spot established that there was no cat's collar in the wastepaper basket, nor anywhere else in the apartment. Miss Paisley was astonished—she knew she had seen it in that basket.

The interview was resumed in her flatlet, where she asserted that she had intended to kill Mr. Rinditch when he returned at 10:30, but was insufficiently prepared at that time. She did not know what time it was when she killed him, but knew that it was not later than a quarter to three in the morning. The weapon had been the knife which she used exclusively for cutting the cat's special meat.

"I have no memory at all of the act itself, Inspector. I can only say that it was fixed in my mind that I must get in close and strike upwards."

The inspector blinked, hesitated, then tried another line.

"It was after 10:30, anyhow, you said—after he had locked up for the night. How did you get in?"

"Again, I can't tell. I can't have hammered on his door, or someone would have heard me. I might have—I must have—got in by his window. I regret to confess that on one occasion I did enter his apartment that way in order to remove my cat, which would not come out when I called it."

"How did you get into the yard? That door is locked at night."

"Probably Jenkins left the key in it—he is very negligent."

"So you have no memory at all of the crime itself?

You are working out what you think you must have done?"

Miss Paisley remembered that she had prayed for calm.

"I appreciate the force of your remark, Inspector. But I suggest that it would be a little unusual, to say the least, for a woman of my antecedents and habits to accuse herself falsely for the sake of notoriety. I ask you to believe that I sat in that chair at about 10:30, that my next clear memory is of being in the chair at a quarter to 3. Also, there were other signs—"

"Right! We accept that you got out of that chair—though you don't remember it. You may have done other things, too, but I'll show you that you *didn't* kill Rinditch. To begin with, let's have a look at the murder knife."

Miss Paisley went to the cupboard.

"It isn't here!" she exclaimed. "Oh, but of course! I must have—I mean, didn't you *find* the knife?"

Inspector Green was disappointed. He could have settled the matter at once if she had produced the knife—which had indeed been found in the body of the deceased. A knife that could be bought at any ironmonger's in the country, unidentifiable in itself.

"If you had entered Rinditch's room, you'd have left fingerprints all over the place—"

"But I was wearing leather riding gloves—"

"Let's have a look at 'em, Miss Paisley."

Miss Paisley went back to the cupboard. They should be on the top shelf. They were not.

"I can't think where I must have put them!" she faltered.

"It doesn't matter!" sighed Green. "Let me tell you this, Miss Paisley. The man—or, if you like, woman—

who killed Rinditch couldn't have got away without some pretty large stains on his—or her—clothes."

"It wouldn't have soaked through the lumber jacket," murmured Miss Paisley.

"What lumber jacket?"

"Oh! I forgot to mention it—or rather, I didn't get a chance. When I sat down in that chair at 10:30 I was wearing a green suede lumber jacket. When I came to myself in the small hours, I was not wearing it."

"Then somewhere in this flatlet we ought to find a ladies' lumber jacket, heavily bloodstained. I'll look under everything and you look inside."

When the search had proved fruitless, Miss Paisley turned at bay.

"You don't believe me!"

"I believe you believe it all, Miss Paisley. You felt you had to kill the man who had killed your cat. You knew you couldn't face up to a job like murder, especially with a knife. So you had a brainstorm, or whatever they call it, in which you kidded yourself you had committed the murder."

"Then my meat knife, my old riding gloves, and my lumber jacket have been hidden in order to deceive you?" shrilled Miss Paisley.

"Not to deceive me, Miss Paisley. To deceive yourself! If you want my opinion, you hid the knife and the gloves and the jacket because they were *not* bloodstained."

Miss Paisley felt a little giddy.

"You don't need to feel too badly about *not* killing him," he said, smiling to himself. "At 7 o'clock this morning a constable found Jenkins trying to sink a bag in the river. That bag was Rinditch's, which was kept under the bed o' nights. And Jenkins had 230-odd quid in cash which he can't account for."

Miss Paisley made no answer.

"Maybe you still sort of feel you killed Rinditch?" Miss Paisley nodded assent. "Then remember this. If the brain can play one sort of trick on you, it can play another—same as it's doing now."

Inspector Green had been very understanding and very kind, Miss Paisley told herself. It was her duty to abide by his decision—especially as there was no means of doing otherwise—and loyally accept his interpretation of her own acts. The wretched Jenkins—an abominable man—would presumably be hanged. Things, reflected Miss Paisley, had a way of coming right. . . .

After a single appearance before the magistrate, Jenkins was committed on the charge of murder and would come up for trial in the autumn at the Old Bailey. Miss Paisley removed her interest.

One evening in early autumn Miss Paisley was sitting in her armchair, reviving the controversy as to whether her father had made a mistake about the croquet lawn. In her eagerness she thrust her hands between the folds of the upholstery. Her fingers encountered a hard object. She hooked it with her finger and pulled up her dead cat's collar.

She held it in both hands while there came a vivid memory of her peering through Mr. Rinditch's window, Jenkins beside her, and seeing the collar in the wastepaper basket . . . The buckle was still fastened. The leather had been cut, as if with a razor. She read the inscription: her own name and address and—*£1 Reward for Return.*

"I took it out of that basket—*afterwards*!" She relived the ecstatic moment in which she had killed Rinditch. Every detail was now clear-cut. Strike *UP*!—as the cat had struck—then leap to safety. She had pulled off a glove, to snatch the collar from the basket and thrust the collar under the neck of her jumper; then she had put the glove on again before leaving the room and making her way to the river. Back in her chair she had retrieved the collar.

Gone was the exaltation which had sustained her in her first approach to the police. She stood up, rigid, as she had stood in the hall while listening to the scratching on the panel, refusing to accept an unbearable truth. Once again she had the illusion of being locked up, aware now that there could be no escape from herself.

There remained the collar—evidence irrefutable, but escapable.

"If I keep this as a memento, I shall soon get muddled and accuse myself of murder all over again! What was it that nice inspector said—'if the brain can play one trick on you it can play another'."

She smiled as she put the collar in her handbag, slipped on a coat and walked—by the most direct route, this time—to the Seventeenth-Century bridge. She dropped the collar into the river, knowing that it would sink under the weight of its metal—unlike the bloodstained lumber jacket and the riding gloves which, Miss Paisley suddenly remembered, she had weighted with stones scratched from the soil of the old cemetery . . .

ARNOLD

Fred Hamlin

I hear the first police car Saturday morning as I am driving back from the drugstore on an emergency run for aspirin and cat food. The aspirin is for me. The cat food is for Arnold, who talks. He has trouble with consonants, and a distinct Siamese accent, but he definitely talks. His favorite word is "chaoowww" which helps to explain why Arnold weighs seventeen pounds, and why I am making an emergency run for cat food.

The aspirin is because the going away party held last night at our apartment building for Sam Archibald was a considerable success. It is a Southern California apartment building, which is to say two stories and U-shaped around a swimming pool, with two palm trees, a tropical name, and frequent parties. I moved in two years ago, right out of college. Sam's party was even noisier than most, and his last official act of residence was a front one-and-a-half off my balcony into the pool. In truth it was a one-and-three-eighths, but he had absorbed enough wine to come up laughing. Sam will be missed. In the meantime, my eyelids ache.

This condition fails to improve when the black-and-white goes by with siren in full shriek. I am relieved to discover that the sound isn't coming from inside my head, a possibility that must not be ruled out. When the second squad car goes by, I try the radio, but am only able to get a rock band that sounds in my present condition like a series of trays being dropped in a restaurant.

As I turn the corner two blocks away from the apartment, I see both of the squad cars, plus two more, forming a rough roadblock between myself and my apartment building. I am waved to a stop.

"I'm sorry, sir, this street is temporarily closed to through traffic," says the officer. He has clear eyes, a thirty dollar haircut and military creases in his tailored uniform shirt.

Sir is not something I'm called very often, and it has a mildly palliative effect on my head.

"I live down at Tropical Towers. Apartment 24."

"Can I see your driver's license, please?"

I dig it out. "What seems to be the problem, officer?"

"An armed robbery at the Palm Paradise Savings and Loan. Witnesses saw the man headed this way. He shot a guard on his way out, so we know he's armed. The guard will live, but we have to be careful. We have the area sealed off."

"Does this mean I can't get to my apartment? I've got Arnold's breakfast, and he turns nasty if he misses a meal."

"Look, mister, I don't know Arnold, but nasty is what we're dealing with here. Our guy has a .44 revolver, armed and dangerous. Yes, you can go through, but be careful, and if you see anything strange, please call us at once. The suspect is about five nine, medium weight. He's wearing jeans and a denim jacket, and had a black watch cap when last seen. Blond hair, thin face. He's also kind of jumpy, probably drugs of some kind. If you see anyone like that, don't take any chances. We'll be coming through to search the area in a few minutes. Here's your license. Remember, call us if you see anything."

I park my van in the regular spot and head up to the apartment, where Arnold is by now probably sitting by his dish yelling, "Naaooww!" With luck he will not be venting his hostility by ripping the grass paper off the walls, a not uncommon form of protest on his part. If cats played football, Arnold would be Dick Butkus.

I open the apartment door and Arnold is hunkered down under the coffee table, with his ears flat against his head, and his tail twice normal size. His eyes look like a couple of solid onyx marbles.

"Knock it off, Arnold," I say, "you are overreacting. Food is forthcoming."

Arnold tends to be moody, no doubt due to kittenhood trauma. I agreed to keep him nine months ago when his former owner went over to Las Vegas for a weekend with her boyfriend. They wound up getting married and she moved into his no-pets-no-kids apartment. I have had Arnold ever since. Neither Arnold nor I are sure who he belongs to. There is the depressing possibility that I belong to Arnold, which he tends to assume.

I put the bag with the cat food cans and aspirin down on the kitchen counter. The open sliding door to the balcony has aired out the worst of the cheap-wine-and-stale-smoke atmosphere that I woke up to. The Formica dinette table that came with the apartment is still littered with glasses from last night, none of which are clean. I dig out the aspirin and head for the bathroom off my bedroom where there may be a clean glass. Arnold glowers from under the coffee table and makes a noise like he's sucking his teeth. Only the noise comes from the bedroom.

I later recreate my thought process at this juncture.

First, maybe Arnold does ventriloquism. Second, there probably isn't anyone in the bedroom. Third, even if there is someone in the bedroom it may be a leftover from last night's party—it was too late to check the closets before I went to bed. Fourth, and here's a great mind in high gear, *the cop on the corner said to call.* Ergo, the phone is in the bedroom, and I have to go in there to call anyway. As I say, we gave Sam a significant party.

The first thing I notice when I go in the bedroom is not that there is anyone there. The first thing I notice is the gun. More specifically the open end of the barrel of the gun, which is level with and about three feet away from my left eye. Forty-four does not begin to describe it. It is more like looking into a railway tunnel that goes straight down, into which I am about to fall.

The railway tunnel shifts slightly, as if moved by a small earthquake, and the sense of vertigo eases somewhat. The gun is held by a pair of hands with white knuckles, and the hands are attached to a person. Give them credit, the police have a very accurate description. I can now add that he is about my age, mid-twenties, and has watery blue eyes and ears that stand out from his head, as if to keep the knit cap from falling over his face. There is something about the eyes that does not quite connect with reality. It occurs to me that Sam's eyes looked a bit like that when he started up to the balcony last night. This is not encouraging.

"Freeze. Don't move. Stay where you are." The voice is somewhere between a croak and a quaver, and I am still not reassured.

He has not asked me to raise my hands, but it couldn't hurt, so I do. Actually, it is a sort of reflex action like the kid's trick where you press the backs of your hands against the inside of a door frame, and then your arms float up by themselves.

"One move, man, and you're wasted. I mean that."

"Okay. Take it easy. I see the gun."

"One move or one sound, dig it? I already wasted one guy today." His eyes are flicking all around the room, almost independently of each other, but one or the other manages to stay on me. He reaches around me and pushes the door nearly closed.

"What's going on out there?"

"There are a lot of cops in the neighborhood. They seem to be looking for somebody."

"You got it, man. How many of them?"

"I don't know. I saw four cars, but there may be more."

"Too many, man, too many. I shouldn't a wasted that guy."

He is shifting from one foot to the other, and the eyes are still doing the pinwheel routine.

"Gotta think, man, gotta be cool. Hey, is this the only phone in here?"

"The only one. It's on an answering machine right now, so anybody who calls gets a message that I'm out."

"That's cool. No, wait, man, pull the plug on it. Pull the jack."

"If I do that and somebody I know calls, they'll know something's wrong. I always leave the machine on when I'm out."

"Yeah, man, stay away from that jack or I'll blow you away."

I am aware of a slight noise and movement behind me, and my new pal crab-hops to one side and drops into a firing crouch with the gun on the door, which is slowly opening. Sweat pops out on his forehead so suddenly you can almost hear it squeak, and his eyes more or less manage to focus on the doorway.

It's Arnold, and we resume breathing. Arnold strolls over and gives the guy's leg a long affectionate rub. Because he is leaning on the guy's leg, the kick he gets in return lacks real force.

"Goddam cat."

"Cloowwwn," says Arnold and dives under the bed. Arnold has not yet learned how to swear convincingly.

The gun is back in my direction again.

"Is there a back way outta here?"

"Not really. Just the front door and the balcony, and that's one floor up."

"I gotta get outta here, dig?"

Needless to say, I am in favor of this, but no suggestions immediately come to mind.

At this point we hear official-sounding footsteps coming up the stairs out front, and shortly a heavy rap on the first apartment door; mine is the third one along. We both figure out what is happening at the same time.

"Okay, dig. When those guys get here you don't know nothing. You seen nobody. I stay here in the bedroom, but the gun is on you all the time. If you try anything funny, you're wasted. If I go down, you go down. Dig it?"

I nod, and we can both hear them move to the second apartment and bang on the door. From there it's close enough to hear them calling into the apartment. "Open up, police."

The foot-to-foot hopping starts up again, and the eyes are slipping in all directions. I am contemplating how large the end of the gun barrel looks, and imagine a hole that size in my back. I do not find this a pleasant fantasy.

"Okay, man, get out there and get rid of them. Fast."

I walk into the living room. The bedroom door is on a wall that runs front-to-back in the apartment, and the door swings into the bedroom. He leaves this open about two inches and is standing a foot or so back, next to the wall. He can't be seen, and like they say at the National Guard meetings, his field of fire is unimpaired.

I hear the footsteps and the banging on my door.

"Open up, police."

It is the same cop I talked to down at the barricade, and he remembers me. He has a partner with him who goes to the same barber.

"Hello again. We're checking the neighborhood. I don't suppose you've seen anything since you got back."

"I've seen nobody," I say, having my lines down pat, "and I'll give you a call if I do. Have a nice day."

"That must be Arnold," the cop says, remembering the name, and at about the same time I feel a familiar rubbing on my ankle.

This is not good news. First, Arnold could not have fit through the two inch gap. Ergo, the door is open wider than it was, which means that the cop may be able to see into the bedroom. It also means that my pal back there has a bigger gap to shoot through. A trickle of sweat starts down my spine. It will no doubt stain a perfect bull's-eye on the back of my shirt.

The cop is bent over scratching Arnold's ears. "Did you get your breakfast, big fellow?"

"Noooooo," says Arnold.

"Arnold," I say, "shut up."

Arnold has rolled over on his back and is getting his stomach rubbed. He is smirking.

"He looks like an Arnold," says the cop. "Palmer, maybe. Or Schwarzenegger."

"Benedict," I say. "Look, don't let me hold you up. I know you want to get your man."

"Right. Remember, call if you see anything unusual. We should be through the neighborhood in a couple of hours. We'll find him. But be careful till we do."

I close the door and look around, but Arnold is out of retribution range under the coffee table. He is looking smug. The bedroom door swings open and my pal comes out.

"You did fine, man, but that cat almost got you killed. And those cops, too. I already wasted one guy."

I don't need to be reminded.

"Listen, maybe the guy isn't dead. Maybe this isn't as bad as you think it is."

"With this piece?" He is waving the gun in my face. "Man, this piece don't make mistakes, and I popped him twice."

I am looking down the barrel again and decide not to press the point.

"You got a car, man?"

"Right. If you would like to borrow it, the keys are right here in my pocket. You could be on your way and . . ."

"Do I look stupid, man? I take your car and you're on the phone the minute I'm out the door."

"So tie me up before you go. Put a gag in my mouth." I am not into bondage as a general rule, but there are always exceptions.

"No, man. I got a better idea. The cop said they would be through the neighborhood in a couple of hours, right? Okay, you and me we just sit tight here until they get it done. Then we both get in your car and just ease out of here. What kind of car you got?"

"It's a VW van."

"Okay, when we drive out of here I'm on the floor in the back and the gun is right behind your spine, dig? And if we run into anyone on the way to the van, the gun is in your neck. That way if we run into any cops they can't shoot without hitting you." His eyes have escalated from pinwheel to Roman candle. He is thinking very hard.

I am in no way enamored of his train of thought.

"So then what happens?"

"If everything stays cool, everything stays cool. I got no argument with you, man. You got rid of the cop. I could probably just let you go after a while."

It occurs to me that "probably" is a key word in this sentence. I am not sure I want to know what alternatives are under consideration.

Still, we now have an agenda and the atmosphere is marginally less tense. The eyes are back to low-grade shifty, and I remember where this whole mess started. I realize I am still holding the aspirin bottle.

"Would you like an aspirin?" I ask. "I could sure use one myself."

"No thanks, man," he says. "I've got my own stuff."

He digs a handful of miscellaneous capsules out of his pocket and swallows them and then follows me into the bathroom. I manage four aspirin, a dosage which seems appropriate.

"Do you mind if I feed the cat? He hasn't eaten since last night."

"Okay, man, but stay away from that window. And nothing cute." The eyes are speeding up again, and the movements are jerkier.

The phone rings, and he bounces about eight inches into the air. The answering machine kicks in.

"This is Arnold," my taped message says, "and the

guy I live with is out right now. If you will leave your number at the tone . . ."

It gets no further than this because my visitor has ripped the jack out of the wall. When he turns back, the gun hand is downright shaky.

"One more trick like that, man, you're dead." I sense that a logical explanation may not help the situation, and also that the glue that is holding him together has begun to melt.

We proceed to the kitchen area with the gun acting as a sort of hyphen between us. He comes past the dinette table and stops at the counter that divides the cooking area from the small dining space. I go around the counter and dig out a can of cat food, stick it in the electric can opener, and push the lever down.

This sound is to Arnold as the bell is to Pavlov's pup. He is out of the living room in full feeding frenzy and leaps for the kitchen table on his way to the counter. He realizes too late that the glassware from last night is in the way, and his claws scrabble desperately for traction on the slick Formica.

"Whoa-oowwww," he yells, which is promptly drowned out by a blast of crashing glass.

This in turn is drowned out by the thunderclap of the .44 as my house guest spins and unloads a couple of rounds at the empty air behind him.

By the time he turns back to where I was, I am through the sliding door and airborne over the railing. I hear two more shots before I hit the pool. Sensing a disturbance, the cops are through the front door of my apartment with guns drawn before I come up for air. My houseguest is still trying to figure out what happened. He has also emptied his gun.

A neighbor later tells me my form was better than Sam's, but that I lost points on degree of difficulty. I attribute this to inadequate planning and preparation and consider it a moral victory.

It's another hour or so before all of the questions are answered and the dust has settled and the cops have hauled their guy away. I get into dry clothes and the first order of business is to get Arnold fed. Fair is fair.

"Sorry for the delay, Arnold. It's been a busy morning."

"Surrrrrrrrrrrre," he says. If there's anything I can't stand, it's a sarcastic cat.

CAT'S-PAW

Mary Reed

"Well, the only way I can think of for doing away with someone by way of a cat is to bash them on the head with a stuffed one!" Neil, resident wit at the Goat and Gamp, downed the remains of his pint at one swallow.

As if on cue, in walked Colin, carrying a box. Everyone propping up the bar-counter burst out laughing, and his normally sallow face flushed scarlet with confusion. Joyce, our buxom and very blonde hostess, leaned over the mahogany expanse of the counter to ask him, with that often-misunderstood easy familiarity of the English barmaid, what it would be. Colin, putting his burden onto the bar, pushed his hair out of his eyes, gave a grateful smile, and ordered the usual. A light scratching sound came from the box as Joyce set down a foaming tankard in front of him and raised fine-penciled eyebrows.

"Present for the wife," Colin said, wiping foam from his upper lip. "A kitten."

He looked startled at the gale of merriment his innocent reply provoked.

Taking pity on his obvious bewilderment, I moved a couple of feet along the bar and explained. He listened carefully, nose buried in the tankard. Poor old devil, I thought, he's always finding himself in unfortunate juxtapositions of unlikely circumstances. His very name, Colin Andrew Thompson, for example. It rolls off the tongue nicely, and sounds properly imposing for an Executive Insurance Director, which is what it says on the nameplate on his office door, but then he went and married a breeder of Calico Persians, so of course, between that and his initials, the local wags had a field day. He had scarcely set foot in the pub after his honeymoon when he was met with a barrage of jokes about cataloguing catastrophic losses from cat burglary, living in a cathouse (bucolic humor can be very coarse), and so on. But he never said much, just kept on pushing his hair out of his eyes and smiling at all and sundry over his nightly pint. He wasn't what you'd call a drinking man, by any means. A couple of refills would last him all night, and Neil often voiced the opinion that Colin only came in every evening to feast his eyes on Joyce.

Joyce and Gerald, the long-suffering landlord of the Goat and Gamp, had been courting for years. People in the village used to say "when Joyce and Gerry get wed" much as others might say "in a blue moon." Neil was always saying that one day someone—with a meaningful glance in Colin's direction—was going to come and sweep Joyce away, right from under Gerry's nose, and then he'd be sorry for procrastinating for so long. Colin just smiled, never rising to the bait, and said nothing.

Anyhow, the rather bizarre discussion we'd been having when Colin arrived that particular evening had arisen in the somewhat convoluted way pub conversations will. It had started when Gerry, leaning on the cash till, mentioned reading about a wealthy local spinster leaving all her money to her pet Pekinese. Needless to say, the grieving relatives were contesting the will, and he asked me what I thought the ruling might be.

As a solicitor myself, I hedged a bit, pointing out that litigation might well drag on for some time, because it would, so far as I could tell, hinge upon whether or not the deceased was of sound mind when she drew up the will. And that was a circumstance that might, at this late date, be a little difficult to prove one way or the other. But offhand, and speaking off the record, I guessed that the will would be proved legal, and thus valid, no matter how odd its bequest.

Neil inquired if I had come across any odd wills myself, but Joyce, polishing a glass, pointed out that I could hardly discuss such confidential matters as that, could I? Then she said: "But the wills you read about fair give you the creeps. What about that woman who left all her money to her husband, as long as she was above ground? Of course, he got round that by putting her into one of them fancy mausoleums. And do you remember that fellow in London who wanted to be stuffed?"

When things quietened down a bit, Ned, a local farmer who only happened to be at the Goat and Gamp that evening because it had been market day and he returned home this way, piped up, saying he had actually seen a photograph of the geezer Joyce mentioned. "It gave me a fair turn, I can tell you," he said, signaling Gerry to refill his glass. "Mind, that were years back, before folk got used to all them horror films and such."

Ned being a well known prankster, his supposed recollection of seeing such a photograph provoked some argument. I knew who he was talking about—it was, in fact, a true case—but held my peace. In the end, Neil was dispatched to the ladies' snug across the corridor to consult Marjory, the village librarian. She was a notorious gossip, but she also knew her business, and he returned with confirmation of the story—and, chortling to himself, he stood everyone a pint on the strength of it.

Neil raised his pint to Ned. "Cheers," he said, taking a big gulp, and then continuing: "Well, I don't know about queer wills or odd bequests, but from what you read in the papers it seems like more folk than ought to get themselves ideas about hastening the reading of the will, if you get my drift. Not but what it usually benefits them very much."

This latter gloomy statement was met with more hilarity. It was common knowledge in the village that for years Neil had been anticipating a small remembrance from his grandmother. When, cantankerous to the last, the old girl had died at the age of ninety-something, it turned out to be just that—a small remembrance. To wit, ten pounds and a lecture on the evils of intemperance. Neil spent the lot on standing everyone drinks. I remember we toasted his granny with them. He was never one to bear a grudge was Neil.

Joyce was wiping the bar absentmindedly. "Yes, but the problem is, Neil, there's few ways you can help folk out of the world undetected, so to say, and get away with it. I mean, there's no such thing as an undetectable poison, like, and guns and knives are so gruesome—and easy to trace, anyhow, aren't they?" Joyce was a great lover of mystery novels, and the more convoluted the better. "Then there's your alibi. You got to be miles away when the murder is committed, don't you? And you can't pay anyone else to do it—there's always a chance of blackmail, right?"

"Well," Gerry commented, "if you can't use someone else, what about *something* else? Like that there Hound of the Basketballs or that Sprinkled Hand? One of them poisonous snakes, it was."

His patrons' general opinion was that poisonous snakes—as well as tarantulas and scorpions—were hard to come by in our neck of the woods. Nor did we have any lonely moors with quicksands over which a devilish dog could hound hapless landowners to death. Though there were several suggestions as to suitable landowners who might be selected for that particular honor, of course. Then someone suggested escaping zoo animals of the fiercer kind, such as tigers, say, or lions.

Surprisingly, it was Ned, the farmer, who addressed that one. "Big cats, you mean," he said from the end of the bar. "Actually, I was once almost frit to death by a small cat. I was having this nightmare about being crushed to death with these huge blocks—like the kind they used to build the Pyramids. It was probably the wife's cooking—her puddings tend to lie a bit heavy, like. Anyhow, I woke up in a bit of a sweat and there *was* this terrible weight on my chest. And when I opened my eyes, there were these huge green ones staring right at me.

Well, you know how it is when you're coming out of a nightmare—you're not sure if you're here or there, so to speak. It was our Tommy, of course. I reckon he were trying to get his revenge on me for having him fixed."

Neil, evidently not a cat lover, suggested putting poison on a cat's claws as a method of poisoning its owner, but Gerry pointed out that the cat would probably scratch itself first, or lick its claws, die, and give the game away. To which Neil made his retort about bashing someone on the head with a stuffed cat, just as Colin made his entrance . . .

Funnily enough, just as Colin walked in, I'd been thinking about his wife, Penelope. We didn't see much of her at the Goat and Gamp. For one thing, she was a martyr to asthma, as well as being allergic to cigarette smoke—or so we understood. Besides which, she was just out of hospital after breaking her leg. This she had managed to do by slipping on one of her numerous cats' many toys, at the top of a darkened stairwell, en route to rendering aid to her oldest cat, Queenie. Fortunately, given the severity of the fall and the length of the stairs, Penelope had come out of it relatively unscathed.

Neil, needless to say, had been quick to talk about cats with nine lives, though, give him his due, he didn't say it in front of Colin. This Queenie was positively ancient by feline standards, something like twenty-three years old, and the daughter of one of the first blue-ribbon winners Penelope bred. Penelope is, in fact, quite famous in the cat-breeding world, as Marjory was telling me the last time I went in to change my library book.

However, it was from my wife Marie that I learned Penelope is hypersensitive to short-hairs. This seems unfortunate, because they form the bulk of your everyday domestic-cat population and must be a major handicap in Penelope's chosen profession. Not that I want you to think we spend our time discussing our neighbors. Marie mentioned it because she goes to the monthly sewing-circle meetings at the vicarage and when Penelope joined them, not long after she and Colin moved to Yew Lodge, the vicar's cat, which rejoiced in the name of Ezekiel, was banned from the meetings. Marie said she felt sorry for the cat, which is unusually friendly for a Siamese, and that she thought Penelope was turning into a professional invalid.

Anyhow, back to Colin explaining that there was a kitten in the box and it was a present for Penelope.

"Oh, yes?" Joyce said. "What a nice thought, especially with poor old Queenie dying last month."

Colin reddened again. I never knew a man who blushed so easily.

"As a matter of fact," he confessed, "I'm sort of responsible for that. I was the one that bought the bad fish, you see. We were going to have it for supper, but as my wife was feeling a bit off-color with her allergies she just gave a bit to Queenie for a treat and put the rest in the fridge for the following day." Pointing out how easily the fish might have made them ill didn't seem very tactful, because Penelope had broken her leg going downstairs to see to the cat the night it was taken sick. I wondered if she was speaking to Colin again yet.

"What sort is the kitten?" Joyce was cooing. "Can I see it?"

Colin opened the box and we all crowded around to look. The kitten reminded me a bit of those cats you see on Egyptian tomb-paintings, only with blue eyes and rather large ears.

"Hey, it looks a bit like Ezekiel," Gerry remarked, leaning over the bar with his nose almost in the box.

"No, this is an Abyssinian—the vicar's is a Siamese," Colin replied, stroking the kitten's head. It was certainly a handsome little thing. Even Neil the cat hater was charmed.

"Not bad-looking, is it?" he said, leaning over the box and breathing beer fumes over the hapless kitten. "So that's why you were borrowing the A–E section of the encyclopedia. And all those cat books. Wanted to surprise the wife, eh?"

Colin shot him a look of real dislike. "Not much chance of that if the whole village knows, is there?"

"Oh, go on, who's going to tell her what you've been reading in your spare time?" Neil cackled. "Besides, our Marjory only happened to notice because she wanted to look up a few things and you had the A-to-E volume. Anyhow, you'll be giving her her present tonight, right? Then the cat will *really* be out of the bag, won't it?" He chortled at his own joke.

Colin put the lid back on the box and finished his drink just as Gerry called ten minutes to time and there was the usual rush to the bar to order the last drinks of the evening. Colin left not long afterward, and I walked part of the way with him.

We strolled along in silence, past the school and across the green, skirting the war memorial. Our paths parted at the bottom of Church Lane, his taking him left through the ornate iron gates of Yew Lodge, mine bearing right, up the darkened lane. It was a fine, clear night, very quiet. Walking up the hill, I could hear Colin's fading footsteps as he crunched over the gravel in the Lodge forecourt.

But going home, I got to thinking. Abyssinians are short-haired cats, and I remembered not only Ezekiel's banishment from the sewing circle but also the time Ned's youngest got stung by a bee. He had an allergic reaction that was so bad he had to be rushed to the County Hospital, where it was really touch and go for a time. And A-to-E might include Abyssinian and Cat, but it also covered Allergies. The tainted fish that did for Queenie. The fall in the dark. The way Colin stared at Joyce when he thought no one was looking. Penelope's hypersensitivity to short-haired cats and her current immobilization in a plaster cast.

But the whole thing was quite fantastic, wasn't it? At least, that's what I tried to tell myself as I approached the house. I hoped Colin wasn't contemplating anything foolish. For one thing, he'd never get away with it. For another, as his wife's solicitor, I had seen the terms of her new will, drawn up while she was still in the hospital. It left the bulk of her not inconsiderable estate to the local humane society. To be sure, there was a small legacy for Colin, but it wasn't much. Not enough to keep Yew Lodge, for one thing. And her estate would pay it for only as long as he looked after the cats.

THE ABOMINABLE HOUSE GUEST

Theodore Sturgeon

Ransome lay in the dark and smiled to himself, thinking about his hostess. Ransome was always in demand as a house guest, purely because of his phenomenal abilities as a raconteur. Said abilities were entirely due to his being so often a house guest, for it was the terse beauty of his word pictures of people and their opinions of people that made him the figure he was. And all those clipped ironies had to do with the people he had met last week-end. Staying a while at the Joneses, he could quietly insinuate the most scandalously hilarious things about the Joneses when he week-ended with the Browns the following fortnight. You think Mr. and Mrs. Jones resented that? Ah, no. You should hear the dirt on the Browns! And so it went, a two-dimensional spiral on the social plane.

This wasn't the Joneses or the Browns, though. This was Mrs. Benedetto's ménage; and to Ransome's somewhat jaded sense of humor the widow Benedetto was a godsend. She lived in a world of her own, which was apparently set about with quasi-important ancestors and relatives, exactly as her living room was cluttered up with perfectly unmentionable examples of Victorian rococo.

Mrs. Benedetto did not live alone. Far from it. Her

very life, to paraphrase the lady herself, was wound about, was caught up in, was owned by and dedicated to her baby. Her baby was her beloved, her little beauty, her too darling my dear, and—so help me—her boobly wutsi-wutsikins. In himself he was quite a character. He answered to the name of Bubbles, which was inaccurate and offended his dignity. He had been christened Fluffy, but you know how it is with nicknames. He was large and he was sleek, that paragon among animals, a chastened alley cat.

Wonderful things, cats. A cat is the only animal which can live like a parasite and maintain to the utmost its ability to take care of itself. You've heard of little lost dogs, but you never heard of a lost cat. Cats don't get lost, because cats don't belong anywhere. You wouldn't get Mrs. Benedetto to believe that. Mrs. Benedetto never thought of putting Fluffy's devotion to the test by declaring a ten-day moratorium on the canned salmon. If she had, she would have uncovered a sense of honor comparable with that of a bedbug's.

Knowing this—Ransome pardoned himself the pun—categorically, Ransome found himself vastly amused. Mrs. Benedetto's ministrations to the phlegmatic Fluffy were positively orgiastic. As he thought of it in detail, he began to feel that perhaps, after all, Fluffy was something of a feline phenomenon. A cat's ears are sensitive organs; any living being that could abide Mrs. Benedetto's constant flow of conversation from dawn till dark, and then hear it subside in sleep only to be replaced by resounding snores—well, that *was* phenomenal.

And Fluffy had stood it for four years. Cats are not renowned for their patience. They have, however, a very fine sense of values. Fluffy was getting something out of it—worth considerably more to him than the discomforts he endured, for no cat likes to break even.

Ransome lay still, marveling at the carrying power of the widow's snores. He knew little of the late Mr. Benedetto, but he gathered now that he had been either a man of saintly patience, a masochist, or a deaf-mute. A noise like that from just one stringy throat must be an impossibility, and yet, there it was.

Ransome liked to imagine that the woman had calluses on her palate and tonsils, grown there from her conversation, and it was these rasping together that produced the curious dry-leather quality of her snores. He tucked the idea away for future reference. He might use it next week-end. The snores were hardly the gentlest of lullabies, but any sound is soothing if it is repeated often enough.

There is an old story about a lighthouse tender whose lighthouse was equipped with an automatic cannon which fired every fifteen minutes, day and night. One night, when the old man was asleep, the gun failed to go off. Three seconds after, the old fellow was out of his bed and flailing around the room, shouting, "What was that?" And so it was with Ransome.

He couldn't tell whether it was an hour after he had fallen asleep, or whether he had not fallen asleep at all. But he found himself sitting on the edge of the bed, wide awake, straining every nerve for the source of the—what was it?—sound?—that had awakened him.

The old house was as quiet as a city morgue after closing time, and he could see nothing in the tall dark guestroom but the moon-silvered windows and the thick blacknesses that were drapes. Any old damn thing might be hiding behind those drapes, he thought comfortingly. He edged himself back on the bed and quickly snatched his feet off the floor. Not that anything was under the bed, but still—

A white object puffed along the floor, through the moonbeams, toward him. He made no sound, but tensed himself, ready to attack or defend, dodge or retreat. Ransome was by no means an admirable character, but he owed his reputation, and therefore his existence, to this particular trait—the ability to poise himself, invulnerable to surprise.

The white object paused to stare at him out of its yellow-green eyes. It was only Fluffy—Fluffy looking casual and easy-going and not at all in a mood to frighten people. In fact, he looked up at Ransome's gradually relaxing bulk and raised a longhaired, quizzical eyebrow, as if he rather enjoyed the man's discomfiture.

Ransome withstood the cat's gaze with suavity, and stretched himself out on the bed with every bit of Fluffy's own easy grace. "Well," he said amusedly, "you gave me a jolt! Weren't you taught to knock before you entered a gentleman's boudoir?"

Fluffy raised a velvet paw and touched it pinkly with his tongue. "Do you take me for a barbarian?" he asked.

Ransome's lids seemed to get heavy, the only sign he ever gave of being taken aback. He didn't believe for a moment that the cat had really spoken—this was, of course, someone's idea of a joke.

Good God—it has to be a joke!

"You didn't say anything, of course," he told the cat, "but if you did, what was it?"

"You heard me the first time," said the cat, and jumped up on the foot of his bed.

Ransome inched back from the animal. "Yes, I thought I did. You know," he said, with an attempt at jocularity, "you should, under these circumstances, have written me a note before you knocked."

"I refuse to be burdened with the so-called social amenities," said Fluffy. His coat was spotlessly clean, and he looked like an advertising photograph for eiderdown, but he began to wash carefully. "I don't like you, Ransome."

"Thanks," chuckled Ransome, surprised. "I don't like you either."

"Why?" asked Fluffy.

Ransome told himself silently that he was damned. He held tight to a mind that would begin to reel on slight provocation, and, as usual when bemused, he flung out a smoke screen of his own variety of glib chatter.

"Reaons for not liking you," he said, "are legion. They are all included in the one phrase—'You are a cat!' "

"I have heard you say that at least twice before," said Fluffy, "except that you have now substituted 'cat' for 'Woman.' "

"Your attitude is offensive. Is any given truth any the less true for having been uttered more than once?"

"No," said the cat with equanimity. "But it is just that more clichéd."

Ransome laughed. "Quite aside from the fact that you can talk, I find you most refreshing. No one has ever criticized my particular variety of repartee before."

"No one was ever wise to you before," said the cat. "Why don't you like cats?"

A question like that was, to Ransome, the pressing of a button which released ordered phrases. "Cats," he said oratorically, "are without doubt the most self-centered, ungrateful, hypocritical creatures on this or any other earth. Spawned from a mésalliance between Lilith and Satan—"

Fluffy's eyes widened. "Ah! An antiquarian!" he whispered.

"—they have the worst traits of both. Their best qualities are their beauty of form and of motion, and even these breathe vile. Women are the ficklest of bipeds, but few women are as fickle as, by nature, any cat is. Cats are not true. They are impossibilities, as perfection is impossible. No other living creature moves with utterly perfect grace. Only the dead can so perfectly relax. And nothing—simply nothing at all—transcends a cat's incomparable insincerity."

Fluffy purred.

"Pussy! Sit-by-the-fire and sing!" spat Ransome. "Smiling up, all bearers of liver and salmon and catnip! Soft little puffball, bundle of joy, playing with a ball on a string, making children clap their soft hands to see you, while your mean little brain is viciously alight with the pictures your play calls for you. Bite it to make it bleed; hold it till it all but throttles; lay it down and step about it daintily; prod it with a gentle silken paw until it moves again, and then pounce. Clasp it in your talons then, lift it, roll over with it, sink your cruel teeth into it while you pump out its guts with your hind feet. Ball on a string! Play-actor!"

Fluffy fawned. "To quote you, that is the prettiest piece of emotional claptrap that these old ears have ever heard. A triumph in studied spontaneity. A symphony in cynicism. A poem in perception. The unqualified—"

Ransome grunted. He deeply resented this flamboyant theft of all his pet phrases, but his lip twitched nevertheless. The cat was indeed an observant animal.

"—epitome of understatement," Fluffy finished smoothly. "To listen to you, one would think that you would like to slaughter earth's felinity."

"I would," gritted Ransome.

"It would be a favor to us," said the cat. "We would keep ourselves vastly amused, eluding you and laughing at the effort it cost you. Humans lack imagination."

"Superior creature," said Ransome ironically, "why don't you do away with the human race, if you find us a bore?"

"You think we couldn't?" responded Fluffy. "We can outthink, outrun, and outbreed your kind. But why should we? As long as you act as you have for these last few thousand years, feeding us, sheltering us, and asking nothing from us but our presence for purposes of admiration—why then, you may remain here."

Ransome guffawed. "Nice of you! But listen—stop your bland discussion of the abstract and tell me some things I want to know. How can you talk, and why did you pick me to talk to?"

Fluffy settled himself. "I shall answer the question socratically. Socrates was a Greek, and so I shall begin with your last questions. What do you do for a living?"

"Why I—I have some investments and a small capital, and the interest—" Ransome stopped, for the first time fumbling for words.

Fluffy was nodding knowingly. "All right, all right. Come clean. You can speak freely."

Ransome grinned. "Well, if you must know—and you seem to—I am a practically permanent house guest. I have a considerable fund of stories and a talent for telling them. I look presentable and act as if I were a gentleman. I negotiate, at times, small loans—"

"A loan," said Fluffy authoritatively, "is something one intends to repay."

"We'll call them loans," said Ransome airily. "Also,

at one time and another, I exact a reasonable fee for certain services rendered—"

"Blackmail," said the cat.

"Don't be crude. All in all, I find life a comfortable and engrossing thing."

"Q. E. D.," said Fluffy triumphantly. "You make your living being scintilliant, beautiful to look at. So do I. You help nobody but yourself; you help yourself to anything you want. So do I. No one likes you except those you bleed; everyone admires and envies you. So with me. Get the point?"

"I think so. Cat, you draw a mean parallel. In other words, you consider my behavior catlike."

"Precisely," said Fluffy through his whiskers. "And that is both why and how I can talk with you. You're so close to the feline in everything you do and think; your whole basic philosophy is that of a cat. You have a feline aura about you so intense that it contacts mine; hence we find each other intelligible."

"I don't understand that," said Ransome.

"Neither do I," returned Fluffy. "But there it is. Do you like Mrs. Benedetto?"

"No!" said Ransome immediately and with considerable emphasis. "She is absolutely insufferable. She bores me. She irritates me. She is the only woman in the world who can do both those things to me at the same time. She talks too much. She reads too little. She thinks not at all. Her mind is hysterically hidebound. She has a face like the cover of a book that no one has ever wanted to read. She is built like a pinch-type whiskey bottle that never had any whiskey in it. Her voice is monotonous and unmusical. Her education was insufficient. Her family background is mediocre, she can't cook, and she doesn't brush her teeth often enough."

"My, my," said the cat, raising both paws in surprise. "I detect a ring of sincerity in all that. It pleases me. That is exactly the way I have felt for some years. I have never found fault with her cooking, though; she buys special food for me. I am tired of it. I am tired of her. I am tired of her to an almost unbelievable extent. Almost as much as I hate you."

"Me?"

"Of course. You're an imitation. You're a phony. Your birth is against you, Ransome. No animal that sweats and shaves, that opens doors for women, that dresses itself in equally phony imitations of the skins of animals, can achieve the status of a cat. You are presumptuous."

"You're not?"

"I am different. I *am* a cat, and have a right to do as I please. I disliked you so intensely when I saw you this evening that I made up my mind to kill you."

"Why didn't you? Why—don't you?"

"I couldn't," said the cat coolly. "Not when you sleep like a cat . . . No, I thought of something far more amusing."

"Oh?"

"Oh, yes." Fluffy stretched out a foreleg, extended his claws. Ransome noticed subconsciously how long and strong they seemed. The moon had gone its way, and the room was filling with slate-gray light.

"What woke you," said the cat, leaping to the window sill, "just before I came in?"

"I don't know," said Ransome. "Some little noise, I imagine."

"No, indeed," said Fluffy, curling his tail and grinning through his whiskers. "It was the *stopping* of a noise. Notice how quiet it is?"

It was, indeed. There wasn't a sound in the house—oh, yes, now he could hear the plodding footsteps of the maid on her way from the kitchen to Mrs. Benedetto's bedroom, and the soft clink of a teacup. But otherwise—suddenly he had it. "The old horse stopped snoring!"

"She did," said the cat.

The door across the hall opened, there was the murmur of the maid's voice, a loud crash, the most horrible scream Ransome had ever heard, pounding footsteps rushing down the hall, another scream, silence.

"What the—"

Ransome bounced out of bed.

"Just the maid," said Fluffy, washing between his toes, but keeping the corners of his eyes on Ransome. "She just found Mrs. Benedetto."

"Found—"

"Yes. I tore her throat out."

"Good God! Why?"

Fluffy poised himself on the window sill. "So you'd be blamed for it," he said, and laughing nastily, he leaped out and disappeared in the gray morning.

THE FAITHFUL CAT

Patricia Moyes

The fact that Hubert Withers decided one Thursday morning not to murder his wife after all should not be ascribed to kindness, change of heart, nor any moral scruples, but to a mixture of squeamishness and cowardice, plus the realization that he could get what he wanted by other means. Hubert was a small man and had always shrunk from violence of any kind. The thought of actually killing Caroline made him feel quite nauseous. Also, there was the risk of being caught. However ingenious his plan, a husband who stood to inherit his wife's fortune would automatically be Suspect Number One.

Nevertheless, he had to have money—and very soon. It would be nice, of course, to have Caroline permanently out of the way and to come into his inheritance—but he now saw that the matter might be dealt with in a less drastic manner. If he could get her removed for even a short while and get a Power of Attorney to act on her behalf—that is, to sign checks and draw cash—all would be well.

It wasn't that Hubert particularly disliked Caroline. She wasn't a bad old thing at all really, although of course he had married her strictly for her money. She was the plain, shy daughter (and only child) of a widower who had made a fortune in the construction business in Washington, D.C., and she stood to pick up the lot when the old man died.

During her life, Caroline Todman had made few friends. At school—an extremely expensive private establishment where all the girls were by definition heiresses—her only real friend had been another girl, also plain but less shy, called Annabel: but Annabel had married the impoverished younger son of a British nobleman and was now Lady Fairley, living in a very grand Elizabethan manor house in southern England—bought with Annabel's money, naturally. Several times Annabel had written suggesting that Caroline should visit England and stay with her and her husband, but Caroline had felt too shy to make the trip alone.

Despite her plainness and shyness, Caroline had had plenty of suitors, as any girl in her position was bound to have, but old Todman, her father, swore he could pick out a fortune hunter at a hundred yards. Even Caroline herself got to be quite good at it, and this tended to increase her timidity and to put her off young men. Thus she had remained unmarried until the age of thirty.

Hubert Withers appeared to be the only man who had ever wanted her for herself alone. He, too, appeared to be very shy, and although he was reasonably good-looking he disguised the fact by wearing unbecoming steel-rimmed spectacles and a wispy moustache. He had been observing Caroline Todman's movements, and so cleverly contrived to meet her for the first time in the Georgetown Public Library. They started talking about books, and he shyly invited her out for a cup of coffee at a cheap cafe, apparently quite unaware of who she was.

Caroline was enchanted, and even old Todman grunted his approval. The young man appeared pleasant enough and seemed stupefied the first time Caroline invited him home to the family mansion, which stood in a couple of acres of garden in superfashionable Georgetown. Hubert had stammered out that he'd had no idea she was the daughter of *the* Arnold Todman. It was an excellent performance—Hubert should really have been an actor.

As it was, however, he confided frankly—but shyly—to his prospective father-in-law that he was simply an impecunious student, several years younger than Caroline, and without any means of visible support except his student grant. He was working, he said, on a definitive thesis on the impact of witchcraft on medieval European thought. As a matter of fact, it was a subject which interested him mildly, and he knew enough about it to talk convincingly to a millionaire who had started life as an unskilled building laborer.

Todman gave his consent—but on one condition. The very condition for which Hubert had been hoping. That young Withers should consign his interest in historical research to the status of a hobby and take a job with The Firm.

"Start at the bottom, my boy, as I did. You'll soon make good."

One look at Hubert had decided Arnold Todman that for this frail intellectual the bottom of the construction industry did not mean a job as a builder's laborer. Instead, Hubert was allotted a place in the more comfortable and less strenuous side of the bottom of the business—a glorified office boy, who happened to be married to the daughter of the boss.

This might have worked out very well, except for one fact. It became painfully obvious within a few months that Hubert was simply no good. It was probably just as well that Arnold Todman dropped dead of a heart attack before any of his senior staff had plucked up the courage to tell him that Hubert was, and always would be, hopeless. Arnold died happy, knowing that Caroline was married and that his son-in-law would soon make his way in The Firm. He left everything he had—including his controlling share in the business—to Caroline.

Caroline herself knew very little about The Firm, except that it provided a handsome income. She took the advice of the senior executives of the company and soon began to get a sound grasp of the business. She suggested tactfully to Hubert that since they no longer needed the extra money he should quit his so-called job and go back to the research on which he had always been so keen. Hubert agreed, with relief. His satisfaction with the situation was tempered only by the fact that Caroline, although as plain and shy as ever, kept a tight hold on the family purse-strings.

In the Todman mansion, where they now lived, the magnificent library had been handed over to Hubert for his research work and space cleared on the shelves for his books of reference. Caroline organized the house, dealt with all finances, and kept in touch with The Firm. Hubert spent lonely and frustrated hours in the library. He was regarded with great deference by the household staff.

"The Master is working on his book," the butler would say with great severity to a giggling maid or a clumsy kitchen boy. "Don't you know that he needs complete quiet?"

So Hubert got complete quiet, and it nearly drove him mad. In fact, what saved his sanity was that he began to fill in his Saharan hours by gambling on horses.

Naturally, as the husband of Caroline (nee Todman), his credit with bookmakers was excellent. Nevertheless, the fact remained that all he had was the pin-money doled out in cash by his wife—"After all, darling, you can charge everything, can't you?"—and matters had now reached a point where his creditors were demanding payment, and that without delay. He had stalled them for a while by quietly selling a valuable picture from the Blue Morning Room—a place Caroline seldom visited—but that was only a sop to the wolves. Soon the crunch must come.

As Hubert saw it, he had two alternatives. He could confess the whole thing to Caroline, who would undoubtedly pay his debts for the sake of family honor: but thenceforth his life would be untenable. Or he could kill her.

The fact that he had a third choice came to him, as has been remarked, on a Thursday morning in spring. Caroline, who had been complaining of internal pains, had been taken to the hospital for tests and observation on the Wednesday, and on Thursday Hubert was telephoned by Dr. Edwards—an old family friend as well as the Todman medical adviser.

"I'm afraid," the doctor said, "that Mrs. Withers must be operated on immediately."

"What is it?" asked Hubert, hoping he sounded suitably worried, for his heart had given an upward leap.

He was quickly disillusioned. "Oh, nothing dangerous, now that we've discovered it in time," the doctor reassured him. "She has a large but happily not malignant growth on her womb. This is undoubtedly why she hasn't had any children. I would like to think it can be removed without a complete hysterectomy, but—"

"A complete what?" said Hubert, who knew little of medical matters.

"Removal of the womb and ovaries," explained Dr.

Edwards. "Not a dangerous operation—but I'm very much afraid, old man, that you'll have to face the fact that Caroline will never be able to have a baby."

This suited Hubert fine, but he made appropriate noises of regret. It was then that Dr. Edwards produced his life-saving bombshell.

"I must impress upon you, Mr. Withers," he said, "that although relatively simple medically, this operation can have quite serious mental aftereffects on a woman. The surgeon, you see, is doing in half an hour what nature does gradually over a period of many years. The result is that some women suffer severe post-operative depression. I don't want to frighten you, but sometimes they may have delusions and even become slightly unbalanced for a while. So I want you to be especially kind and considerate to your wife when she comes home from the hospital."

"Of course," said Hubert.

"The best thing," the doctor went on, "is for the woman to get a pet of some sort—a surrogate child, if you like. She may well transfer to it the pent-up affection for the child she now knows she can never have."

"Caroline has a pet already," said Hubert. "A Siamese cat." He tried to keep the dislike out of his voice. He had always hated the creature, with its steady blue eyes and supercilious manner.

"And she's fond of it?" pursued Dr. Edwards.

"She dotes on it," said Hubert. "She's even found a Siamese name for it—Pakdee, which means the faithful cat."

"Then it's splendid," said the doctor. "The cat will probably be able to do more for her than either you or I can."

A plan was forming in Hubert's mind. He said, "I

was just thinking—when she's strong enough, it might be a good thing for her to take a vacation."

"Excellent. Excellent."

"I won't be able to get away myself," said Hubert, "but Caroline has an old school-friend who is married and lives in England. Lady Annabel Fairley. Annabel has been begging her to go and visit."

"A most satisfactory scheme, if Caroline agrees," said the doctor. "I wouldn't have liked her to go to some hotel on her own, but a visit to a friend and a complete change of scene—yes, by all means."

So, in a couple of weeks, Caroline was back from the hospital and recovering rapidly. She appeared to suffer from none of the ill effects the doctor had predicted, but this didn't prevent Hubert's fertile imagination from inventing them.

Each time the doctor called—for even today doctors will pay house calls on people like Caroline—Hubert managed to have a word with him alone before he left.

"Our patient seems to be making excellent progress," the doctor would say.

"Well—yes and no, Doctor."

"How do you mean?"

"Of course you wouldn't notice it just visiting, but you did warn me, and I think you ought to know that the thing is becoming an obsession."

"Thing? What thing, Mr. Withers?"

"This business of the Siamese cat. She won't let him out of her sight." Indeed, Pakdee had been snuggled up with Caroline on the daybed where she was resting when the doctor arrived. Hubert went on, "She even has this crazy idea that somebody is out to harm the cat. I can't help feeling it's not healthy for somebody to be so wrapped up in a mere animal."

"I told you, Mr. Withers, it's quite natural." Dr. Edwards was reassuring. "It will pass."

A few days later, while Benson, the butler, was serving cocktails, Hubert suggested to Caroline that she might visit the Fairleys in England. Caroline was enthusiastic. Since her marriage and her involvement with the business, she had become much more self-reliant. "What a good idea, Hubert. I'll call her tomorrow. You'll come, too, won't you?"

"I wish I could, darling," said Hubert, "but I've had a word with Bentinck"—Bentinck was The Firm's managing director—"and he doesn't feel we should both be out of the country at the same time. Besides, I've never even met Annabel. You'll have much more fun on your own."

"Yes, perhaps I will," said Caroline cheerfully. "I wish I could take Dee-Dee, but one can't, with the silly British quarantine regulations. Still, you'll look after him for me, won't you, Hubert?"

Dee-Dee was Caroline's pet-name for Pakdee. It revolted Hubert almost as much as the cat's parlor trick, which he would perform for nobody but Caroline. Every time Caroline returned home after an outing, she would stand in the hallway and call "Dee-Dee!" in a particular tone of voice. Wherever the cat might be, he would come hurtling at the sound and with one leap would be in Caroline's arms, his dark-brown front legs embracing her and his face buried in the hollow of her neck. The whole thing made Hubert feel slightly sick.

Now, however, all that he said was, "Of course I will, darling, you know that." Soon he was able to report to Dr. Edwards that Caroline seemed much better and had agreed to go and visit her friend in England.

It was on the morning of the doctor's final checkup visit, while Caroline was sitting on the sofa with Pakdee on her lap, that Hubert said, "So it's all fixed? You go to England on the twentieth?"

"That's right," said Caroline. "The agency has made me a first-class booking on the lunchtime flight."

In the same pleasant, even tone, Hubert said, "I may as well tell you now that as soon as you've gone I intend to get rid of that cat."

"It should be—" Caroline did a double-take. "You intend to *what*?"

"Get rid of Pakdee," said Hubert. "I shall have him destroyed. Make no mistake about that, my dear." He left the room.

Dr. Edwards found his patient in near-hysterical tears. As far as he could make out, her husband had threatened to have the cat destroyed as soon as she left for England. She absolutely refused to go. Nothing would make her. Hubert must have gone mad. When the doctor suggested that she might have misunderstood her husband, Caroline clasped the cat even more firmly to her heart and sobbed that the doctor was as bad as Hubert and probably in league with him. Dr. Edwards persuaded her to take a sedative and went in search of Hubert.

Hubert sighed deeply. "Oh, dear," he said. "So it's started all over again. How very distressing. I suppose it's the idea of going abroad that's upset her. She's seemed so much more rational lately."

Edwards cleared his throat. "I don't suppose, Mr. Withers, that you might inadvertently have made any remark that might have led her to think—"

"Of course not!" Hubert was suitably indignant.

"Why, only the other day I assured her I would do everything to care for the cat while she was away. I believe Benson was there, serving drinks. He must have heard me. I'll ring for him now."

The doctor was deeply embarrassed. "My dear Mr. Withers, there's no need. Of course I believe what you say."

Hubert, however, was adamant. "No, no, I insist." His finger was already on the bell. "This is all so worrying in its implications that I think you should feel convinced about poor Caroline's delusions."

Benson appeared, and dutifully confirmed what Hubert had said. Of course, he added, in answer to the doctor's questions, the cat was Madam's, and Madam had a special affection for him. On the other hand, he had never known the Master to be other than most kind and considerate to the animal. When he saw him, that was. Madam and the cat spent most of their time together.

The cat was not allowed in the kitchen, but Madam always fed him herself in the butler's pantry. While Madam was away, he, Benson, would be happy to undertake this duty personally. Benson was an English butler of the old school, inherited with the house from Arnold Todman, and he had known and been fond of Caroline since her childhood. In listing Caroline's scant number of friends, Benson should have been included.

"Well," said Dr. Edwards when Benson had withdrawn, "this is, as you say, a sad setback. I feel it more important than ever that she should get away for a vacation. On the other hand, since she can't take the cat with her, we must somehow convince her that she simply imagined your threat. Shall we talk to her together?"

* * *

They talked to Caroline together, and they talked to her separately. Hubert protested over and over again that he would cherish Pakdee. Benson promised to hand-feed him and to let Caroline know at once by telephone if anything seemed to be the matter with him.

Finally, Caroline was convinced. In fact, she was more than convinced, she was frightened—for she now truly believed she had been suffering from delusions. It's always a little scary to feel that one may be going slightly mad.

Dr. Edwards, speaking privately to Hubert, said that he had high hopes that Caroline's vacation in England would put an end to any further symptoms, especially when she returned to find her cat in good health. However, he added, changing to a more somber vocal gear, if delusions still persisted on her return, it might be necessary for her to take a cure in a quiet nursing home for a few weeks.

Hubert saw Caroline off at Dulles Airport, making all the right gestures and saying all the right things. Just as the doors were closing on the mobile lounge which was to take London-bound passengers to their waiting jumbo jet, he said, softly and pleasantly, "I shall have Pakdee destroyed this evening. Goodbye, darling. Have a wonderful time."

Caroline cried all the way to London, despite—or perhaps because of—the excellent champagne with which the air hostess plied her, hoping to cheer her up. As soon as she arrived at Fairley Hall, which was after midnight by British time, she insisted on telephoning home and speaking to Benson. He assured her that Pakdee was hale and hearty and enjoying his supper—it was seven o'clock in the evening, Washington time.

"I'm delighted you had a smooth journey, Madam," said Benson. "I'll fetch the Master to speak to you right away."

"No. No, don't do that, Benson," said Caroline. "Don't tell him I called." She rang off.

Early next morning, Hubert said to Benson, "I've been looking up Pakdee's health card. He's due for his yearly shots very soon."

"Yes, sir," said Benson. "Madam was remarking the same thing only the other day."

"Well, no time like the present. Call the Animal Hospital, will you, and make an appointment for this morning? Then find me the cat basket and I'll take him along."

So a couple of hours later Hubert drove to the Animal Hospital with a surly, silent Pakdee glaring from his wicker basket on the passenger seat of the Jaguar. The cat was duly given his inoculations and the details entered on his health card. On the way home, however, Hubert took a side street, doubled back, and drove to an entirely different address. It was that of a veterinarian he'd never met but had picked from the Yellow Pages on account of the fact that he lived in an outlying suburb to the south of the city, in Virginia. His name was Michaelson, and Hubert—identifying himself as Mr. Robinson—had made an appointment with him from a public phonebooth before leaving Dulles Airport the previous day.

Dr. Michaelson was a tall, thin man with a long, slightly vague face and long-fingered, sensitive hands. Pakdee calmed down as soon as he got into the surgery and allowed himself to be lifted out of the basket.

"Well," said Michaelson admiringly, "you sure have a beautiful and valuable cat here, Mr. Robinson. He seems in fine fettle. Is anything wrong, or does he just need shots?"

"He needs more than shots," said Hubert. "He's to be destroyed."

"You can't mean that, Mr. Robinson."

"Oh, it's nothing to do with me," said Hubert crossly. "It's my wife. She bought him as a toy and now she's tired of him. He's got to go."

"And there's nothing the matter with him?"

"Not that I know of."

The vet looked thoughtful. He said, "I never like to destroy a young, healthy animal. Especially such a fine specimen. Are you sure you wouldn't like me to find a good home for him?"

"I want to see that cat killed," said Hubert with unattractive firmness. "I'm paying you to do it. The cat is mine, and I can do as I like with him. Come on, get it over with."

"You're absolutely adamant, Mr. Robinson?"

"Absolutely. And I want to see it done."

Michaelson sighed. "Very well," he said. He went to a cupboard and began to prepare a syringe. "Do you want to take the body away with you?"

"Certainly not."

"Some people," said Michaelson, gently ironic, "care enough about their pets to bury them in their gardens. However, if you wish me to dispose of him—"

"Yes, I do. Do what you like—just get rid of him."

"Very well." Michaelson stroked Pakdee gently. "Come on then, old fellow. This won't hurt."

Hubert tried not to look as the needle went in, but somehow he couldn't keep his eyes off the cat. Pakdee turned his head with his last strength and gave Hubert such a look of concentrated hatred from his deep-blue eyes that Hubert took an instinctive step backward. Then Pakdee keeled over and lay still.

Hubert pulled himself together. Averting his eyes from the body, he said, "Well, that's that. Thank you. What do I owe you?"

Michaelson said, "Nothing, Mr. Robinson. I never make a charge for destroying animals—whether it's to put them out of their misery or whether they're in perfect health." The tone of his voice exactly matched Pakdee's dying stare.

Hubert picked up the basket and made his escape. As he passed through the waiting room, he felt acutely conscious of the empty basket he was carrying. The only occupant waiting to see the doctor was a severe-faced middle-aged lady who also held a cat basket, which was occupied by a nondescript tabby.

"I'm sorry to see you've had to leave your cat with the doctor," she remarked. "Is it something serious or is he just boarding?"

Hubert muttered something about just boarding and hurried out to the car. He didn't for the moment feel up to anything more than finding a bar and having a stiff drink. Everywhere he looked, he seemed to see Pakdee's eyes. It was unfortunate that in the course of his so-called research he had just been reading a book on the connection between cats and witchcraft. Perhaps Caroline was a witch and Pakdee had been her familiar spirit. He ordered another drink and told himself not to be a fool. After all, his plan was only half complete. Pakdee had gone forever, but there was the question of his successor.

After an hour or so, Hubert felt strong enough to resume his journey, with the empty cat basket as passenger. This time he drove around the Beltway and off into the northernmost Maryland suburbs to another address he'd found in the Yellow Pages. This was a private humane society, which he'd picked as being as far as possible distant from the Michaelson surgery. The society, which announced in its advertisement that it never destroyed a healthy animal, acted as a lost-and-found agency and a sort of adoption society for cats. Hubert had also telephoned them from Dulles, giving his name as Mr. Green. His wife, he said, had set her heart on having a seal-point Siamese cat, having just lost her elderly but much-loved one. Did they have any for adoption?

"We don't have any kittens at the moment." Hubert had been surprised to hear a masculine voice on the line. He had always supposed that these places were run by cranky old ladies.

"Oh, we don't want a kitten," said Hubert quickly. "We want an adult cat. About two years old."

"Ah, then I think we can help you. Adult animals are always more difficult to place. Seal-point Siamese, you said? Yes, we have no less than three."

"I'll be along after lunch tomorrow," Hubert said.

He lunched in a small Maryland restaurant where he knew he wouldn't be recognized, and then drove to the Society's address, which turned out to be a small suburban house with half an acre of garden.

The whole place seemed to Hubert to be swarming with cats of all ages, sizes, and colors—some in spacious wire runs, some roaming freely. A covey of them were gently shooed away by the benign elderly gentleman who opened the front door, introducing himself as Mr. O'Donnell.

"Ah, Mr. Green," he beamed. "So nice to see you. Please come in. I'll take you to the drawing room—that's the one place cats are not allowed." He ushered Hubert into a small, shabbily furnished room. "I daresay you find this a rather strange establishment, but it's very worthwhile work. Makes a contribution, you know."

Hubert felt sure that he, too, would be expected to make a contribution. He had the money with him.

Mr. O'Donnell was still talking. "A seal-point Siamese, I think you said. About two years old."

"That's right," said Hubert. "A neutered male."

"A neutered male? You didn't mention that. That cuts down the choice a little, but, yes, we do have two. I'll fetch them and you can choose."

Left alone, Hubert ran over his plan in his mind. It seemed to him a good one. All Siamese cats, in his view, looked very much alike—except perhaps to the eye of love. Certainly none of the domestic staff—not even Benson—knew Pakdee well enough to be able to identify him positively. Dr. Edwards had only seen the cat on a couple of fleeting occasions. Only Caroline would accept no substitutes—especially in view of the fact that the new cat would certainly not respond to her call with Pakdee's parlor-trick. He knew—because he'd been listening in—about Caroline's call to Benson the previous evening, and guessed that a similar call would be made daily. Benson would be uniformly reassuring. So when Caroline returned and claimed that the cat in the house was not her cat—well, Dr. Edwards would certainly prescribe the quiet nursing home, which would enable Hubert to get the Power of Attorney he needed. Even a couple of weeks would be long enough.

He was aroused from his reverie by the return of Mr. O'Donnell, carrying a cat under each arm.

"There we are," he said, putting the animals down on the floor. "Delightful creatures, both of them. Take your choice."

There was never any doubt. One of the cats was noticeably larger than Pakdee, and his points were a much lighter shade of brown. The other, however, was perfectly possible. True, his whole coat was paler than Pakdee's, fluffier and less sleek, and his eyes were not only lighter blue, but mild and amiable. However, he was just about the right size and Hubert felt sure he would fool everybody except Caroline.

"There's no charge for the cat, of course," Mr. O'Donnell assured him, "but any little donation you feel inclined to make—"

Hubert made his donation and popped the counterfeit Pakdee into the basket, where he sat purring, his gentle eyes half shut. In fact, by the time Hubert had reiterated to Mr. O'Donnell that they had owned a Siamese before and therefore did not require the leaflets on care and feeding the Society provided, the cat had curled up in Pakdee's basket and was sound asleep.

Benson met Hubert at the front door and took the basket from him. "I hope the little fellow is quite all right, sir," he said. "We were a mite worried when you didn't return for luncheon."

"Sorry about that, Benson," said Hubert. "Matter of business I had to attend to, which involved lunching out." He hesitated. "Pakdee seems a little lethargic," he added. "Probably the effect of the shots. But the doctor says he's in excellent health. Just give him a light meal tonight."

"As you say, sir."

Hubert had been right. Caroline telephoned again that evening and spoke to Benson. When she heard that Pakdee had been taken to the hospital for shots, she panicked again—to the consternation of her friend

Annabel. Only after she had phoned her veterinarian at his home and learned from him that Mr. Withers had indeed brought Pakdee in that morning for his inoculations did Caroline calm down. Annabel had a word with her husband and together they decided to write to Hubert and tell him they were worried about Caroline's nerves and her apparent obsession about her cat.

The letter arrived the day before Caroline's return, and was even more than Hubert could have hoped for. He called Dr. Edwards at once—he had intended to do so, anyway, but this gave him a God-sent opportunity. He suggested that the doctor should arrange to be at the house to welcome Caroline home and see her reunion with her beloved cat. The doctor agreed.

During Caroline's absence, Hubert had barely set eyes on the Siamese, who had been entirely in Benson's care. He had taken pains, however, to inquire frequently about the cat's well being and had been assured by Benson that the little fellow was fine, eating well and quite his old self. Very satisfactory.

On the day Caroline was due back, Hubert entertained the doctor to lunch and left him to his post-prandial coffee as he went off to Dulles to meet his wife.

Caroline was looking remarkably well. She inquired at once about Pakdee and Hubert assured her that he was in good form. "He missed you, of course, darling," he said, "but Benson and I tried to make it up to him. He'll be thrilled to see you."

On the drive back down the lovely George Washington Parkway, Caroline chattered happily about England and her friends. Hubert was silent. He was bracing himself, with a mixture of emotions, for the scene that would shortly follow. It was bound to be unpleasant, and he disliked unpleasantness. There would be hysterics, and he disliked hysterics. Nevertheless, his plan would work. It couldn't fail. And Dr. Edwards himself would be there to see it.

Benson heard the car in the drive and had the front door open before Caroline had reached the top step.

"Welcome home, Madam!"

"Oh, Benson, it's nice to be back." Caroline came into the big hallway as the doctor came out of the drawing room. "Why, Dr. Edwards, I didn't know you'd be here! How very kind of you! Yes, I feel splendid—I had a marvelous vacation!" She put down her handbag and as Hubert came in through the front door she called, "Dee-Dee! I'm home, Dee-Dee!"

The cat must have been waiting on the stairs, on the landing where there was a window overlooking the front door. He came down the last flight like a flying bomb and leapt into Caroline's arms, purring his delight. And, as Caroline caressed him, he looked at Hubert over her shoulder. The old hard-blue eyes now gleaming with triumph. The old sleek coat. Pakdee.

"My Dee-Dee," Caroline was murmuring, "my Pakdee! My faithful cat."

It was Hubert who spent the next few weeks in the quiet nursing home. Soon after his release from it, he and Caroline were divorced. When last heard of, Hubert was in California, looking for another heiress. He was somehow managing to live on the meager allowance Caroline's lawyers sent him every month. The allowance would have been much larger—for Caroline was a generous soul—had Hubert not, in his frenzy, declared that she was a witch and that he had seen Pakdee die with his own eyes.

Dr. Edwards tried to put in a good word for

Hubert. "He was mentally deranged, Mrs. Withers. How could he possibly have seen the cat die when it was obviously alive and well? I think you must make allowances."

"He had the intention," said Caroline. "That is what matters."

Funnily enough, it was only a few days after Caroline's return that Dr. Michaelson visited the private humane society in Maryland, bringing with him half a dozen delightful kittens for adoption.

"By the way," he said, "I suppose you had no difficulty in finding a home for that beautiful Siamese?"

"Which one?" asked Mr. O'Donnell.

"Oh," said Mrs. O'Donnell, her severe face softening into a very sweet smile, "John means the one I picked up from his surgery. Some miserable man had brought him in to be destroyed because he said his wife was tired of him—the cat, I mean."

"I suppose I should have destroyed him," said John Michaelson, "but he was an absolute beauty, and in perfect health. I took no money and got Robinson's permission to dispose of the cat as I wished. By that time I'd given him a pre-operation anesthetic shot and the man went away convinced he was dead. I knew Grace was in the waiting room and could bring him back here right away."

"That's right," said Grace O'Donnell. "I gave him a bath and blow-dry—he emerged several shades lighter, I can tell you—and some eyedrops I thought he needed. Then I went out shopping and, believe it or not, by the time I came back Patrick had found a home for him with a—a Mr. Green, wasn't it, Patrick?"

"Yes, my dear. A nice guy, he seemed. Had had Siamese before. Wanted this one as a present for his wife, who'd just lost hers."

"Mr. Green seems to have a much nicer wife than Mr. Robinson," said Grace O'Donnell. "I'm sure the poor creature is in a very happy home now."

He is, Mrs. O'Donnell. He is.

THE LADY WORE BLACK

Hugh B. Cave

Ignoring the familiar rustle of leather being dragged over the living room carpet, eighty-year-old Emma Bell continued to watch the six o'clock evening news on television. A cat's harness was dropped at her feet, and the bearer gazed up at her with demanding blue eyes.

Without even looking down, Emma stubbornly wagged her head. "Not this evening, Tai-Tai. My arthritis is acting up."

The cat, a Siamese blue point, replied with an indignant meow that, if translated—and, of course, Emma could always translate—clearly said, "This can't go on! It's been three days now and we need our exercise, all three of us!"

"No, Tai-Tai."

Tai-Tai looked toward the bedroom doorway and summoned the old lady's other companion, a much younger Siamese seal point. Yum-Yum, named by Emma after the character in her favorite Gilbert and Sullivan operetta, obediently appeared from that room with *her* harness, and dropped it beside the one at Emma's feet.

Both cats—the large blue-gray and white one with lavender ears, and the smaller, light brown one with a chocolate-colored face and paws—then sat like statues in front of Emma's sofa, gazing relentlessly at her.

And would continue to sit, the old lady knew, until they had their way.

"Oh, all right, my darlings. If you insist. But only a short one because I really do hurt."

They understood her—they always did—and meowed in unison.

At eighty, Emma Bell had been without a husband for nine years, but having had Tai-Tai for eight years and Yum-Yum for five, she no longer suffered acutely from loneliness. She had loved her husband dearly, though, and still always wore black, and vowed she always would.

They lived, the three of them, in total harmony in a small cottage in rural South Carolina. What they lived on was the monthly social security check Emma received as a widow, plus the interest from a modest nest egg lodged in the local bank. That paid the taxes and bought food for the three of them.

It also financed the daily sip of brandy Emma's aging doctor had prescribed to help her endure the pain of her arthritis.

The harnesses buckled and leashes attached, Emma led the cats out the front door, transferring both leashes to her left hand so she could make sure the door locked itself behind her. It was certainly not a crowded neighborhood, but there had been a number of break-ins of late. "We have to be extra careful, darlings."

At the end of the driveway she turned to the right, along a road that curled attractively through pine woods, with shallow ditches on either side. In some places the ditches held water, and water harbored frogs that filled the evening with their throaty music. The clean country air smelled of wild honeysuckle and pine needles. Tai-Tai walked sedately on one side of her and Yum-Yum strained to accelerate the pace on the other.

The younger Siamese was always the more impetuous. Looking down at her, the old lady wagged her head in mild reproach. "Can't you see I'm limping? Please, darling, have a little consideration." The cat actually stopped straining. "There, that's better. Thank you."

At the first intersection Emma, as always, carefully looked both ways before starting across. Her eyes were still sharp; she wore glasses only when reading; but her aging legs grew stiffer every day, it seemed. Of course, with so few houses around, there was not much danger from cars. But the neighborhood was home to one young man, the son of the town's police chief, who seemed to think he owned every road he raced his pickup over. Twice in the past month neighborhood dogs had been run down and killed by someone. If not by him, then by whom?

The young man in question was not driving his pickup this evening, however. When Emma and her companions approached his house, he was seated on his front porch steps with a bourbon bottle in one hand. His slack face twisted into a grin under its shock of blond hair. He flapped his empty hand in a salute. "Evenin', Mrs. Bell. Out for your conshatutional?"

Emma politely nodded. "Good evening, Maynard." One must always do the proper thing. But to her cats, after they were past, she said with a frown, "Did you see that, darlings? Always a bottle. Always. He even drives his truck with a bottle or a beer can in one hand. And he uses drugs, too; I'm sure he does. I don't know what kind, but he uses them. He's dangerous, that young man is."

The cats meowed to let her know they were being attentive.

"And he's the one breaking into people's houses around here, too," Emma declared. "I'm sure of *that.* Where else would he get all the money he must spend on his drugs and drinking? He never does a lick of honest work, and his folks wouldn't be giving him money to ruin his life with, you can be certain. If they know what-all he does, of course. Maybe they don't."

Tai-Tai and Yum-Yum declared their agreement. The walk continued.

"All right," the old lady announced at the next crossroad. "We'll go down here and back home along Linden because I don't want to have to say 'good evening' to that man again. Come, darlings." And so she added a quarter mile to the length of the return journey, pleasing her two companions enormously but increasing her own torment.

Because she had difficulty sleeping, Emma usually stayed up and watched television at night, at least until the eleven o'clock news ended. If the programs happened to be of interest to Tai-Tai and Yum-Yum, they too sat on the living room sofa, one on each side of her, and watched with her. If they were bored with what they saw, they left her and went to bed. All three used the same double bed, the two cats sleeping outside the covers, at Emma's feet.

Tonight, tired and in more pain than usual from her unwise walk, the old lady stayed up late. It was after midnight when she at last turned off the TV and shuffled into the kitchen for her ounce of brandy, then went to the bedroom. The cats were already there.

Gazing down at them for a moment, she thought how fortunate she was to have two such loyal and loving creatures to keep her company. Then, knowing she would not sleep and would have to walk about from time to time to ease the pain, she simply lay down on the bed in her black dress and closed her eyes.

But she could not even doze. From ankle to hip, her left leg ached like an infected tooth. No matter how she turned, seeking a position of relief, the ache persisted.

The luminous, snail-slow hands of the electric clock on the chest of drawers near the bed stood nearly at two A.M. when she heard a door creak open.

In the whole house there was but one door that creaked. It led from the back yard into the small laundry room off the kitchen, and it had been creaking now for at least two years, in spite of her oiling the hinges. It must be warped, the man at the local hardware store had said. At the bottom of it was a small swinging gate by which the cats went in and out. But the gate didn't creak; the door itself did.

A glance at the foot of the bed assured the old lady the cats were still with her. Unafraid but puzzled, she wriggled painfully off the bed and went padding through the house to the kitchen.

There stood the intruder at the sink—the same young man she had spoken to earlier when passing the police chief's house. He had the cupboard door above the sink open and was reaching for the bottle of brandy she kept there.

How had he known she kept it there? Had he watched her at times through the sliding glass doors leading to the back porch when she poured her bedtime drink? Even tonight, perhaps?

Emma jerked to a halt and put her hands on her hips. "Young man, what do you think you're doing?"

He took the bottle from the shelf anyway, before turning to face her. His features, all slack, took on the unwholesome gray of spoiled liver and shaped themselves into something one might find in an ape-house at a zoo. His white shirt was almost as gray with grime. His khaki pants were urine-stained. His bare feet were as nasty as the rest of him.

Drunk, Emma decided. And probably high on drugs, as well. That was the word they used, wasn't it? High? She fixed him with her gaze. "So you *are* the one who's been breaking into houses." Not very often did her voice go shrill like that. "Well, you won't get away with it this time, even if your father *is* the chief of police! You'll have *me* to deal with."

Something brushed against her ankle and she glanced down. It was the blue point, Tai-Tai, rubbing against her but peering warily at the intruder. Suddenly Yum-Yum appeared from the bedroom, too.

The cat with the chocolate-colored face and paws voiced a shrill meow of disapproval and launched herself like a furry rocket at the intruder's chest. It was ever thus with the seal point. Act on instinct; think later.

Too tardily the old lady cried. "No, Yum-Yum, no!"

The leer on the thief's face widened as he swung the bottle by its neck. There was a crunch as the weapon made contact with the cat's head. Deflected in mid leap, Yum-Yum must have been dead before she crashed into the refrigerator door. At least, she uttered no cry but simply fell to the floor, a twisted brown ball with a shattered head or broken neck or both, while Emma Bell stood there gazing down at her in horror.

"You beast! You filthy beast!" Emma screamed, and with arms outflung and fingers twitching, hurled *her* frail body at the intruder.

He lashed out with the bottle again. Again there was a dull crunch, but with a difference. As her legs melted under her and she slumped to the floor, Emma moaned and put her hands to her head.

The young man took one look at what he had accomplished and sucked in a sputtering breath. The bottle, falling from his hand, struck Emma on the hip and rolled onto the floor without shattering. He retrieved it. Clutching it by the neck again, he backed slowly out of the room and into the laundry, where he had left open the door to the yard. On reaching that, he wheeled and ran stumbling into the night.

Emma Bell somehow succeeded in turning her head a few inches, looking for the cat that was still alive. The blue point was in a crouch ten feet away, ready to leap. Her quivering tail was twice as bushy as usual. Her shoulders were coiled springs. Her haunches had never looked more powerful. But she seemed uncertain of what to do, and her gaze flicked back and forth, back and forth, from the old lady to the crumpled body of Yum-Yum.

"Tai-Tai." Emma's voice was barely audible, not even a whisper. "Come here."

The cat crawled to her with nostrils twitching, and sniffed at the ooze of blood now coloring Emma's face. She peered into the woman's glazed eyes, her own bright ones only inches away.

The old lady struggled to move one arm and at last, with a tremendous effort, she touched the cat with her fingertips. "Did you . . . did you see what he did to our Yum-Yum?" she breathed. "He killed her, Tai-Tai. Oh, darling, make him pay!"

"Mrrreeoouw!"

The eyes of Emma Bell closed then. Her fingertips were still. But the blue point remained there for another hour or so, peering into her dead face, before departing.

* * *

Knowing he had killed the old woman, Maynard Albro did not return home by way of the road. He took to the pine woods instead. This was not exactly his style; he was more used to driving hell-for-leather along that road in his pickup. As a consequence, when he finally emerged from the woods into his own back yard, he was exhausted. Dragging his feet, he staggered to the back door and clawed it open.

He had not locked the house on leaving it, even though he was temporarily alone in it. His parents had gone that morning to the state capital, where his father was to attend a seminar for police chiefs. They would be away for several days.

Once in the house, however, he did lock the back door behind him, then went to the front and locked that. Then he went to the windows and secured those. Finally, in the living room, he slumped into a chair with Emma Bell's bottle of brandy and drank deeply from the bottle and reflected on what he had done.

Stupid . . . he shouldn't have left the old lady there on the kitchen floor. Sooner or later someone was bound to wonder where she was, and investigate. "You dumb jerk, Albro, what's the matter with you? Go back there and clean up!"

He went back through the pine woods, still carrying the bottle because he guessed he would need it. Along with the brandy he carried a long-handled shovel, and before going into the house, the back door of which was still open as he had left it, he groped his way into Emma Bell's flower garden and began to dig a grave.

Fortunately, the earth there was soft enough for even a drunken man to handle with ease. First Emma's beloved husband, then Emma herself had lovingly grown flowers there. In half an hour the grave was ready, and he went into the house for the body, with an eye peeled for the big gray and white cat lest it attack him as the smaller one had done.

The cat was not in the kitchen, however. Either it was someplace else in the house—he wasn't about to look—or it had ducked out. To hell with it. Lifting the old lady, he carried her to the garden, marveling at how light she was. Then he returned for the cat he had killed, and laid it beside her.

After filling the grave, he put back the clumps of zinnias, petunias, and marigolds he had carefully removed before digging it. No one would ever in the world suspect a body was laid to rest there. "You're pretty smart, Albro, you know that? And you done it in the dark, with only a quarter moon up there to see by. So finish up now and clear out, you hear?"

Back in the kitchen he pulled a strip of paper towels off a roll above the counter, wet it under a tap, and on hands and knees rubbed up every last spot of blood from the woman and cat. Then with the towels in his pants pocket and the brandy bottle in one hand again, he departed.

Twice on the way home he tipped the bottle to his mouth and deeply drank. When he got there and slumped again into his chair in the living room, he drank more. Earlier that evening, on the porch steps, he had emptied a nearly full bottle of bourbon. Now the room's off white walls and green curtains began to spin, and he closed his eyes to keep from spinning with them, and reviewed what he had done.

It was okay. Nobody would look for a grave in the old lady's flower garden. Folks would think she just wandered off somewhere. Plenty of people thought she was a little crazy anyway, still wearing black for a husband that died all that long ago.

Miserable old black-dress widow woman, why hadn't

she been asleep like she ought to've been, instead of causing all this trouble?

He heard his mother's antique clock, on the bookcase, chime thrice. Then with his eyes closed against the undulations of the room, he slept.

When he awoke, the lamp by his chair was still on and the clock's hands stood at ten past seven. It had to be ten past seven in the evening because there was no daylight at the windows.

At one of the windows something was scratching.

Not only scratching; it was meowing. And even more than meowing. *Howling*. Where had he heard a sound like that before? He remembered. It was the night he went to the local graveyard to swipe some fresh flowers off a grave, to give to Mom next day for her birthday. There'd been a high wind wailing through the big trees there. And among the stones. Now it was a cat.

The lamp beside his chair had a three-way bulb. He turned it up bright, and the cat's image appeared behind the window pane as if by magic. *Her* cat, the gray and white one, the one he hadn't killed.

The light touched its eyes and they were like Fourth of July sparklers. The howling increased to an accusation that lanced his eardrums and filled him with fear.

"Shut up!" He stormed to the window and banged on the glass almost hard enough to break it. "Shut up, damn you! Get out of here!"

The cat leaped from the sill and disappeared into the dark of the yard.

Maynard Albro returned to his chair. The pounding in his head was all but unbearable, and so was the wrenching cramp in his gut. He shouldn't have hit the booze so hard after so many joints of pot; the combination was stupid. It wasn't his fault, though, was it? What the hell had they expected, leaving him alone like this with no one to fix a meal for him, no one for him to talk to, no one even to nag him for drinking too much. He lifted the brandy bottle and gulped another long drink. The cat was back.

"Mrrreeoouw!" God, that howl! It was enough to tear a man's scalp off.

Up from his chair, he went reeling into his parents' bedroom. No way was any stupid cat going to drive him out of his mind while there was a shotgun in the house. Even if it was only a cheap twelve-gauge single-shot his miserly old man had owned for years. It would damn well blow a cat away.

With the weapon in his hands he staggered back through the living room, accompanied by a chorus of cat-screams from the thing at the window. Stealthily he unlocked the front door.

But when he lurched out onto the wooden front porch, he stumbled over something there, and before he could regain his balance, he crashed into the porch railing. When he recovered from that and went plunging down the steps and around the house to the window where the cat was, the cat had disappeared again.

Cursing his own clumsiness, Albro returned to the porch and sought the thing that had tangled his feet and tripped him. Picking it up in anger, he saw by the light from the living room that it was a dress. A black dress. In a hand that wouldn't stay steady he held it away from him and walked into the living room. Halting by the lamp, he looked at it.

A black dress. The same dress the old lady was wearing when he buried her. It was damp all over and blotchy with earth. Pine needles and bits of dead leaves clung to the fabric. As if she had crawled here in it.

Dropping it on the carpet, he sank into his chair

and sat there staring at it like one hypnotized. Not for half an hour did he stop shaking. Even then his eyes stayed bigger than normal and his heart continued its scary pounding.

That cat did not come back. But the dress was there at his feet and he had to do something with it. Had to get rid of it. Leaning from his chair, he gingerly picked it up, then rose and walked very slowly with it, holding it at arm's length, through the kitchen to the back door and out into the yard. At the end of the yard was a concrete incinerator his father had built to burn rubbish in. But the dress was too damp to catch fire when he held matches to it.

After using up half a book of paper matches and growing more panicky with each failure, he forced himself to stop. "Use your head, stupid. Get some newspaper!" That morning's paper lay on the kitchen table, still in its plastic wrapper. It had been tossed onto the front lawn by the carrier after his folks left for the capital, and he had brought it in. He hadn't looked at it, of course. He never messed with newspapers.

The paper did it. The dress caught and burned, and he stood there watching it. The smoky orange light flickered on his face and the terror slowly faded from his eyes. But had he looked beyond the incinerator to where the yard merged into the pine woods, he would have seen other eyes watching him, close to the ground.

Under the influence of alcohol and marijuana, Maynard Albro slept most of the following day. Because he'd been afraid to take off his soiled clothes and crawl into bed properly, he did his sleeping on top of the covers. On waking just before dark, he fed himself from the refrigerator with cold meatloaf his mother had left, a raw egg in beer, and half a loaf of bread layered with peanut butter.

Then, feeling better and convinced he no longer had anything to fear, he looked for the brandy bottle and finished what was left in it.

Not enough. A three-mile ride in the pickup carried him to the town's only liquor store, where he spent his last few dollars on two more bottles. Not brandy this time. The cheapest on-sale whisky the store had to offer.

They knew him in this town where his father was chief of police. The young woman who took his money looked with unconcealed distaste at his stubbled face and filthy clothes, but offered no comment.

On his way home he drank from the bottle, arriving there just after dark. Ten minutes later, while sprawled in his living room chair, he heard the cat at the window again.

"Mrrreeoouw!"

"Oh no you don't, damn you! Not tonight!" The nearest weapon at hand was the bottle he was drinking from, on the lamp table beside his chair. Lurching to his feet, he seized and hurled it. It exploded against the wall a foot from the window and fell to the floor in a rain of shattered glass. The cat did not even leap from the sill, but continued to peer in at him.

"Mrrreeoouw!"

This time he wasn't drunk, he told himself. He would know how to be stealthy. The shotgun was leaning in the corner by the front door, where he had left it last night after his unsuccessful attempt to kill the cat. Elaborately pretending he was not even aware of the cat's keening, he strolled to the door. One hand reached for the weapon; the other silently pushed the door open.

But he did not step out. On the porch in front of

him, right where the other had been, was a second black dress. Or was it the same black dress? Anyway, it was hers, the one he had buried her in. Like the first, it lay there in a soggy heap and was smeared with earth, as though she had crawled here in it.

He didn't pick this one up. His hands, his whole body, shook so hard he couldn't. Like something made of wooden parts and activated by springs and gears, he backed away from it and jerked up the twelve-gauge and squeezed the trigger.

The black dress moved a foot or so toward the porch steps, leaving a jagged rent in the porch flooring.

Scarcely able to breathe, Albro slammed the door shut. Then he ran with the gun into his bedroom and slammed that door, too.

Seated on the bed, staring wide-eyed at a blank wall, he told himself the old woman couldn't have crawled here. Not tonight, not last night. There was no *way* she could have done such a thing. She was dead. Dead, dead, dead. In the ground. Rotting.

But the dress. How had it *got* here?

A scratching sound behind him made his turn his head in panic. That wall was not blank; it was an outside wall with two windows. At one of them something gray and white, on the sill, peered in at him and scratched the glass with sharp claws.

"Mrrreeoouw!"

His hands still gripped the shotgun. They jerked it up and again he squeezed the trigger, but nothing happened. He had not reloaded it. The cat looked in at him with what had to be a sneer, its face clearly visible in the light from the lamp on his dresser. Then, with languid lack of haste, it leaped from the sill and vanished.

All right, the dress. No matter how it had got here,

he had to get *rid* of it. And this time he would make *sure*.

He went to the front porch and gingerly picked it up. Walked around to the back yard with it. In the toolhouse there his father kept a container of gasoline for the lawn mower. He carried that to the incinerator and this time soaked the garment after dropping it in. Then he returned the can to the toolhouse because everything had to be done right.

Returning to the incinerator, he stood a few feet away from it and held a lighted match to a crumpled ball of newspaper. When the paper caught fire, he tossed it onto the fuel-soaked dress.

No question this time. After the first big *whoof* of flame and smoke, the dress burned brightly until nothing was left but ash. Even though drunk he couldn't be mistaken. This time it would not reappear.

Still, there was no real reprieve in store for him tonight. Every few minutes, hour after hour, that accusing meow pursued him. Though the doors and windows were again locked, no matter where he went in the house he heard it. Living room, kitchen, his bedroom, his parents' bedroom, there was no escaping it anywhere. And whenever he heard it, it reminded him of the sound in the cemetery the night he had swiped the flowers.

A cat cry but not *only* a cat cry. Something more. Something meant to drive him crazy.

It was after four in the morning when he at last succeeded in drinking himself to sleep.

His room was dark when he again struggled up from the depths of his liquor haze into a murky kind of awareness. The light was on. In fact, all the lights in the house were on, he discovered when he went stumbling about in an effort to orient himself. He must have turned them on last night when the cat was trying to get to him, and left them on when he finally hit the bed. Well, okay. With the lights on he felt safer. What time was it, anyway?

He peered at the watch on his wrist. He'd neglected to wind it. There was a battery wall clock in the kitchen, he vaguely remembered. He blinked up at it. Seven forty.

Something was scratching at the kitchen door. A *door* this time, not a window.

"Mrrreeoouw!"

"I'll *kill* you!" The gun. Where had he put the gun? For hours last night he'd carried it around with him while he prowled the house, hoping to see the damned thing at a window and get a shot at it. The gun must be *somewhere*.

He searched the house. Found the weapon at last under his bed. Loading it, he went back to the kitchen. But the scratching at the door had ceased.

A drink. He had to have a drink. Where was the bottle?

He had bought two, he distinctly remembered. Had killed one last night before falling asleep. The other had to be around somewhere.

No. He'd hurled one at the window where the cat was, and missed, and watched it explode against the wall. He was out of liquor. Out of money, too. And anyway, he wouldn't dare leave the house now and drive to the store.

He licked his dry lips and began sobbing. Then heard a scratching sound at the *front* door.

This time, by God . . . !

Shotgun in hand, he stole through the living room and jerked the door open. And despite a backward leap, the old lady's gray-white cat was a perfect target, facing him halfway across the porch with only another of those damned black dresses between them. The gun was loaded. All he had to do was fire it.

But a town police car was at the foot of the front walk, by the mailbox, and its door was open, and one of his father's cops, Andy Cramer, was stepping out of it. With a triumphant "Mrrreeoouw!" the old lady's cat fled into the night.

The cop strode up the walk, climbed the steps, and scowled at the shotgun in Albro's hands. He was a man of forty or so, with long arms and big shoulders. "You fixin' to *shoot* that cat, Maynard?"

"I—no, I—well, it was drivin' me crazy!"

"Drivin' you crazy, Maynard? I know that cat well. Belongs to old Emma Bell down the road, and it's a purebred Siamese, one of the best-behaved cats you'll ever meet. What you talkin' about, drivin' you crazy? You drunk again?"

Reaching out, he took the shotgun from Albro's hands and checked it. Removing the shell, he handed the weapon back. Then, stooping to pick up the black dress on the porch floor between them, he said, scowling, "What's this?"

Maynard Albro took a backward step and began shaking again. His hands were so unsteady, the barrel of the gun beat a tattoo against the doorframe.

"A dress?" Andy Cramer's gaze lifted to the youth's face again. "What's a dress doin' here on your porch?"

"I—dunno."

"By God, it's one of *hers*." Andy turned to peer into the dark of the yard, where Tai-Tai had disappeared. "What's goin' on here, Maynard? *Her* cat, *her* dress, you with a gun this time of night . . . Looks like it's a good thing I stopped. Wouldn't have, except I seen all the lights on and knew your folks was away. Are you stoned?"

Albro's mouth uncontrollably twitched now. "N-n-no, I'm n-n-not."

"What's this dress doin' here, then? Tell me!" Andy held the garment up between them by its shoulders. "It's hers, all right. She never wears anything different. Why's it here on your porch, all wet and dirty like this?"

"I d-d-don't know."

"Get in the car, Maynard. I think we better call on that little lady and see what you been up to."

It was at Emma Bell's house that Maynard Albro broke down. Two reasons. One: when they got into the car, the cop thrust the black dress at him, saying, "Here, *you* hold this," and of course to Maynard it was like being ordered to hold *all* of what he had buried. And two: when they were almost to Emma's house, he couldn't help but look toward the back yard flower garden, and there where he had dug the grave he saw the gray and white cat again. It was just sitting there in the light of the quarter moon, its eyes aglow, watching as the car slowed down to make the turn into the driveway.

He confessed in the driveway, so instead of going into the house or even the garden, Andy Cramer drove him to the police station. But a little while later, with another man from the station, Andy did go into Emma's house to complete his investigation.

In Emma's bedroom closet he found three black dresses hanging, all identical to the one he had discovered on the Albros' porch. Alongside them was an empty hanger, and under that, on the floor, were two more hangers that must have fallen from the same rod.

Shaking his head at this discovery, Andy said to his companion, "These dresses are what she always wore, and it looked like she had quite a few of them, all alike. I can see how finding one on his front porch three nights running would scare young Albro into talking. But how do you suppose those dresses *got* from here to there, Joe?"

The man spoken to merely stared at the dresses in the closet and shrugged his shoulders.

Andy struggled to answer his own question. "They were all wet and dirty, the kid said. So was the one I seen. There's plenty of bare ground between here and there, and water in some of those roadside ditches. If some animal was to drag a thing like a dress from here to there and didn't want to be seen, it wouldn't travel on the road, either, would it?"

Silent for a moment, he tugged at an ear while concentrating on the problem. Then with a frown he said, "Joe, you suppose that cat of Emma's . . . ? It's a whole heap smarter'n most cats, you know. I swear it understood everything the old lady said to it—always."

HARDROCK

Gary Erickson

The cat needed killing. He was old, mean, smelly, toothless, covered with grey hairs matted into indistinguishable piles. He hissed at me when I came home.

Times were tough. Bill Brewster told me he'd had his cat put to sleep by the vet and it had cost him thirty dollars. Not to mention the impersonality of it all.

"I'll tell you," he said, a cigarette dangling from his lips, "if I had to do it again, I'd do the job myself. Save the thirty bucks and feel like I'd seen Hubie through to the end."

I decided to profit from Bill's experience. I'd take Hardrock out to a deserted road, put a single, nearly painless bullet through his senile head, and save the trouble and expense of the vet.

It wouldn't be easy—Hardrock and I had been together over ten years. Still, he wasn't the same. He'd forgotten what his litter box was for, and instead of purring I got hissing. Why pay the vet to do what I was responsible for doing? Besides, I was a good shot, had taken first place in the annual turkey shoot last fall. Almost painless, certainly fast.

He looked suspicious as we drove. It had been a while since we'd gone for a drive together, mainly because of Hardrock's constant diarrhea. The rifle was in the trunk. As I found the deserted road and hit the turn signal, a brief, unhappy impulse told me to go home—to forget it—to pay the thirty bucks and spare myself. I didn't pay any attention to it.

Of course, I haven't told you the worst. I was married once. Maria never liked the cat: That is, until our divorce—then she acted as if it were her firstborn and an inconsolable loss. Her actual firstborn, *our* firstborn, Stanley—now, he was the second problem. He did like the cat. Always.

If my ex-wife knew what I was about to do, she'd try to get custody of Stanley—which is what she did every time she didn't like what I was doing. First it was the live-in girlfriend. The judge dropped that one, but did give me a look. Then it was visitation, and she gained ground there. The judge said I *had* to let her see Stanley. I suppose I could go into all the reasons why I didn't agree, but I won't; I figured I was lucky to get custody at all, so I let that slide. She didn't want Stanley any more than she wanted Hardrock but she insisted she did, and between her job and her inheritance she had enough money and enough charm to convince numerous lawyers to pursue numerous suits, numerous movements against me. She claimed I was unfit, cruel, unstable, a drunk, a drug addict, a philanderer, a philistine, a bad manager, a poor cook, a god-dammed *man*, for christsake. But I still had Stanley and I still had Hardrock, and even though I'd always "won," I was just about broke from defending myself in court. Lawyers aren't cheap, especially good ones, and I hadn't messed around.

Hardrock hissed at me, interrupting my visions of Maria's finger wagging at me across a courtroom floor. He crawled into the back seat and defecated on the vinyl seats. It began to smell.

The last time.

He hissed in a sort of off way as if to draw my attention to what he'd done, but I ignored him.

Stanley and Hardrock had grown up together, and if Stanley knew what I was about to do, he'd never forgive me. When he was older he might, but not now. And Maria! She'd say it was "cruelty to animals," "mental cruelty" to Stanley, "murder." "Typical," she'd say, bursting at the judge like before, and for a brief moment I again saw myself in court, Maria's finger pointed at me accusingly with Stanley half huddled behind her skirts, crying, his eyes stained red with disbelief and betrayal. An eight-year-old doesn't understand getting old, getting slow, losing control over your bowels, feeling little pains all over.

"I'm doing this because I love you, Hardrock. I'm sorry, but it's better I do it than somebody who doesn't know you." *And hasn't cleaned up after you for the last three years.*

The smell got worse, and any remaining doubts vanished. I was going to kill the cat. My cat. Stanley's cat. The cat that used to curl around my neck and purr. And worse, I was going to do it to save thirty dollars. To save the cost of an injection, I was going to dispatch the cat I'd lived with for over a decade. I was going to do a hit on a housecat. My cat. Hardrock.

I stopped the car where the road narrowed into open country roads of gravel and fine dust.

"Come on, Hardrock. Let's go for a walk."

He hissed loudly at me and deftly crawled into the back window ledge, seemingly daring me to try to catch him. I grabbed at him.

Had he still had his teeth I'm sure he would have displayed them at that moment, for as I grabbed at him, Hardrock—old, mellow, hard-sleeping, heavy-eating, not-a-care-in-the-world Hardrock—suddenly revealed his true wolverine soul and with an amazing amount of agility, zoomed from the ledge to the top of the front seat, then bounded out the open window. With a single, beastly, backward snarl, he began trotting down the road, the fur on his tail looking like fudge stuck to a snow bunny's tail. *He knows*.

I threw open the trunk, snatched the rifle from it, slammed a full clip into it, and took aim at his backside. He was wobbling down the road like an overloaded squirrel and I almost had him in my sights, but I decided that a mercy killing must be merciful and to shoot him in the back would be, somehow, weirdly unfair.

This was not going the way I'd planned it at all. I'd imagined a long monologue full of sound purpose; and a sort of pre-eulogy, with Hardrock understanding everything, perhaps even nodding.

But here he was—running. Running away!

It didn't take long to catch up with him, and I soon found him sitting against a pile of gravel like a furry grey bull's-eye, and afraid of not having another chance, determined that quick was best, aimed and fire.

And missed.

But not entirely. When the bullet hit him, Hardrock instantly discovered that life is sweetest when most threatened and his heart got the message and he came to full alert and vanished in a blur of grey fur. Escaped. Gone. Missing.

I found blood, but I didn't find Hardrock. By the time I gave it up it was dark. In the rear view mirror I peered into the face of a monster under the dome light. A wanton cat killer who had used the lure of trust to murder . . . no, that was too kind . . . to *wound* a domestic cat and leave it at the edge of the civilized world, bleeding, old, tired; shot, for God's sake! To save thirty dollars, an animal's life, no, a *friend's* life had been exchanged. A Judas with thirty saved dollars and a single bullet casing left. That was me.

I drove home in silence, the windows down. Hardrock's essence still with me.

I lied to Stanley when he asked where I'd been. I said I'd been to the store, not out ten miles in the country trying to kill his best friend.

I lied again when his mother called the next day.

"Stanley said Rocky ran off." Her voice indicated disbelief.

"Yeah. He's not here. You know how cats are. They come back."

"He hasn't stayed away overnight for years! You never should have had that cat anyway. I sure as hell hope you're taking better care of my boy than my cat. If anything happens . . ."

Maria went on with clear and vague threats both, and in time I simply listened, fearing that any statement I made would be taken down and produced in some future courtroom. At times I suspected she recorded our conversations. I knew she kept notes.

I dreamt about Hardrock that night. I saw him driving up in a police car with the sirens going. I dreamt that he'd bitten my face and clawed my eyes while a dozen judges in billowing black robes held me down.

The next morning, tired and shaken, I found myself lying again before I'd had coffee.

"Dad, do you think Hardrock will come home today?"

"He might, Stan. He might."

But Hardrock was dead. Or dying a horrible death, perhaps lying barely conscious while field mice bit deeply into his flesh. Hardrock could barely handle walking across the room to stuff himself, much less survive the wilderness wounded.

In my original scenario, I'd buried him under high piled rocks—a sort of frontier burial—but his running away had spoiled his painless, good death and I now imagined maggots and worms fighting flies where once his eyes had been: decay instead of warmth. Hardrock wasn't coming home. His blood was on the sand. I'd seen it, touched it. I glanced at my hands—sure they were covered with blood—sure that Stanley could see it.

But, of course, there was no blood. Still, the way Stanley looked at me haunted me.

That night as I tried to go to sleep I remembered in painful detail the day I'd purchased him. How I'd brought him home. And the bed and the toys, the collar with our names on it, the bell and the scratching post . . . the trips to the vet, the kitty litter, the tons of food. Hardrock would only eat Mrs. Pamper's cat-food. Nothing ordinary for him. Or cheap. Besides the thirty, I thought coldly, I'm saving at least two bucks a day in expenses. Murder was profitable.

And then I heard sobbing from the end of the hall.

I found Stanley lying at the end of his bed, crying softly, curled like a . . . yes, cat.

"What's wrong, Stan?"

"I miss Hardrock," he bellowed, his face a terrible image of sorrow, trembling lips, tears crawling down his face. I was consumed with shame. "Dad, I think he might be dead," he sobbed. "He wouldn't run away from home, would he? We were never mean to him." He shot me a questioning look through his tears as if to say, "I know *I* wasn't mean to him."

I held him.

"He might have been hit by a car," and this brought a fresh howl, "but I'm sure he didn't run away. Or maybe somebody kidnapped him. He was awfully cute," I lied. And both of these might have happened. I didn't think for a second that either one of them had, but it was possible.

"He was old."

"He wasn't *that* old, Dad. You wouldn't run away when you got old, would you?"

And I had an image of an older Stanley driving me, old, wheezing, half-blind, poop in my shorts, down a gravel road with a rifle in the trunk.

"No, but cats aren't people," I said to reassure myself, "and Hardrock wasn't really himself. I'm sure some nice people found him. He's probably sleeping right now." *In the belly of a bear.*

"But he's got his collar on with his name and stuff." He looked at me with hope.

Oh my God! I'd forgotten to remove his collar. I was going to do it after I'd shot him.

"Yes, his collar," I said as calmly as possible. "Maybe it fell off."

We got nostalgic then and talked about cute things Hardrock had done over the years and in time Stanley fell asleep.

Maria's lawyer called the next day. He hinted darkly that Maria was extremely concerned about my ability to exercise proper care in my supervision of "disputed property" and that "God knows" he didn't want to end up going to court again over a cat but he had promised Maria that he would call and say what he had to say, and he had but we both knew his heart wasn't in it. I said little, wishing I'd had an attorney on retainer to refer him to.

As soon as we hung up I went to look for Hardrock's body . . . and collar. I combed heavy brush, deep woods, looked in the treetops. Not a trace. The blood was still there, fading into nothingness, but I found not a single track, nor a clue as to where he might have gone off to die. I lied to Stanley again that night when I returned.

Stanley was having another dream. I heard the crying right away because I couldn't sleep. I had visions of my name in the newspaper—MAN MURDERS SON'S PET FOR MONEY—and saw Hardrock's body with the incriminating collar on it in a plastic bag on a table with my rifle lying next to it with a tag on it, plaster casts of my footprints, charts of blood samples. I imagined eyewitness testimony from Maria about the time I'd kicked him—saw Stanley tearful, surrounded by woeful looking psychiatrists shaking their heads and pointing at me.

I thought I heard a funny noise as I was walking to his bedroom, a sort of scratching sound. Then it went, just as quickly, away. *The wind.*

"Dad, I was dreaming that Hardrock was hungry and alone."

I comforted him, promising, *almost*, that we might get another cat, something I saw as extremely unlikely.

His head suddenly shot up away from my chest. "Did you hear that?" he said sharply.

"What?"

"I thought I heard a meow."

The poor kid hears cats in his mind. What have I done?

But then I heard it. A scratching sound again. On the screen door downstairs. Then a meow.

Stanley got to the door first and jerked it open.

A three-legged cat with an infected stump stood there. It was Hardrock.

"We've got to get him to the vet, Dad."

And we did.

He needed surgery, medication, "in-house treatment," "follow-up care." The bill came to four hundred and thirty-six dollars.

That was five years ago. He still lives with us.

Everybody suspects that I was the one who blew his leg away—they look at me in a strange way sometimes when I'm near the cat. I have to be extra careful that nothing happens to him.

Hardrock looks at me sometimes late at night as if he knows he's safe. He limps over and craps at my feet.

Maria and I have been to court over summer vacations, medical records, and parent-teacher conferences, and although she has tried to bring up the "maiming" of Hardrock, my lawyer (the latest) won't let her. He's good. Not cheap, but good.

Stanley hardly ever does anything with the cat, having developed interests in other things, like video games and girls. So mainly it's just the two of us. The vet says that it's almost a miracle the way Hardrock hangs on. She says she's never seen anything like it. She told me once that she thought he would have to be put to sleep years ago, but that his "accident" seemed to have instilled in him a fierce desire to live. I only smiled.

I took a pillow once and put it over him, but as soon as he woke up I couldn't go through with it. I had my chance and blew it. So we go on, both getting older. Some days I think he'll always be here. Maria would like that.

THE BEAST WITHIN

Margaret B. Maron

Early summer twilight had begun to soften the harsh outlines of the city when Tessa pushed open the sliding glass doors and stepped out onto the terrace. Dusk blurred away the grime and ugliness of surrounding buildings and even brought a kind of eerie beauty to the skeletal girders of the new skyscraper going up next door.

Gray haired, middle-aged and now drained of all emotion, Tessa leaned heavily-fleshed arms on the railing of the penthouse terrace and let the night enfold her.

From the street far below, the muffled sounds of evening traffic floated up to her, and for a moment she considered jumping—to end it all in one brief instant of broken flesh and screaming ambulances while the curious stared. What real difference would it make to her, to anyone, if she lived another day or year, or twenty years?

Still, the habit of life was too deeply in her. With a few cruel and indifferent words, Clarence had destroyed her world; but he had not destroyed her will to live. Not yet.

She glanced across the narrow space to the uncompleted building. The workmen who filled the daylight hours with a cacophony of rivets and protesting winches were gone now, leaving behind, for safety, hundreds of tiny bare light bulbs. In the warm breeze, they swung on their wires like chained fireflies in the dusk.

Tessa smiled at the thought. How long had it been since she had seen real fireflies drift through summer twilight? Surely not more than half a dozen times since marrying Clarence. She no longer hated the city, but she had never forgiven it for not having fireflies—or for blocking out the Milky Way with its star-quenching skyscrapers.

Even thirty years ago, when he had married her and brought her away from the country, Clarence had not understood her unease at living in a place so eternally and brilliantly lit. When his friends complimented them on the penthouse and marveled at the size of their terrace (enormous even by those booming wartime standards of the Forties), he would laugh and say, "I bought it for Tessa. Can't fence in a country girl, you know; they need 'land, lots of land 'neath the starry skies above!' "

It hadn't taken her long to realize that the penthouse was more a gift to his vanity than to still her unspoken needs. After a while, she stopped caring.

If the building weren't high enough above the neon glare of the streets to see her favorite stars, it at least provided as much quiet as one could expect in a city. She could always lie back on one of the cushioned chaises and remember how the Milky Way swirled in and out of the constellations; remember the dainty charm of the Pleiades tucked away in Taurus the Bull.

But not tonight. Instead of star-studded skies, memory forced her to relive the past hour.

She was long since reconciled to the fact that Clarence did not love her; but after years of trying to fit his standards, she had thought that he was comfortable with her and that she was necessary to him in all the other spheres which hold a marriage together after passion is gone.

Tonight, Clarence had made it brutally clear that not only was she unnecessary, but that the woman she had become, to please him, was the antithesis of the woman he'd chosen to replace her.

In a daze, Tessa had followed him through their apartment as he packed his suitcases. Mechanically, she had handed him clean shirts and underwear; and, seeing what a mess he was making of his perfectly tailored suits, she had taken over the actual packing as she always did when he had to go away on business trips. Only this time, he was going to a hotel and would not be back.

"But why?" she asked, smoothing a crease in his gray slacks.

They had met Lynn Herrick at one of Alison's parties. Aggressive and uninhibited, she wore the latest mod clothes and let her straight black hair swing longer than a teenager's although she was probably past thirty. Tessa thought her brittle and obvious, hardly Clarence's type, and she had been amused by the girl's blatantly flirtatious approach.

"Why?" she demanded again and was amazed at the fatuous expression which spread across Clarence's face: a blend of pride, sheepishness and defiance.

"Because she's going to bear my child," he said pompously, striking a pose of chivalrous manhood.

It was the ultimate blow. For years Tessa had pleaded for a child, only to have Clarence take every precaution to prevent one.

"You always loathed children. You said they were encumbrances—whining, slobbering nuisances!"

"It wasn't my fault," Clarence protested. "Accidents happen."

"I'll bet!" Tessa muttered crudely, knowing that

nothing accidental ever happens to the Lynn Herricks of this world; but Clarence chose to ignore her remark.

"Now that it has happened, Lynn has made me see how much I owe it to myself and to the company. A 'pledge to posterity' she calls it, since it doesn't look as if Richard and Alison are going to produce an heir, as you know," Clarence said.

Richard Loughlin was Clarence's much younger brother. Together, they had inherited control of a prosperous chain of department stores. Although Tessa had heard Richard remark wistfully that a child might be fun, his wife Alison shared Clarence's previous attitude toward offspring; and her distaste was strengthened by the fear of what a child might do to her size eight figure.

With Clarence reveling in the newfound joys of prospective fatherhood, Tessa had straightened from his packing and snapped shut the final suitcase. Still in a daze, she stared at her reflection in the mirror over his dresser and was appalled.

In her conscious mind, she had known that she would soon be fifty, that her hair was gray, her figure no longer slim; and she had known that Clarence would never let her have children—but deep inside, she felt the young, half-wild girl she had been cry out in protest at this ultimate denial, at this old and barren woman she had become.

The siren of a fire engine on the street below drew Tessa to the edge of the terrace again. Night had fallen completely and traffic was thin now. The sidewalks were nearly deserted.

She still felt outraged at being cast aside so summarily—as if a pat on the shoulder, the promise of lavish alimony, and an "I told Lynn you'd be sensible about everything" were enough to compensate for thirty years of her life—but at least her brief urge toward self-destruction had dissipated.

She stared again at the bobbing safety lights of the uncompleted building and remembered that the last time she had seen fireflies had been four years ago, after Richard and Alison returned from their honeymoon. She and Clarence had gone down to Pennsylvania with them to help warm the old farm Richard had just bought as a wedding surprise for Alison.

The hundred and thirty acres of overgrown fields and virgin woodlands had indeed been a surprise to Alison. Her idea of a suitable weekend retreat was a modern beach house on Martha's Vineyard.

Tessa had loved it and had tramped the woods with Richard, windblown and exhilarated, while Alison and Clarence complained about the bugs and dredged up pressing reasons for cutting short their stay. Although Alison had been charming, and had assured Richard that she was delighted with the farm, she found excellent excuses for not accompanying him on his infrequent trips to the country.

Remembering the farm's isolation, Tessa wondered if Richard would mind if she buried herself there for a while. Perhaps in the country she could sort things out and grope her way back to the wild freedom she had known thirty years ago, before Clarence took her away and "housebroke her"—as he'd expressed it in the early years of their marriage.

A cat's terrified yowl caught her attention. She looked up and saw it running along one of the steel girders which stuck out several feet from a higher level of the new building. The cat raced out on it as if pursued by the three-headed hound of Hell, and its momentum was too great to stop when it realized the danger.

It soared off the end of the girder and landed with

a sickening thump on the terrace awning. Awkwardly writhing off the awning, the cat leaped to the terrace floor and cowered under one of the chaises, quivering with panic.

Tessa watched the end of the girder, expecting to see a battle-scarred tomcat spoiling for a fight. Although cats seldom came up this high, it was not unusual to see one taking a shortcut across her terrace from one rooftop to another, up and down fire escapes. But no other cat appeared.

The night air had roused that touch of arthritis which had begun to bother Tessa lately, and it was an effort to bend down beside the lounge chair. She tried to coax the cat out, but it shrank away from her hand. "Here, kitty," she murmured, "it's all right. There's no one chasing you now."

She had always liked cats, and for that reason, refused to own one, knowing how easy it would be to let a small animal become a proxy child. She sensed Richard's antipathy and sympathized with him whenever Alison referred to Liebchen, their dachshund, as "baby."

Patiently, she waited for the cat to stop trembling and sniff her outstretched hand. She kept her tone low and soothing, but it would not abandon its shelter. Careful to make no sudden moves, Tessa stood up and stepped back a few feet.

The cat edged out then, suspiciously poised for flight, and the light from the living room beyond the glass doors fell across it. It was a young female with crisp black and gray markings and white paws; and judging by its leggy thinness, it hadn't eaten in some time.

"Poor thing," Tessa said, moved by its uneasy trust. "Wait right there, kitty—I'll get you something to eat." As if it understood she meant no harm, the cat did not skitter aside when she moved past it into the apartment.

In a few minutes, Tessa returned, carrying a saucer of warm milk and a generous chunk of rare beef which she'd recklessly cut from the heart of their untouched dinner roast. "You might as well have it, kitty. No one else will be eating it."

Stiff-legged and wary, the young cat approached the food and sniffed; then, clumsily, it tore at the meat, almost choking in its haste.

"Slow down!" Tessa warned, and knelt beside the cat to pull the meat into smaller pieces. "You're an odd one. Didn't you ever eat meat before?" She tried to stroke its thin back, but the cat quivered and slipped away beneath her plump hand. "Sorry, cat. I was just being friendly."

She sat down heavily on one of the chaises and watched the animal finish its meal. When the meat was gone, it turned to the saucer of milk and drank messily with much sneezing and shaking of its small head as it inadvertently got milk in its nose.

Tessa was amused and a bit puzzled. She'd never seen a cat so graceless and awkward. It was almost like a young, untutored kitten; and when it finished eating and sat staring at her, Tessa couldn't help laughing aloud. "Didn't your mother teach you *any*-thing, silly? You're supposed to wash your paws and whiskers now."

The cat moved from the patch of light where it had sat silhouetted, its face in darkness. With purposeful caution, it circled the chaise until Tessa was between the cat and the terrace doors. Light from the living room fell full in its eyes there and was caught and reflected with an eerie intensity.

Uneasily, Tessa shivered as the cat's eyes met her

own with unwavering steadiness. "Now I understand why cats are always linked with the supernatu—"

The cat's eyes seemed to bore into her brain. There was a spiraling vortex of blinding light. Her mind was assaulted—mauled and dragged down and under and through it, existence without shape. She was held by a roaring numbness which lasted forever and was over instantly, and she was conscious of another's existence, mingling and passing—a being who was terrified, panic-stricken, and yet fiercely exultant.

There was a brief, weird sensation of being unbearably compacted and compressed; the universe seemed to tilt and swirl; then it was over. The light faded to normal city darkness, the roaring ceased and she knew that she was sprawled upon the cool flagstones of the terrace.

She tried to push herself up, but her body would not respond normally. Dazed, she looked around and screamed at the madness of a world suddenly magnified in size—a scream which choked off as she caught sight of someone enormous sitting on the now-huge chaise.

A plump, middle-aged woman held her face between trembling hands and moaned, "Thank God! Thank God!"

With a shock, Tessa realized she was seeing her own face for the first time, without the reversing effect of a mirror. The shock intensified as she looked down through slitted eyes and saw neat white paws instead of her own hands. With alien instinct, she felt the ridge of her spine quiver as fur stood on end. She tried to speak and was horrified to hear a feline yowl emerge.

The woman on the chaise—Tessa could no longer think of that body as herself—stopped moaning then and watched her warily. "You're not mad, if that's what you're wondering. Not yet, anyhow. Though you'll go mad if you don't get out of that skin in time."

Snatching up one of the cushions, she flung it at Tessa. "Shoo! G'wan, scat!" she gibbered. "You can't make me look in your eyes. I'll never get caught again. Scat, damn you!"

Startled, Tessa sprang to the railing of the terrace and teetered there awkwardly. The body responded now, but she didn't know how well she could control it, and twenty-eight stories above street level was too high to allow for much error.

The woman who had stolen her body seemed afraid to come closer. "You might as well go!" she snarled at Tessa. She threw a calculating glance at the luxurious interior beyond the glass doors. In the lamp lights, the rooms looked comfortable and secure. "It's a lousy body—too old and too fat—but it seems to be a rich one and it's human and I'm keeping it, so *scat!*"

Her new reflexes were quicker than those of her old body; and before the slipper left the woman's hand, Tessa had dropped to the narrow ledge circling the outside of her apartment. Residual instinct made her footing firm as she followed the ledge around the corner of the building to the fire escape, where it was an easy climb to the roof. There, in comparative safety from flying shoes and incipient plunges to the street, Tessa drew up to consider the situation.

Cat's body or not, she thought wryly, *it's still my mind*. She explored the sensations of her new body, absentmindedly licking away the dried milk which stuck to her whiskers, and discovered that vestigial traces of former identities clung to the brain. Mere wisps they were, like perfume hanging in a closed room, but enough to piece together a picture of what had happened to her on the terrace below.

The one who had just stolen her body had been young and sly, but not overly bright. Judging from the terror and panic so freshly imprinted, she had fled through the city and had taken the first body she could.

Behind those raw emotions lay a cooler, more calculating undertone and Tessa knew *that* one had been more mature, had chosen the girl's body deliberately and after much thought. Not for her the hasty grabbing of the first opportunity; instead, she had stalked her prey with care, taking a body that was pretty, healthy, and, above all, young.

Beyond those two, Tessa could not sort out the other personalities whose lingering traces she felt. Nor could she know who had been the first, or how it all had started. Probing too deeply, she recoiled from the touch of a totally alien animal essence struggling for consciousness—the underlying basic *catness* of this creature whose body she now inhabited.

Tessa clamped down ruthlessly on these primeval stirrings, forcing them back under. This must be what the girl meant about going mad. How long could a person stay in control?

The answer, of course, was to get back into a human body. Tessa pattered softly to the edge of the roof and peered down at the terrace. Below, the girl in her body still cowered on the chaise lounge as if unable to walk into the apartment and assume possession. She sat slumped and looked old and defeated.

She was right, thought Tessa, *it is a lousy body. She's welcome to the joys of being Mrs. Clarence Loughlin.*

Her spirits soaring, Tessa danced across the black-tarred roof on nimble paws. Joyfully, she experimented with her new body and essayed small leaps into the night air. No more arthritis, no excess flab to make her gasp for breath. What bliss to think a motion and have lithe muscles respond!

Drunk with her new physical prowess, she raced to the fire escape, leaped to the railing and recklessly threw herself out into space. There was one sickening moment when she felt she must have misjudged, then she caught herself on a jutting scaffold and scrambled onto it.

Memories it had taken thirty years to bury were uncovered as Tessa prowled through the night and rediscovered things forgotten in the air-conditioned, temperature-controlled, insulated environment which had been her life with Clarence.

Freed of her old woman's body, she felt a oneness again with—what? The world? Nature? God? The name didn't matter, only the feeling. Even here in the city, in the heart of man's farthest retreat into artifice, she felt it.

What it must be like to have a cat's body in the country! Tessa thought, and then shivered as she realized that it would be too much. To be in this body with grass and dirt underneath, surrounded by trees and bushes alive with small rustlings, and uncluttered sky overhead—a human mind would go mad with so much sensory stimulation.

No, better the city with its concrete and cars and crush of people to remind her that she was human, that this body was only temporary.

Still, she thought, descending gracefully from the new building, *there can be no harm in just a taste.*

She ran west along half-deserted streets, heading for the park.

On the cross-town streets, traffic was light; but crossing the avenues terrified her. The rumble and throb of all those engines, the glaring lights and impatient horns kept her fur on end. She had to force herself to step off the curb at Fifth Avenue; and as she darted across its wide expanse, she half-expected to be crushed beneath a taxi.

The park was a haven now. Gratefully, she dived between its fence railings and melted into the dark safety of its jumble of bushes.

In the next few hours, Tessa shed all the discipline of thirty years with Clarence, her years of thinking "What will Clarence say?" when she gave way to an impulsive act; the fear of being called "quaint" by his friends if she spoke her inmost thoughts.

If Pan were a god, she truly worshipped him that night! Abandoning herself to instinctual joys, she raced headlong down grassy hills, rolled paws over tail-tip in the moonlight; chased a sleepy, crotchety squirrel through the treetops, then skimmed down to the duck pond to lap daintily at the water and dabble at goldfish turned silver in the moonbeams.

As the moon slid below the tall buildings west of the park, she ate flesh of her own killing; and later—behind the Mad Hatter's bronze toadstool—she allowed the huge ginger male who had stalked her for an hour to approach her, to circle ever nearer . . .

What followed next had been out of her control as the alien animal consciousness below surged into dominance. Only when it was over and the ginger tom gone, was she able to reassert her will and force that embryonic consciousness back to submission.

Just before dawn, her neat feline head poked through the railing at Fifth and East 64th Street and hesitated as she surveyed the deserted avenue, emptied of all traffic save an occasional green and white bus.

Reassured, Tessa stepped out onto the sidewalk and sat on narrow haunches to smooth and groom her ruffled striped fur. She was shaken by the night's experiences, but complacently unrepentant. No matter what lay ahead, this night was now part of her past and worth any price she might yet have to pay.

Nevertheless, Tessa knew that the strength of this body's true owner was growing and that another night would be a dangerous risk. She had to find another body, and soon.

Whose?

Lynn Herrick flashed to mind. How wickedly poetic it would be to take her rival's body, bear Clarence's child, and stick Lynn with a body which quite probably, after last night, would soon be producing offspring of its own! But she knew too little about Miss Herrick to feel confident in that role.

No, she was limited to someone familiar; someone young and financially comfortable; someone unpleasantly deserving; and, above all, someone *close*. She must be within transferring distance before the city's morning rush hour forced her back into the park until dark—an unthinkable risk.

As Tessa formulated these conditions, the logical candidate came into focus. *Of course!* She grinned. *Keep it in the family*. Angling across Fifth Avenue, she trotted uptown toward the luxurious building which housed the younger Loughlins.

Her tail twitched jauntily as she scampered along the sidewalk and elation grew as she considered the potentials of Alison's body, which was almost twenty-five years younger than her old body had been.

It might be tricky at first, but she had met all of Alison's few near relatives; and as for the surface friends who filled the aimless rounds of her sister-in-law's social life, Tessa knew they could be dropped without causing a ripple of curiosity. Especially if her life became filled with babies. That should please Richard.

Dear Richard! Tessa was surprised at the warmth of her feelings for her brother-in-law. She had always labeled her emotions as frustrated maternalism, for Richard had been a mere child when she and Clarence married.

Since then, somewhere along the line, maternalism seemed to have transmuted into something stronger. Wistful might-have-beens were now exciting possibilities.

Behind the heavy bronze and glass doors of Richard's building, a sleepy doorman nodded on his feet. The sun was not yet high enough to lighten the doorway under its pink and gray striped awning, and the deep shadows camouflaged her gray fur.

Keeping a low silhouette, she crouched beside the brass doors. As the doorman pushed it open for an early-rising tenant, she darted inside and streaked across the lobby to hide behind a large marble ash stand beside the elevator.

The rest would be simple as the elevator was large, dimly lit, and paneled in dark mahogany. She had but to conceal herself under one of the pink velvet benches which lined its sides and wait until it should stop at Alison's floor.

Her tail twitched with impatience. When the elevator finally descended, she poised ready to spring as the door slid back.

Bedlam broke loose in a welter of shrill barks, tangled leash and startled, angry exclamations. The dog was upon her, front and back yipping, and snapping before she knew what was happening.

Automatically, she spat and raked the dog's nose with her sharp claws, which set him into a frenzy of jumping and straining against the leash and sent his master sprawling.

Tessa only had time to recognize that it was Richard, taking Liebchen out for a pre-breakfast walk, before she felt herself being whacked by the elevator boy's newspaper.

All avenues of escape were closed to her and she was given no time to think, to gather her wits, before the street doors were flung open and she was harried out onto the sidewalk.

Angry and disgusted with herself and the dog, Tessa checked her headlong flight some yards down the sidewalk and glared back at the entrance of the building where Liebchen smugly waddled down the shallow steps and pulled Richard off in the opposite direction.

So the front is out, thought Tessa. *I wonder if their flank is so well-guarded?*

It pleased her to discover that those years of easy compliance with Clarence's wishes had not blunted her initiative. She could not be thwarted now by a Wiener schnitzel of a dog.

Halfway around the block, she located a driveway leading to the small courtyard which serviced the complex of apartment buildings. From the top of a rubbish barrel, she managed to spring to the first rung of a fire escape and scramble up.

As she climbed, the night's physical exertion began to make itself felt. Paw over paw, up and up, while every muscle begged for rest and her mind became a foggy treadmill able to hold only the single thought: paw in front of paw.

It seemed to take hours. Up thirteen steps to the landing, right turn; up thirteen steps to the landing, left turn, with such regular monotony that her mind became stupid with the endless repetition of black metal steps.

At the top landing, a ten-rung steel ladder rose straight to the roof. Her body responded sluggishly to this final effort and she sank down upon the tarred rooftop in utter exhaustion. The sun was high in the sky now; and with the last dregs of energy, Tessa crept into the shade of an overhanging ledge and was instantly asleep.

When she awoke in the late afternoon, the last rays of sunlight were slanting across the city. Hunger and thirst she could ignore for the time, but what of the quickening excitement which twilight was bringing?

She crept to the roof's edge and peered down at the empty terrace overlooking the park. An ivied trellis offered easy descent and she crouched behind a potted shrub to look through the doors. On such a mild day, the glass doors of the apartment had been left open behind their fine-meshed screens.

Inside, beyond the elegant living room, Alison's housekeeper set the table in the connecting dining room. There was no sign of Alison or Richard—or of Liebchen. Cautiously, Tessa pattered along the terrace to the screened doors of their bedroom, but it too was empty.

As she waited, darkness fell completely. From deep within, she felt the impatient tail-flick of awareness. She felt it respond to a cat's gutteral cry two rooftops away, felt it surfacing against her will, pulled by the promise of another night of dark paths and wild ecstasy.

Desperately, she struggled with that other ego, fought it blindly and knew that soon her strength would not be enough.

Suddenly the terrace was flooded with light as all the lamps inside the apartment were switched on. Startled, the other self retreated; and Tessa heard Alison's light voice tell the housekeeper, "Just leave dinner on the stove, Mitchum. You can clear away in the morning."

"Yes, Mrs. Loughlin, and I want you and Mr. Loughlin to know how sorry I was to hear about—"

"Thank you, Mitchum," came Richard's voice, cutting her off.

Tessa sat motionless in the shadows outside as Liebchen trotted across the room and scrambled onto a low chair, unmindful of a feline.

As Richard mixed drinks, Alison said, "The dreadful thing about all this is Tessa. Those delusions that she's really a young girl—that she'd never met Clarence—or either of us. Do you suppose she's clever enough to fake a mental breakdown?"

"Stop it, Alison! How can you have watched her wretchedness and think that she's pretending?"

"But, Richard—"

"What a shock it must have been to have Clarence ask for a divorce after all these years. Did you know about Clarence and Lynn?" His voice was harsh with emotion. "You introduced them. Did you encourage it?"

"Really, darling! You sound as if Tessa were the injured party." Alison's tone held scornful irony.

"Well, really, she is!" Richard cried. "If you could have seen her, Alison, when Clarence first married her—so fresh and open and full of laughter. I was just a child, but I remember. I'd never met an adult like her. I thought she was like an April breeze blowing through this family; but everyone else was appalled that Clarence had married someone so unsuitable. I remember her face when Clarence lectured her for laughing too loudly."

Richard gazed bleakly into his glass. "After Father died, it was years before I saw her again. I couldn't believe the change; all the laughter gone, her guarded words. Clarence did a thorough job of making her into a suitable wife. He killed her spirit and then complained that she was dull! No wonder she's retreated into her past, to a time before she knew him. You heard the psychiatrist. He said it often happens."

"Nevertheless," Alison said coolly, "you seem to forget that while Clarence may have killed her spirit, he's the one who is actually dead."

In the shadows outside the screen, Tessa quivered. So they had found Clarence's body! That poor thieving child! At the sight of Clarence lying on the bedroom floor with his head crushed in, she must have panicked again.

"I haven't forgotten," Richard said quietly, "and I haven't forgotten Lynn Herrick either. If what Clarence told me yesterday is true, she's in an awkward position. I suppose I should make some sort of arrangement for her out of Clarence's estate."

"Don't be naive, Richard," Alison laughed. "She merely let Clarence believe what he wanted. Lynn is far too clever to get caught without a wedding ring."

"Then Clarence's request for the divorce, his death, Tessa's insanity—all this was predicated on a lie? And you knew it? You *did!* I can see it in your face!"

"You're being unfair," Alison said. "I didn't encourage his affair with Lynn. I introduced them, yes; but if it hadn't been Lynn, it would have been someone else. Clarence wanted a change and he always took what he wanted."

As she spoke, Alison moved between the kitchen and living room, arranging their dinner on a low table in front of the couch. Liebchen put interested paws on the edge of the table, but Richard shoved him aside roughly.

"There's no need to take it out on Liebchen," she

said angrily. "Come along, baby, I have something nice for you in the kitchen."

On little short legs, the dachshund trotted after Alison and disappeared into the kitchen. Relieved, Tessa moved closer to the screen.

When Alison returned from the kitchen, her flash of anger had been replaced by a mask of solicitude. "Must you go out tonight, darling? Can't the lawyers wait until morning?"

She sat close to Richard on the couch and tried to interest him in food, but he pushed the plate away wearily.

"You know lawyers," he sighed. "Clarence's will can't be probated as written, so everything's complicated. There are papers to sign, technicalities to clear up."

"That's right," Alison said thoughtfully. "Murderers can't inherit from their victims, can they? Oh, Richard, don't pull away from me like that. I'm not being callous, darling. I feel just as badly about all this as you do, but we have to face the facts. Like it or not, Tessa did kill Clarence."

"Sorry," he said, standing up and reaching for his jacket. "I guess I just can't take it all in yet."

Alison remained on the couch with her back to him. As Richard took papers from his desk and put them in his briefcase, she said with careful casualness, "If they decide poor Tessa killed him in a fit of insanity and she later snaps out of it, would she then be able to inherit?"

"Probably not, legally," he said absently, his mind on sorting the papers. "Wouldn't matter though, since we'd give it back to her, of course."

"Oh, of course," Alison agreed brightly; but her eyes narrowed.

Richard leaned over the couch and kissed her

cheek. "I don't know how long this will take. If you're tired, don't bother to wait up."

"Good night, darling. Try not to be too late." She smiled at him as he left the apartment; but when the door had latched behind him, her smile clicked off to be replaced by a grim look of serious calculation.

Lost in thought, she gazed blindly at the dark square of the screened doorway and was unaware when Tessa slowly eased up on narrow haunches to let the lamplight hit her eyes—eyes that glowed with abnormal intensity . . .

It was after midnight before Richard's key turned in the lock. Lying awake on their wide bed, she heard him drop his briefcase on the desk and open the bedroom door to whisper, "Alison?"

"I'm awake, darling," she said throatily and switched on a lamp. "Oh, Richard you look so tired. Come to bed."

When at last he lay beside her in the darkness, she said shyly, "All evening I've been thinking about Tessa and Clarence—about their life together. I've been a rotten wife to you, Richard."

He made a sound of protest, but she placed slim young fingers against his lips. "No, darling, let me say it. I've been thinking how empty their marriage was and how ours would be the same if I didn't change. Richard, let's pretend we just met and that we know nothing about each other! Let's completely forget about everything that's happened before now and start anew. As soon as the funeral is over and we've settled Tessa in the best rest home we can find, let's go away together to the farm for a few weeks."

Incredulous, Richard propped himself on one elbow and peered into her face. "Do you really mean that?"

She nodded solemnly and he gathered her in his

arms, but before he could kiss her properly, the night was broken by an angry, hissing cry.

"What the devil is that?" Richard asked, sitting up in bed.

"Just a stray cat. It was on the terrace this evening and seemed hungry, so I gave it your dinner." With one shapely arm, she pulled Richard back down to her and then pitched her voice just loud enough to carry through the screen to the terrace. "If it's still there in the morning, I'll call the ASPCA and have them take it away."

THE THEFT OF THE MAFIA CAT

Edward D. Hoch

Nick Velvet had always harbored a soft spot for Paul Matalena, ever since they'd been kids together on the same block in the Italian section of Greenwich Village. He still vividly remembered the Saturday afternoon when a gang fight had broken out on Bleecker Street, and Paul had yanked him out of the path of a speeding police car with about one inch to spare. He liked to think that Paul had saved his life that day, and so, being something of a sentimentalist, Nick responded quickly to his old friend's call for help.

He met Paul in the most unlikely of places—the Shakespeare garden in Central Park, where someone many years ago had planned a floral gathering which was to include very species of flower mentioned in the works of the Bard. If the plan had never come to full blossom, it still produced a colorful setting, a backdrop for literary discussion.

" 'There's rosemary, that's for remembrance,' " Paul quoted as they strolled among the flowers and shrubs. " 'And there is pansies, that's for thoughts.' "

Nick, who could hardly be called a Shakespeare scholar, had come prepared. " 'A rose by any other name would smell as sweet,' " he countered.

"You've gotten educated since we were kids, Nick."

"I'm still pretty much the same. What can I do for you, Paul?"

"They tell me you're in business for yourself these days. Stealing things."

"Certain things. Those of no great value. You might call it a hobby."

"Hell, Nick, they say you're the best in the business. I been hearing about you for years now. At first I couldn't believe it was the same guy."

Nick shrugged. "Everyone has to earn a living somehow."

"But how did you ever get started in it?"

The beginning was something Nick rarely thought about, and it was something he'd never told another person. Now, strolling among the flowers with his boyhood friend, he said, "It was a woman, of course. She talked me into helping her with a robbery. We were going to break into the Institute for Medieval Studies over in New Jersey and steal some art treasures. I got a truck and helped her remove a stained-glass window so we could get into the building. While I was inside she drove off with the window. That was all she'd been after in the first place. It was worth something like $50,000 to collectors."

Paul Matalena gave a low whistle. "And you never got any of it?"

Nick smiled at the memory. "Not a cent. The girl was later arrested, and the window recovered, so perhaps it's just as well. But that got me thinking about the kind of objects people steal. I discovered there are things of little or no value that can be worth a great deal to certain people at certain times. By avoiding the usual cash and jewelry and paintings I'm able to concentrate on the odd, the unusual, the valueless."

"They say you get $20,000 a job, and $30,000 for an especially dangerous one."

Nick nodded. "My price has been the same for years. No inflation here."

"Would you do a job for me, Nick?"

"I'd have to charge you the usual rate, Paul."

"I understand. I wasn't asking for anything free."

"Some say you're a big man in the Mafia these days. Is that true?"

Matalena shot him a sideways glance. "Sure, it's true. I'm right up with the top boys. But we don't usually talk about it."

"Why not? I'm an Italian-American just like you, Paul, and I think it's wrong to act as if organized crime doesn't exist. What we should do is admit it, and then go on to stress the accomplishments of other Italian-Americans—men like Fiorello LaGuardia, John Volpe, and John Pastore in government, Joe DiMaggio in sports, and Gian Carlo Menotti in the arts."

"I stay out of policy matters, Nick. I've got me a nice laundry business that covers restaurants and private hospitals. Brings me in a nice fat income, all legit. In the beginning I had to lean on some of the customers, but when they found out I was Mafia they signed up fast. And no trouble with competition."

"You must be doing well if you can afford my price. What do you want stolen?"

"A cat."

"No problem. I once stole a tiger from a zoo."

"This cat might be tougher. It's Mike Pirrone's pet."

Nick whistled softly. Pirrone was a big man in the Syndicate—one of the biggest still under 50. He lived in a country mansion on the shore of a small New Jersey lake. Not many people visited Mike Pirrone. Not many people wanted to.

"The cat is on the grounds of his home?"

Matalena nodded. "You can't miss it. A big striped tabby named Sparkle. Pirrone is always being photographed with it. This is from a magazine."

He showed Nick a picture of Mike Pirrone standing with an older, white-haired man identified as his lawyer. The Mafia don was holding the big tabby in his arms, almost like a child. Nick grunted and put the picture in his pocket. "First time I ever saw Pirrone smiling."

"He loves that cat. He takes it with him everywhere."

"And you want to kidnap it and hold it for ransom?"

Matalena chuckled. "Nick, Nick, these wild ideas of yours! You haven't changed since schooldays."

"All right. It's not my concern, as long as your money's good."

"This much on account," Matalena said, slipping an envelope to Nick. "I need results by the weekend."

They strolled a bit longer among the flowers, talking of old times, then parted. Nick caught a taxi and headed downtown.

Mike Pirrone's mansion was a sprawling ranch located on a hill overlooking Stag Lake in northern New Jersey. It was a bit north of Stag Pond, in an area of the state that boasted towns with names like Sparta and Athens and Greece. It was fishing country, and the man at the gas station told Nick, "Good yellow perch in these lakes."

"Might try a little," Nick admitted. "Got my fishing gear in back. How's Stag Lake?"

"Mostly private. If you come ashore at the wrong spot it could mean trouble."

Nick thanked him and drove on, turning off the

main road to follow a rutted lane that ran along the edge of the Pirrone estate. The entire place was surrounded by a wall topped by three strands of electrified wire. As he passed the locked gates and peered inside, he saw the large sprawling house on its hill about two hundred feet back. The lake lay at the end of the road, and a chain-link fence ran from the end of the wall into the water. Mike Pirrone was taking no chances on uninvited guests.

Nick was studying the layout when a girl's voice spoke from very close behind him. "Thinking of doing some fishing?"

He turned and saw a willowy blonde in white shorts and a colorful print blouse standing by the back of his car. He hadn't heard her approach and he wondered how long she'd been watching him. "I might try for some yellow perch. I hear they're biting."

"It's mostly private property around here," she said. Her face was hard and tanned, with features that might have been Scandinavian and certainly weren't Italian.

"I noticed the wall. Who lives there—Howard Hughes?"

"A man named Mike Pirrone. You probably never heard of him."

"What business is he in?"

"Management."

"It must be profitable."

"It is."

"You know him?"

She smiled at Nick and said, "I'm his wife."

After his unexpected encounter with Mrs. Pirrone, Nick knew there was no chance for a direct approach to the house. He rented a boat in mid-afternoon and set off down the lake, trolling gently along the shoreline. No one was more surprised than Nick when he hooked a large fish almost at once. It could have been a yellow perch, but he wasn't sure. Fishing was not his sport.

The boat drifted down to a point opposite the Pirrone estate, and Nick checked the shoreline for guards. No one was visible, but through his binoculars he could see a group of wire cages near the main house. Since the cat Sparkle could be expected to sleep indoors, the cages seemed to indicate dogs—probably watchdogs that prowled the grounds after dark.

Working quickly, Nick filled his jacket pockets with fishhooks, lengths of nylon leader, and a folded and perforated plastic bag. A few other items were already carefully hidden on his person, but the binoculars and fishing pole would have to be abandoned. He used a small hand drill to bore a tiny hole in the bottom of the boat, then watched while the water began to seep in. He half stood up in the boat, giving an image of alarm to anyone who might have been watching, then threw the drill overboard and quickly headed the boat toward shore. In five minutes he was beached on the Pirrone estate; the boat was half full of water.

For a few minutes he stood by it as if pondering his next move. Then he looked up toward the house on the hill and started off for it, carrying his fish. Almost at once he heard the barking of dogs and suddenly two large German shepherds were racing toward him across the expanse of lawn. Nick broke into a run, heading for the nearest tree, but as the dogs seemed about to overtake him they stopped dead in their tracks.

Nick leaned against the tree, panting, and watched a white-haired man walking across the lawn toward him. It was the man in the picture—Pirrone's lawyer—and he held a shiny silver dog whistle in one hand.

"They're well trained," Nick said by way of greeting.

"That they are. You could be a dead man now, if I hadn't blown this whistle."

"My boat," Nick said, gesturing helplessly toward the water. "It sprang a leak. I wonder if I could use your phone?"

The man was well dressed, in the sporty style of the town and country gentleman. He eyed Nick up and down, then nodded. "There's a phone in the gardener's shed."

Nick had hoped to make it into the house, but he had no choice. As the lawyer led the way, Nick held up his fish and said, "They're really biting today."

The man grunted and said nothing more. He led Nick to a small shack where tools and fertilizer were stored and pointed to the telephone on the wall. Nick put down his fish and dialed information, seeking the number of a taxi company. He'd just got the operator when the fish by his foot gave a sudden lurch. He looked down to see a large striped tabby cat pulling at it with a furry paw.

"Sparkle," Nick whispered. "Here, Sparkle."

The cat lifted its head in response to the name. It seemed to be awaiting some further conversation. Nick bent to stroke it under the chin and saw the legs of a man in striped slacks and golf shoes. His eyes traveled upward to a broad firm chest and the familiar beetle-browed face above. It was Mike Pirrone, and he wasn't smiling. In his hand he held a snubnosed revolver pointed at Nick's face.

"To what do I owe this pleasure, Mr. Velvet?"

The house was fit for a don, or possibly a king, with a huge beamed living room that looked out over the lake. The furniture was expensive and tasteful, and Pirrone's blonde wife fitted the setting perfectly. She was much younger than her husband, but seeing them together one quickly forgot the difference in ages. Pirrone was approaching 50 gracefully, with a hint of youth that occasionally broke through the dignified menace of his stony face.

"He's the fisherman I told you about," Mrs. Pirrone said as they entered. Her eyes darted from Nick to her husband.

"Yes," Pirrone said softly. "It seems he was washed up on our shore, and I recognized him. His name is Nick Velvet."

"The famous thief?"

"None other."

Nick smiled. He still held the fish at the end of a line in one hand. "You have me at a disadvantage. I don't believe we've ever met."

"We met. A long time ago at a political dinner. I never forget a face, Velvet. It costs money to forget faces. Sometimes it costs lives. I'm Mike Pirrone, as you certainly know. This is my wife, Frieda, and my lawyer, Harry Beaman."

The white-haired man nodded in acknowledgment and Nick said deliberately, "I thought he was your dog trainer."

Mike Pirrone laughed softly and Beaman flushed. "He does have a way with the dogs," Pirrone said. "He's trained them well. But they only guard the place. I'm a cat fancier myself." As if to illustrate he bent and cupped his arms. Sparkle took a running leap and landed in them. "This cat goes everywhere I go."

"Beautiful animal," Nick murmured.

Pirrone continued to stroke the cat for a few moments, then put it down. "All right, Velvet," he said briskly. "What do you want here?"

"Merely to use the phone. My boat sprang a leak."

"You're no fisherman," Pirrone said, pronouncing the words like a final judgment.

"Here's my fish," Nick countered, holding it up; but the don was unimpressed.

"You scouted my place and you managed to get inside. What for?"

"Even a thief needs a vacation now and then."

"You don't take vacations, Velvet. I investigated you quite closely a few years back, when I almost hired you for a job. I know your habits and I know where you live. Who hired you, and why?"

"I didn't even know this was your place till I met your wife this morning."

"I heard you call my cat by name, out in the shed."

Nick hesitated. Mike Pirrone was no fool. "Everybody knows Sparkle. You're always photographed with him."

"Her. Sparkle is a her."

Harry Beaman cleared his throat. "What do you plan to do with him, Mike? If you try to hold him against his will it could be a serious legal matter. So far you've been within your rights to treat him as a trespasser, but that could change."

Pirrone threw up his hands. "Lawyers! Things were simple in the old days—right, Velvet?"

"I wouldn't know."

A maid appeared with cocktails and Pirrone waved his hand. "You're a guest here, Velvet. You arrived in time for the cocktail hour." He took a glass himself and went off to an adjoining study to make some phone calls. Nick wondered what Pirrone had in mind for him.

Frieda Pirrone rose from the sofa and came to sit by him. "You should have told me you wanted to meet my husband. I could have arranged it much more easily. Are you really a thief?"

"I steal women's hearts, among other things."

Her eyes met his for just an instant. "It would take a brave man—or an idiot—to steal anything from Mike Pirrone."

"I'm neither of those." He watched Sparkle move slowly across the carpet, stalking some imaginary prey.

"Just what sort of thief are you?"

"Sometimes I'm a cat burglar."

"Really? You mean one of those who climbs across rooftops?"

Before he could answer, Pirrone returned and handed his lawyer a sheaf of papers. "Business can be a bore at times, Velvet. I'm being a poor host."

"Perfectly all right. Your drinks are very good."

The dark-browed don nodded. "My chauffeur will be driving Harry to the train shortly. You're free to leave with them."

"Thank you."

"But one word of advice. If anything turns up missing from this house—now or later—I'll know just where to look. I'll send somebody for you, Velvet, and it'll be just like the old days. Understand?"

"I understand."

"Good! Whoever paid you, tell them the deal is off."

Nick nodded. He needed to be careful now. There would be no other chance to enter the Pirrone domain. Whatever the risk, he had to take Sparkle out of the house with him. He glanced at his watch. It was just after five. "Could I use your bathroom?"

Mike Pirrone nodded. "Go ahead. The maid will show you." Then, as Nick started to follow her, the don called out, "Taking your fish with you? Now I've seen everything!"

The maid waved him into a large tiled bathroom and departed. Nick checked his watch again. He had perhaps three minutes before they would grow suspicious. Quickly he crossed to the door and opened it. As he'd hoped, Sparkle had followed the trail of the fish and was hovering in the hall. With a bit of coaxing Nick had her in hand. He only hoped Pirrone wouldn't come looking for her right away.

Close up, Sparkle was a handsome feline, uniquely spotted and with a curious expression all her own. Perhaps that was why Pirrone liked her—because she was one of a kind. Nick held her firmly and injected a quick-acting sleeping drug. Sparkle gave one massive yawn and curled up on the floor. Then, working fast, he wrapped the disposable syringe in a tissue and put it in his pocket. He lifted Sparkle's limp body and slipped it into the perforated plastic bag.

Carrying the cat in one hand, Nick opened the bathroom door again and glanced down the hall toward the living room. No one was in sight. He crossed the hall quickly, entering a spare bedroom which he hoped was the room he sought. From the road he'd observed the telephone line running up the hill to the house and he thought it reached the wall just outside this room. Opening the window he saw that he'd been correct. The phone wire was just above his head, about a foot beyond the window.

He removed two fishhooks from his pocket and attached one to each end of a length of nylon leader. Reaching up he looped the fishing leader over the telephone wire and left it dangling there while he lifted the plastic-bagged cat. The fishhooks snagged two of the perforations in the bag and held it dangling beneath the telephone wire.

Nick tested it for weight, drew a deep prayerful breath, then gave the bag a shove. It began to slide slowly down the phone line, across the wide side yard, and finally over the wall to the telephone pole by the road. Near the pole the bag came to a stop, but by carefully tugging on his end of the wire Nick was able to propel it over the last few feet.

He sighed and closed the window. The whole operation had taken him four minutes—one minute more than he'd planned. He went back to the living room, still carrying his fish, and saw at once that Pirrone and Frieda and the lawyer were waiting for him. A large man in a chauffeur's uniform stood by the door.

Mike Pirrone smiled slightly and brought out the snubnosed revolver once more. "I hope you'll excuse the precaution, Velvet, but we don't want you leaving with anything that doesn't belong to you. Search him, Felix."

Nick raised his arms and the chauffeur ran quick firm hands over his body. After a few seconds he yanked one hand away; it was bleeding. "Damn! What's he got in there?"

"Fishhooks," Nick answered with the trace of a smile. "I should have warned you."

Felix cursed and finished the search. "He's clean, Mr. Pirrone."

"All right." The don put away his gun. "You can go now, Velvet."

"Thanks," Nick said, and started to follow the chauffeur and Beaman to the car.

He was halfway down the front walk when he heard Pirrone ask his wife, "Where's Sparkle?"

Nick kept walking steadily, glancing across the wall at the distant telephone pole and its hanging plastic bag. "I think she went outside," Frieda answered.

Suddenly Pirrone called, "Velvet! Hold it!"

Nick froze. The chauffeur, Felix, had turned toward the don, waiting for instructions. "What is it?" he asked as Pirrone came down the walk.

"That fish—let me have it. You could have hidden something small inside it. And if you didn't it'll make a nice supper for Sparkle."

Nick handed it over with feigned reluctance, then climbed into the car with Beaman. On the drive into town the white-haired lawyer tried to smooth things over. "You have to understand Mike. He's a real gentleman, with a heart of gold, but he lives in constant fear of rivals trying to take over what he's spent his life building."

"I assumed he had something to fear when I saw the gun," Nick said, nodding.

Beaman went on, "Frieda doesn't like it. She doesn't like anything connected with his old life, but Mike has to be careful."

"Of course."

Beaman dropped him at the marina and went on to the station. Shortly after dark Nick drove back to the Pirrone estate, climbed the telephone pole outside the wall, and removed the perforated plastic bag from the overhead wire. The cat was still sleeping peacefully. From inside the wall Nick could hear one of the servants calling for Sparkle.

Paul Matalena was overjoyed. "Nick, I never thought you could do it!" He stroked the cat on his lap and listened to it purr. "How in hell did you manage it?"

"I have my methods, Paul."

"Here's the rest of your money. And my thanks."

"You realize that Sparkle is a unique cat. She's been photographed with Pirrone a hundred times, and could hardly be mistaken for anyone else's pet. When people see it they'll know it's Pirrone's."

"That's exactly the idea, Nick."

"If you're planning to hold Sparkle for ransom you're playing with dynamite."

"It's nothing like that. In fact, I only want the cat for a meeting tomorrow afternoon. Then you can have her back. If Pirrone recovers his pet within a day, the whole thing shouldn't upset him too much."

"You mean you only want Sparkle for one day?"

"That's right, Nick." Matalena went to the phone and started making calls. The hour was late, but that didn't seem to bother him. Sparkle watched for a time, then ran over to Nick and rubbed against his leg. Suddenly, listening to Paul's words on the telephone, Nick knew why his old schoolmate was willing to pay $20,000 to have Sparkle for one day. He looked at Paul Matalena and chuckled.

"What's so funny, Nick?"

"Paul, you always were something of a phony, even back in school."

"What?"

Nick got to his feet and headed for the door. "Good luck to you."

The following evening, as Nick sat on his front porch drinking a beer, Gloria called to him. "Telephone for you, Nicky."

He went in, setting down his beer on the table near the phone. She grabbed it up at once and wiped away the damp ring. Grinning, he said, "You're acting more like a wife every day."

The voice on the phone was soft and feminine. "Nick Velvet?"

"Yes."

"This is Frieda Pirrone. My husband is on his way

to kill you. He thinks that somehow you stole Sparkle."

"Thanks for the warning."

"I don't want him to go back to killing, back to the way it used to be."

"Neither do I," Nick said. He hung up and turned to Gloria.

"Trouble, Nicky?"

"Just a little business problem." He bit his lip and pondered. "Look, Gloria, I've got a man coming over to see me. Why don't you go to a movie or something?"

"That was no man on the phone, Nicky."

"Come on," he grinned. "Ask no questions and I'll buy you that little foreign sports car you've been wanting."

"Will you, Nicky? You really mean it?"

"Sure I mean it."

When she'd gone he turned out all the lights in the house and sat down to wait. Just before ten o'clock a big black limousine pulled up and parked across the street. Nick had always considered his home to be forbidden territory, away from the dangers of his career; but this time it was different. Two men left the car and crossed the street to his house. One was the chauffeur, Felix. The other was a burly hood Nick didn't recognize. Mike Pirrone would be waiting in the car.

As they reached the porch Nick opened the door. Felix's hand dived into his pocket and the hood grabbed Nick, who didn't resist when they forced him back into the house. "I want to see Pirrone," Nick said.

"You'll see him." While the hood pinioned Nick, Felix went to the door and signaled across the street.

Mike Pirrone left the car and came slowly up the walk, studying the house and the tree-lined street.

"Nice little place you have here, Velvet."

"Good to see you again so soon."

"Did you think you wouldn't?" He stepped close to Nick. "Did you think I'd let you get away with Sparkle?"

"No. Not really."

"Where is she?"

"Right here—I'll get her."

"No tricks." Pirrone had drawn his gun again, and this time he looked as if he meant to use it.

"No tricks," Nick agreed. He stepped into the kitchen with Felix at his side and called, "Sparkle!"

The big striped tabby came running at the sound of her name, rubbed briefly against Nick's leg, then bounded into Pirrone's waiting arms. He put away the gun and stroked her fur while he carefully examined her.

"All right," he said quietly. "Sparkle is all right, so I'll let you live. But Felix and Vic here are going to teach you a little lesson about stealing from me."

"Wait!" Nick said, holding up his hand. "Can't we talk this over?"

"There's no need for talk. You were warned, Velvet."

"At least let me tell you a story first. It's about the man who hired me to steal Sparkle."

"Tell me. We'll want to pay him a visit, too."

Nick started to talk fast. "You might almost call this a detective story in reverse. Instead of discovering a guilty person, I found one who's innocent."

"What are you talking about, Velvet?" Pirrone's patience was wearing thin.

"The man who hired me, who shall be nameless, runs a highly profitable business in New York City. He was able to establish the business, and maintain it profitably for years, mainly by convincing both his customers and his competitors that he is an important member of the Mafia."

Mike Pirrone frowned. "You mean he isn't one?"

"Exactly," Nick said. "He is not a member of the Mafia, never has been. He's a simple hard-working guy who took advantage of his Italian name and the fact that many people are willing to believe that any Italian in business must be in the Mob. By fostering the idea that he had important Syndicate connections, he got a lot of business from people who were afraid to go elsewhere.

"But recently some of his customers began to have doubts. The word started circulating that he wasn't a big Mafia man at all. Faced with the loss of his best customers he decided to call a meeting to keep them in line. Ideally, he would have liked someone like Mike Pirrone with him at the meeting. But since he didn't even know Mike Pirrone he settled for the next best thing—Mike Pirrone's cat."

"What?" Pirrone's mouth hung open. "You mean he had the cat stolen so he could con people into thinking he was a friend of mine?"

Nick Velvet smiled. "That's right. It was worth my fee of $20,000 to keep his customers in line. He showed up at the meeting today with Sparkle in his arms. Naturally, in an audience like that, all of them knew the cat by sight—and they knew that Mike Pirrone couldn't be far away. It convinced them."

"Didn't he think I'd hear about something like that?"

"Possibly. But by that time you'd have Sparkle back safe and sound, and you'd probably be reluctant to admit the theft to anyone."

"Tell me this guy's name."

"So you can beat him up or kill him? Where's your

sense of humor? You have Sparkle back and the man has his customers back. No one's been harmed, and there's a certain humor in the situation. At a time when the Mafia is taking great pains to deny its existence, here is someone cashing in on the false story that he belongs to the Mafia. In fact, it was his open talking about it that made me suspicious in the first place. The real dons don't brag about it."

Felix shifted position. "What should I do, Mr. Pirrone?"

Pirrone studied Nick for a moment, then smiled slightly. "Let him go, Felix. You've got one hell of a nerve, Velvet—you and the guy who hired you." He started out of the house, but then paused by the door. "How did you do it? How did you get Sparkle out of my house?"

"Sorry. That's a trade secret. But I'll give you a tip about something else."

"What sort of tip?"

"Your watchdogs have been well trained by Harry Beaman."

Pirrone shrugged. "He likes them, I guess."

"He called them off me, and he could call them off his friends, too, if they happened to come visiting you late some night."

"I trust Harry," Pirrone said quickly, but his eyes were thoughtful.

"Think it over. You might live a few years longer."

Pirrone took a step forward and shook Nick's hand. "You've got a brain, Velvet. I could use someone like you in the organization."

Nick smiled and shook his head. "Organizations aren't for me. But remember me if you ever need anything stolen. Something odd or unusual"—Nick grinned—"or valueless."

THE OLD GRAY CAT

Joyce Harrington

"I should kill her. I should really kill her."

"Yeah, yeah. But how, how?"

"I could find a way. I bet I could."

"Oh, sure."

"You don't think I could? I could put poison in her cocoa."

"What kind of poison?"

"Ah, you know, arsenic. Something like that."

"Sure. You gonna go down to the store, say, 'Gimme a pound of arsenic, something like that.' Nobody's gonna ask what you want to do with it?"

"I could push her down the stairs. She'd die."

"Maybe not. She could break all her bones and still live. She'd say, 'Ellie pushed me down the stairs.' Then what?"

"She lies. Everybody knows she tells lies."

"Somebody would believe her. A thing like that, why would she lie?"

"Everybody knows she hates me. She steals my things. Remember the time I had that box of chocolate-covered cherries and she took a bite out of every one and put them all back in the box? Even you said she was the one."

"Probably she was. But everybody knows you hate her right back."

"You think I shouldn't kill her? You think I should just let her get away with this?"

"I didn't say that, did I? You want to kill her, go ahead. Only be smart. Don't get caught."

"I don't care if I get caught."

"You'll care. If you have to spend the rest of your life in jail, you'll care all right."

"Is this better than a jail? Listen, if I get caught I'll play crazy. You think I can't play crazy? Watch this."

Ellie crossed her eyes, let her tongue loll out of her mouth, and waggled her head. "Glah-glah-glah," she said.

"Nobody would believe that for a minute. You need some lessons in playing crazy."

"That's funny. You know, you're really funny. Ha, ha, see how I'm laughing? You don't think I'm crazy enough. I suppose you think you're crazier than I am?"

"The whole world is crazy. Just act normal. Then everybody'll think you're crazy."

"Margo, you're my best friend. But you're wrong. Anyway, if I really do kill her, which maybe I won't, but if I do, nobody will know I did it. Not even you."

"Will you tell me?"

"I guess so. Maybe. I could put a deadly snake in her bed. I read that in a book once."

"Where would you get a deadly snake?"

"That's a problem."

A bell rang. The door banged open and Miss Swiss marched into the room.

"Lunchtime, girls," she announced. Her voice was brassy and her hair was the color of tarnished trumpets, stiff and shiny with hair spray. She wore a pink ruffled pinafore over a green nylon dress. The ruffles flapped over her bulging frontage lending a quivering vitality to the corseted flesh beneath.

"Put your games away," she blared. "Books and magazines back on the shelf. Let's keep this room tidy, girls." Her eyes swept the room like twin beacons, flashing malice.

Ellie picked up a fistful of marbles from the Chinese checkerboard that lay on the table between them. She aimed at the back of Miss Swiss's metallic coiffure. Margo grabbed her arm across the table.

"Don't be stupid," she whispered.

Miss Swiss turned. "Fighting again, girls? Margo, I'm surprised at you. Ellie, you've been warned before. I'll have to report you to the Director. No dessert for either one of you." She smiled widely, showing gold inlays. "It's apple brown Betty today."

"Damn your apple brown Betty!" Ellie shouted, throwing marbles onto the worn wine-colored carpet. "And damn you, you fat elephant!"

"Shut up, you dummy," Margo whispered more urgently.

"Language, Ellie. Shocking," said Miss Swiss with an even more complacent smile. "The Director will be terribly disappointed. Margo, leave the room. Ellie will stay and pick up all those marbles. She will get no lunch at all. She will go to her room and stay there until I tell her she may come out. After lunch there will be a movie. I believe it is a film about Hawaii. Move along, girls."

Margo joined the drift of others toward the door of the recreation room. The smell of over-baked fish and boiled potatoes crept in at the door as the group of 20 or so trickled out. In the doorway Margo turned and mouthed silently at Ellie, "I'll bring you some food later."

Ellie shook her head and blinked back tears. Suddenly she felt hungry. The food was usually tasteless but now that it was being withheld, she felt a gnawing in her stomach that could only be assuaged by large helpings of hot food.

"I'm hungry," she whined.

"You should have thought of that before," snapped Miss Swiss, no longer smiling. "Pick up those marbles."

Ellie hunkered down on her heels, her thin legs disappearing into the folds of her wrinkled cotton skirt. She dropped her head onto her bony knees and folded her arms over both.

"I'm really going to kill you," she muttered into the flower-printed fabric.

"What was that?" demanded Miss Swiss. And, "What did you say?" when she got no answer. "Look at me!"

Ellie said nothing and did not raise her head. She remained folded into an unresponsive mound on the floor.

Miss Swiss reached down and prodded Ellie's shoulder with a sharp forefinger. Her nails were filed into curving talons and were painted a frosted pink.

"Pick. Up. Those. Marbles." said Miss Swiss, forming each word as if it were a stone falling from her lips onto Ellie's head.

Ellie grunted and toppled over. She lay on the floor, amid the brightly colored marbles, gazing up with hatred at Miss Swiss.

"Where's the cat?" she said.

"What cat?" Miss Swiss stepped back, looking surprised. "You know we don't allow cats in here. Or dogs, for that matter."

"My old gray cat. That's what cat. The one that came to my room." Ellie knew that Miss Swiss was only pretending to be surprised. She knew Miss Swiss was somehow responsible for the non-appearance of the rangy gray tomcat who had the habit of leaping onto Ellie's window sill and wolfing down whatever tidbit she had left for him there, favoring her with a wicked leer and departing with an arrogant flirt of his crooked tail. All summer long the cat had appeared with the first morning light while Ellie lay sleepless, with no reason to get up and no company but her hatred for Miss Swiss.

"If you've had a cat in your room, you've been breaking the rule. I don't know what we're going to do with you, Ellie. You're a very disruptive influence on the other girls. Do you think I like to be always punishing you? Wouldn't you like to be friends?"

"What did you do to him? Did you poison him? Or did you send him to the A.S.P.C.A.? They put cats in gas chambers there. Did you know that? I'd like to put you in a gas chamber."

Ellie felt tears rising again and rolled over to hide her face from Miss Swiss's inquisitory stare. She felt a marble under her hip and concentrated on that small pain to keep the tears in check.

"Ellie, Ellie," said Miss Swiss, her voice wheedling now, placatory. "That's a terrible thing to say. But I won't hold it against you. I won't even report it to the Director. But you've really got to get up now and pick up those marbles. I'll help you. And then later on, when I take my break, you can come and have cocoa in my room and we'll talk about this cat."

Ellie sat up. So, she thought, she does know about the cat. She can't fool me. She's trying to get around me so I won't kill her. Fat chance, the fat slob. Ellie picked up a red marble and then a yellow one. Miss Swiss was on her hands and knees, her green rump in the air, gathering marbles.

"Maybe I can even save you some apple brown Betty," she said.

"With whipped cream," said Ellie. "I like whipped cream."

"We'll see," said Miss Swiss.

Ellie made a rude gesture toward Miss Swiss's backside . . .

Ellie waited in her room for Miss Swiss's summons. It wasn't much of a room, but as Miss Swiss often reminded her, it was one of the best in the house. It had a window that looked out over the little park across the street. The leaves were falling now from the spindly trees that dotted the shriveled grass, and a gusty wind blew the leaves in erratic spirals between the benches.

Ellie lay on her bed and let her mind drift. Her pillow smelled musty and the smell evoked a memory, not of an event, but of a life lived in a house where a dark closet under a staircase smelled just that way and fetching galoshes on a rainy day was an occasion for terror. But the tall woman with the soft brown hair and the long strong hands were there to dispel morbid fancies with raisin cookies, a song, and the certainty of love.

"Ma. Oh, Ma," Ellie sighed.

Ellie had no memory of the death of her mother; she had been too young. There was only the unbearable absence, the loss of love, the vacancy that could never be filled no matter how hard she tried. And she had tried.

The cat had been her latest attempt. Too well she realized that the cat's attachment to her had been cupboard love. His first visit had coincided with half a tuna sandwich smuggled into her room from the regular Sunday evening cold supper. She had wrapped it in a paper napkin and placed it on the window sill to eat later before she went to bed. But a quarrel over the television set had brought a scolding from Miss

Swiss, and Ellie had gone to bed spurting wrathful tears. The tuna sandwich had been forgotten.

A rustling had awakened her to a gray dawn and a gray shape on the window sill. The cat, sensing her movement, had looked up from his feast and hissed a warning at her. Then he had resumed his marauding, ignoring her as the sandwich disappeared and the napkin fell, limp and shredded, from his claws.

From her bed, Ellie had watched the cat's thin sides heave in and out as he chomped voraciously. She'd heard a sound, not quite a purr, yet not a growl, as the cat broadcast his ownership of the food. As the light gradually increased, she saw his tattered ear, his patchy fur, a scab, a clouded eye. He's like me, she thought. Alone and hungry. He left abruptly, not stopping to preen as house cats do after eating.

After that she always left something on the window sill. And always the cat came in the still hour of dawn. After a few visits he permitted Ellie to approach the window, each time a little closer until, by midsummer, he presented his scruffy head to be scratched. Ellie scratched diligently. She fondled his torn ear and passed her fingers gently over the milky eye. The first time she did that, the cat moved swiftly, clamping her hand between sharp yellow teeth.

Ellie was startled, but she didn't flinch. The cat held on for a minute. Two minutes. Ellie stood very still, sweating in her thin nightgown. Then the cat released her hand and nuzzled it with his damp, scarred nose. It was as close as they ever became to each other. The cat would not permit himself to be picked up. Ellie never thought of a name for him. He was just "the old gray cat."

Ellie told no one about the cat. No one but Margo. After her transistor radio disappeared, Ellie had to talk to someone.

"Bet I know who took it," said Margo.

"You think she did? Ooh, I could kill her!"

"She took my Snoopy dog away, didn't she? Said I was too old for baby toys. I bet she has a closet full of stuff she's taken away from people here. She's bad news."

"Well," said Ellie proudly, "I've got something she can't take away from me." And she told Margo about the visits of the cat in the early morning.

"Of course," she added, "he's ugly as sin, and probably dirty and diseased. Nobody would want him but me, and she couldn't keep *him* in any closet. He'd scratch her eyes out." Ellie giggled. "Serve her right," she said.

"Be careful," Margo had warned her. "Don't let her find out. She'll figure out some way to spoil it for you. She's a genius that way."

Ellie had been careful. But somehow Miss Swiss had found out. The cat had been absent for over a week now. Almost ten days. At first she told herself that a tomcat might have gotten into a fight and gone away to heal himself. She waited and watched every morning, wishing he might feel safe enough with her to come and have his injuries tended. Then she thought he might have been hit by a car. She envisioned him lying stiff and bedraggled in a filthy gutter somewhere in the city. But that didn't feel right to her. The cat was too wary, too wise, to be the victim of an accident.

No, she decided, the cat had been intercepted on one of his morning visits. The cat had been on his way to her and had been trapped because of his faithfulness. Trapped and killed, and who would have been mean enough, ruthless enough, cruel enough to do such a thing? Only Miss Swiss.

Ellie rummaged in her bureau drawer and failing to

find her embroidery scissors remembered she had loaned them to Margo. She crept out of her room and down the hall to Margo's room. Everyone was at the movie. Hawaii! All hula dancers and pineapples and surfing. As if any of them could ever hope to go there.

Margo's room was dark, even in the middle of the day, and it smelled bad. Margo wasn't very clean. And her window looked out on an alley where the garbage cans were kept. She found her scissors lying on the floor where Margo had been cutting up magazine pictures for a decoupage project. The floor was littered with scraps of paper and there were dollops of dried glue on the rug. Ellie hurried back to her own room, the embroidery scissors safe in her pocket.

Back in her room, she cast about for some other weapon against Miss Swiss. The embroidery scissors was sharply pointed, but short-bladed. Miss Swiss was thickly clothed in fat. The short blades might not be equal to the task. But search as she might, there was no other possibility in her room; no pills, potions, or powders. Certainly not a knife, and Ellie had never seen a real gun. She considered wrenching one of the iron railings from the foot of her bedstead, but knew without trying that she lacked the strength. Maybe there would be something lying about Miss Swiss's room, some innocuous object that she could use if the right moment came.

If the moment came. But it probably would not come. Ellie would drink cocoa in Miss Swiss's room and listen to the lecture that would accompany it. She would nod and smile and promise to be good, all the while thinking deadly thoughts at the pink and falsely smiling Miss Swiss. But thoughts, however deadly, couldn't kill. Ellie's hand groped in the folds of her skirt, pressing the hard sharp outline of the small scissors against her thigh.

There was no knock at the door. Miss Swiss never knocked. The doorknob turned and the door opened just wide enough to admit the stiff curls and the painted smirk.

"Come along now, Ellie. The cocoa's ready and that movie's good for another half hour. At least we'll have some privacy for our chat."

"Coming, Miss Swiss."

With her hand still pressing the scissors against her thigh, Ellie followed the fluttering pink pinafore down the hall. Miss Swiss had, undoubtedly, the best room in the house, if you discounted the Director's office on the second floor which was paneled in glowing rosewood and draped in burgundy velvet. But the Director didn't live on the premises and Miss Swiss did.

Miss Swiss opened the massive door and ushered Ellie into her sanctum.

"Take the rocking chair, Ellie, dear. Pull it right up to the table. I'll pour the cocoa. There's the dessert I saved for you. *And* a bowl of whipped cream. We can have some in our cocoa, too. Although I really shouldn't, should I? Not with my weight problem."

While Miss Swiss babbled on, Ellie glanced round the room appraisingly. There were china animals everywhere. Quaint mice were pursued by cunning cats who were chased in turn by winsome dogs across the top of a bookcase. A pyramid of owls perched wisely in a whatnot by the window. Beasts of prey were restricted to a bureau where lions, leopards, and bears indiscriminately stalked each other across a long lace doily. A barnyard group browsed placidly atop a console television set. Ellie sneered inwardly at Miss Swiss's execrable taste, while envying both her freedom and her privacy to indulge her whims.

"I see you're admiring my menagerie. I've been collecting them for years. I just love animals, don't you?"

"No," said Ellie, and shifted her gaze to the fireplace. More animals paraded across the mantel: elephants, deer, and a particularly ugly version of a camel complete with howdah.

"No? But I thought that was why we're here. Something about a cat. Help yourself to cream, dear."

Ellie did, and spooned dessert in her mouth before answering. "One cat," she said, while taking careful note of the brass andirons and the iron poker that stood beside the firescreen.

"Well? What about this cat? You know we can't allow you girls to keep animals."

"I wasn't keeping him. Nobody could keep him. He came to visit. He was my friend, and now you've gone and done something to him." Ellie continued spooning up cream and chunks of apple.

Miss Swiss sipped cocoa and licked chocolate foam from her plump pink lips. "But I never saw this cat, Ellie, dear. If I had, I could not have allowed you to continue having him in your room. I would have spoken to you about it. Fair is fair."

"Fair is fair," mocked Ellie. "You killed him, didn't you?" She finished her dessert and stuck her finger into the remaining cream in the bowl.

"Ellie," chided Miss Swiss, "don't eat with your fingers. Use a spoon. I most certainly did not kill your cat. I love animals. I understand how you feel. Suppose I give you one of these?"

She set down her cocoa mug and walked across to the bookcase.

"Now, which one shall it be? A Siamese? Or would you like to have this dear little fluffy white kitten? I can't give you the tabby. She's my absolute out-and-out favorite, given to me by a girl who left us seven years ago. But any of the others. You may take your pick."

While Miss Swiss stood fondling each china cat in turn, Ellie took a final swipe at the bowl of cream and noiselessly left the rocking chair. She felt that the moment had come. If she didn't do it now, she never would. And after all her talk to Margo, she felt obliged to carry out her intentions. She sidled closer to the fireplace. And closer.

Miss Swiss continued to hover lovingly over the glossy representations of cat antics. "Now here's a cutie. I call him my Manx cat because his tail broke off, but he looks so lifelike playing with his tiny ball of yarn."

Ellie picked up the poker. It dragged at her arm and she wondered if she would have the strength to raise it. Her heart pounded and her head felt as if it would float off her shoulders with excitement. She felt an odd drawing together in her stomach almost as though all her vital organs were gathering themselves for one enormous effort. With both hands she raised the poker over her head. Her feet started traveling across the braided rug.

Miss Swiss looked over her shoulder and screamed. The poker flew from Ellie's hands. Miss Swiss stepped to one side, quickly for a woman of her size and weight. The ruffles on her pinafore fluttered wildly and her normally pink face turned the color of used chewing gum. The poker smashed into the bookcase and devastated the prim line of smirking cats.

Ellie's hand fumbled in the folds of her skirt, but before she could find her pocket her knees buckled and she fell to the floor with a thump. She fought for breath and fought the pain that scuttled like a trapped animal through her body. She gritted her teeth and closed her eyes. Her hand found its way into her pocket and she clutched the cold steel scissors.

"My cat," she gasped. "I'll kill you for that."

And she died. Ellie died.

Miss Swiss had seen death before. She recognized its awful presence on Ellie's face, bluish now and set forever in a snarl. But never had she come so close to death herself. If she hadn't moved quickly, she might have been lying on the rug beside Ellie with her head smashed in. Shakily she tiptoed around the pitiful corpse and opened the heavy door.

In the hall wondering eyes stared at her.

"We heard a noise," said Margo. "Anyway, the movie's over. It wasn't any good."

"Ellie has suffered a collapse," said Miss Swiss in answer to their unspoken question. "I shall have to call the doctor and the Director. And that son of hers."

"Is she dead?" asked Margo.

"She is," said Miss Swiss softly, and then resuming her trumpet-like tone, "Go to your rooms, girls. This is no time to be wandering about."

Gray and white heads nodded and carpet-slippered feet shuffled away. There were a few disheartened whispers, but for the most part there was silence as each old woman reflected on the nearness of her own inescapable end.

Only Margo remained.

"Miss Swiss," she said. "May I have Ellie's room? I know this may not be the right time to ask, but it is a much nicer room than mine, and if I wait someone else might get it. So may I, please?"

"Yes, yes," said Miss Swiss. "Margo, you were her friend. Do you know why . . .? No, never mind. Go along now."

Margo lurched down the hall, scarcely needing to

lean on the cane that was never out of her hand these days. In her room she began hauling things out of her bureau drawers and piling them on her bed in preparation for moving into Ellie's room: flannel nightgowns, warm winter underwear, a transistor radio. Too bad about Ellie, she thought, but if she hadn't died she would have got herself tossed out one of these days.

When she came to the closet, she paused. The smell was getting rather bad. She groped on the floor of the closet and came up with a plastic bag. The bag sagged heavily and Margo handled it gingerly, holding it away from her body with stiff fingertips.

It had been so easy to lure the cat onto her own window sill. All it took was a morsel of greasy hamburger. So easy to pretend insomnia and get a sleeping capsule from Miss Swiss. One capsule taken apart and its contents mixed with the meat. The cat, disarmed by Ellie's kindness, had allowed Margo to come close. One swift blow with her cane, and then pop into the plastic bag. Margo never knew whether the cat had died from the capsule or from a crushed skull. Or whether he had suffocated inside the plastic bag. Maybe all three.

But now she had no further use for him. Ellie was dead, too. If Ellie hadn't died this afternoon, or at least provoked Miss Swiss into having her removed, Margo had one final scheme in mind. Early tomorrow morning she would have placed the dead cat on Ellie's window sill. That would surely have done the trick. Ellie would have gone on a rampage and they would have had to get rid of her. But none of that was necessary now.

Margo carried the reeking plastic bag to the open window and dropped it into a lidless garbage can below. Then she cheerfully set about removing her clothes from the closet.

It had been worth it. The best room in the house was now hers. Next to Miss Swiss's, of course.

THE HIGHWAYMAN'S HOSTAGE

A Story of the Detector's Cat (as told by James Boswell)

Lillian de la Torre

A golden harvest moon was rising that evening when I donned my bloom-coloured breeches and my gold-laced three-cornered hat and set forth to pay my devoirs to my philosophical friend. Dr. Sam: Johnson, detector of crime and chicane, at his lodgings in Waterfield Square. There I found Frank, his dark domestick, lounging by the doorpost.

"Is Dr. Johnson within?" said I. Frank was looking sour. "He is, sir. You will find him in the kitchen," (wryly adding) "opening oysters." Curious to see the great philosopher at such a labour of Hercules, thither I hastened. There I found him, sure enough, hunkered down on his massive hams, opening oysters with a rusty knife.

As fast as he released a bivalve, he offered it to a large tiger-striped grey tomcat, whose little pink mouth quickly made away with it. There sat the tom-cat, erect as a grenadier, accepting his meed of oysters with stately condescension.

"That's a fine cat, sir," I remarked. "Oh," said Dr.

Johnson carelessly, "I have had much finer cats than this one." Then, as if perceiving that the creature was put about by so cavalier a dismissal, he added hastily, "But Hodge is a fine cat, Hodge is a very fine cat."

He regarded his pet with that smile of benevolence that always softened the harsh lines of his rugged face, with its scars of the king's evil, and let the warm good will of the sage shine through, drawing to him man and cat alike.

Rising from among his oyster shells, with his own grave stately courtesy, he made me welcome.

"You come in good time, Bozzy. Do but stay and take a dish of tea with me and I will make you acquainted with the prettiest young lady in London."

"With all my heart, sir. How comes it that you have acquired so valuable an acquaintance?"

"Easily. You must know, sir, that my humble lodgings lie jig-by-jowl with the town house of his Majesty's judge. My Lord Stanfield."

"Stanfield, eh?" said I. "It is all the talk among the benchers that within the week Stanfield will have Natty Jack in the dock and must sentence him to the gallows."

"A notorious highwayman!" said Dr. Johnson. "Stanfield will not spare him." "Speaking of Stanfield," said I, "here he comes now."

I had glimpsed the judge's party approaching. To a frequenter of the criminal courts, the judge's hawk's profile was unmistakeable, and his women-folk proved their quality by their fashionable attire. Hastily polishing up at the scullery tap, we soon were making them welcome in the above-stairs withdrawing room.

Dr. Johnson had not exaggerated. Miss Bess was the daintiest little porcelain figurine it had been my good fortune to encounter in many a year. Long black lashes shadowed a pair of melting violet eyes. And little white teeth smiled from the shapely red mouth like snow-flakes in the heart of a rose. She bore in the crook of her arm a little creature as dainty as herself, a snow-white cat, with sea-blue eyes, which she set down at her feet, saying, "I present my friend, Powder Puff."

"Bess!" said Lady Stanfield sharply, glaring at Hodge. "Take up Powder Puff, we are among rakes!"

Across the room, Hodge had stiffened to attention, his green eyes intent upon Powder Puff. Powder Puff simpered and returned his gaze.

As I eyed Miss Bess, I felt a fellow feeling for the grey tomcat. With a cat's uncanny instinct for recognizing an unfriend to cats, Hodge now asserted himself.

He suddenly ascended my Lady's French silk stocking, planted himself on her purple-velvet lap, and fell to "kneading biscuits" with his sharp little claws on her fashionable knee. My Lady screamed and cast him from her, and the tea party broke up in confusion.

I watched them depart, my Lord handing Lady Jean, Miss Bess carrying Powder Puff.

The last I saw of the little cortege, passing homewards along the square, was the long grey tail, erect as a lance of Hodge, escorting his new lady friend home.

Peace descended on Waterfield Square.

But not for long.

"Great heavens!" I cried suddenly. "What is that? A banshee?" "What, Bozzy," smiled Dr. Johnson, "have you never an amorous tomcat at Auchinleck?" "Yes, sir," I replied with a conscious grin, "but I don't yowl like that."

"Sir, it is no laughing matter," replied my moral mentor. "No, sir," I replied meekly. The yowling was broken off suddenly by a yip of pain. A moment later a frantic clawing shook the kitchen door, and Dr. Johnson hastened to open up. In shot Hodge, hackles bristling, tail distended, and flattened himself among the oyster shells under the kitchen table. A figure of wrath followed close upon him—the judge, brandishing his silver-shod staff in fury.

"Pray be seated, my Lord," said Dr. Johnson easily. "You honour my domestick offices with an informal visit. You will find the fireside settle not too uncomfortable." "Humph, that disturber of the peace is yours?" the judge countered, jerking his staff at Hodge, who flattened his ears and shewed his teeth.

"Yes, sir, what then?"

"Then I desire you'll keep him at home and away from my daughter's lap-cat Powder Puff. He is making night hideous with his caterwaulering."

"I grant you that Hodge is no Italian soprano," said Dr. Johnson, "but consider, my Lord, the same passions inflame the hearts of beast and man. Hodge here is protesting his attachment to his fair inamorata in his own way, as it were in Shakespeare's own immortal words, 'Shall I compare thee to a summer's day?' "

"Twaddle!" snapped the judge. "Sir," said Johnson sternly, "the words of immortal Shakespeare are not twaddle." "Hodge's protestations are becoming a publick nuisance," snapped Judge Stanfield, "and I demand that they be put an end to." "They shall be so, my Lord," said my friend.

The episode ended with mutual courtesies and Hodge, deprived of his oyster, moping under the kitchen table.

Calling in Waterfield Square the next morning, I was shocked to receive bad news. Miss Bess had been stolen away out of her bed by ill-intentioned persons!

They had taken her up in her blanket, together with Powder Puff, who slept in her arms. The town was abuzz with the news, and it soon transpired that the kidnappers were Natty Jack's robber crew.

I saw aghast the paper they had pinned to the judge's door:

> BLOODY STANFIELD
>
> If Natty Jack hangs, so will Miss Bess. Wee got her hid safe whare you ull never find her til shee is a swinging.
>
> "BANDY-LEGGED BART"

"Natty Jack's second-in-command, another dangerous scoundrel," commented Dr. Johnson. "The Bow Street men, have searched in vain every evil den in their vicinity. Miss Bess must be found and fast. Come, Boswell, we must hasten to the judge to offer our services."

We were admitted by the liveried butler with his long face even longer than ever.

In the withdrawing room, we found the judge and his Lady in anguished consultation. "If you condemn Natty Jack," milady was sobbing out, "then you condemn your own daughter!" "God help me," groaned my Lord, "I can do no otherwise." "Alack, what are we to do?" cried Lady Jean.

"Be patient, milady, the law will protect her," I said in a vain attempt to console. "How can they protect her," said milady angrily, "when they can not even find her?"

"I'll send to Auchinleck for the cleverest couple of hounds on the estate and we will soon have her back," I cried. "Good of you, Boswell," said the judge without hope.

"She shall be found, milady, I pledge you my word

on it," said Dr. Johnson. "Come, Boswell, there is no time to lose." He made a leg and we betook ourselves homeward. There we found Hodge still moping under the table.

Instructed by fast courier, my factor sent the dogs up by waggon—Flasher and Dasher, my smartest couple. The cart rattled up to Dr. Johnson's door as the sun was setting.

"Huzzah!" I cried. "The hounds are here."

"Hounds!" snorted Dr. Johnson. "What use are hounds?"

"You shall see, sir," I replied. "I'll fetch them from the cart." I opened the door. In a flash, Hodge was out and away.

"So," smiled Dr. Johnson, "the feline gets the start of the canine."

"Not by much," I smiled back, seizing my pair's sturdy leathern lead and steering a course for the mansion next door.

My heart was wrung as the judge put into my hand the tiny red-satin slipper. So small to be in such peril! Flasher and Dasher took in the new scent.

They barked all around the square, and then fell to yapping on the judge's doorstep. An irate householder across the square thrust his head out at window, bawling: "Be off or I'll call the watch!"

Flasher and Dasher pulled me hither and thither about the square wherever the little red shoes had trod. They caught a scent that interested them. With a jerk that set me on my breech, they were off Hell-for-leather. Loose cobble and brickbats told their tale on my posterior as my involuntary steeds dragged me wildly down to the foot of Water Lane Hill. They had treed a cat.

Unfortunately for us, the cat was Hodge. Before the skirmish was over, he had wounded Dasher's nose, ripped out Flasher's ear, and landed with all four feet, claws unsheathed, on my best gold-laced hat.

Over the hysterical yelping of the dogs, from somewhere above our heads rang out Hodge's song of victory. The love-notes of a courting cat ascended to the harvest moon.

A bulky shape crossed my vision. Twas Dr. Sam: Johnson, and he took up a stand under the back wall of a disreputable-looking tumbled-down house of resort. I picked myself up and hastened to his side.

"Mr. Boswell, can you climb?"

I considered the house wall above me. "Yes, sir, I can. You observe the window embrasures are like a flight of stairs. I can climb them."

"Are you armed?" "I wear a sword." "Then climb. There is a rushlight burning in the topmost chamber. The sash-window is open a crack. Slip through, draw your sword, and stand guard over the sleeper."

I began to climb, feeling like a knight of old saving a princess in a tower. The ground looked alarmingly far below me. I hastily adverted my gaze, to where I caught sight of a dusky shape legging it across the square in the moonlight.

Above my head, Hodge's victory song soared. There he sat on the window ledge, peering intently through the pane. Fending off Hodge, I eased open the window and slipped through. There she lay asleep, on her rude pallet. She wore a shift of sheer French gauze embroidered with strawberries, not redder than the tight little crimson rosebuds that tipped her white bosom. So precious was my charge! I drew my sword and took up my post beside the chamber door.

From the attick descended a bandy-legged man. He carried a dagger. With a lunge, I shewed him the bare steel of my rapier edge, and put him to flight. At the stair foot, a door burst open and I heard the feet of the Bow Street men. Then pandemonium erupted—curses and the sound of blows. I started down the stair, sword in hand, just as the constables had the villains laid by the heels.

A burly Bow Street man—no, it was Dr. Sam: Johnson—emerged from the chamber carrying the girl and Powder Puff in his arms.

At the foot of the stair, Dr. Johnson eased himself and his burden into the curve of the entry-way sofa, supporting the slight form against his sturdy shoulder. Miss Bess opened wide violet eyes upon her rescuer.

"Oh, Dr. Johnson," she breathed, "they kept moving us, Powder Puff and me—for I never let loose my hold on Powder Puff—they kept moving us from hiding place to hiding place." "Where?" Dr. Johnson asked. "I know not, sir," she replied. "They kept me under. I think they gave me a sleepy draft. In all of London, how did you ever find us?"

"Why, my dear," said the great detector, "it was Hodge who found you. Once a tomcat has his lady's perfume stuck fast in his nostrils, you may depend upon it, love will found out the way." "How true," said I.

"Thus it fell out, my dear," went on Dr. Johnson, "that Hodge found out Powder Puff, and by his song told me where she was. Thus it fell out that Mr. Boswell mounted the wall to where you were and guarded you at sword's point."

"Dear Mr. Boswell," breathed Miss Bess tenderly.

"And," concluded Dr. Johnson, "when my messenger had informed the Bow Street men, they did the rest."

"Hodge is a good cat," said Miss Bess, reaching down and caressing the velvet ears.

"Hodge is a very good cat," said Dr. Johnson. "He shall hereinafter be known as the 'Detector Cat.' We'll have a neat sign set up in the square curiously lettered: 'Johnson and Hodge, Detectors.' "

"And what about me?" I asked.

"So, Mr. Boswell, you would join the firm—in what capacity?"

"Write it thus: 'J. Boswell, Rapparee.' "

"Pray, Dr. Johnson, you are our lexicographer. What is a rapparee?" asked Miss Bess.

"A bully-huff, who wields a rapier."

"And how valiantly," exclaimed Miss Bess, clasping her hands, and regarding me much as Powder Puff was regarding Hodge.

I took out my tablets and, at Natty Jack's fireside escritoire, I sketched in the new sign.

I thought it looked well—so well that I resolved to affix it to the kitchen door as soon as sunrise gave light for the operation.

I created the new sign on a shingle with fireplace charcoal. Hodge, inquisitive like every cat, supervised my proceeding. When I nailed the shingle above the kitchen door, the unwanted din brought Dr. Johnson down in his shirtsleeves to see what was toward.

We were drinking our breakfast tea at the kitchen table, and Hodge was lapping his milk under it, when a thunderous rapping at the kitchen door broke the morning calm.

I hastened to open the door. Instantly Hodge scooted under the table.

It was our neighbour the judge, in slippers and purple brocaded morning gown. He carried a large covered basket. Seating himself on the kitchen doorstep, uncovered his basket and fell to opening oysters. Allured by the rich fishy aroma, Hodge warily edged towards it, and a morsel of oyster in the judge's hand quickly won him over.

As man and cat sat amicably on the kitchen doorstep sharing oysters, the party-gate creaked and an apparition appeared, wearing a pink dimity pinafore over her dainty white ruffles. She seated herself beside Hodge and began to ply him with morsels of oyster as fast as her father pried them loose.

"A pretty sight," said Dr. Johnson, appearing beside me. He bent his warmest smile of loving kindness upon the group: the judge in his purple, his beautiful daughter rosy as the dawn, and handsome Hodge between them in amity.

And over all my sign:

JOHNSON & HODGE
DETECTORS

J. Boswell, Rapparee

Author's Note: It was inevitable that Dr. Sam: Johnson's favorite cat, Hodge, should play a part in his master's detections. This is his story.

Many people have made this story possible, and I thank them with a full heart.

To my nephew, Dr. José de la Torre-Bueno, I owe the concept of cat psychology that makes Hodge a "Detector Cat."

To my brother Theodore de la Torre-Bueno and his wife Evelyn and their fine cats Tuxedo and Leon, I owe the cat lore that rounds out Hodge's story.

I am indebted to my dear friend Jackie Bellmyer for all kinds of moral support, for her critical judgment, for her intimate knowledge of cats, and for putting together and typing a very patched-up manuscript.

To my valued long-time friend Vincent O'Brien, I owe my thanks for his knowledgeable criticism and much help and encouragement, and for reading Dr. Johnson onto tape with the most pungent sense of his character.

There are many other friends who gave me help and encouragement. To each and all I say, "Thank you, good friends."

THE BLACK CAT

Edgar Allan Poe

For the most wild, yet most homely, narrative which I am about to pen, I neither expect nor solicit belief. Mad indeed would I be to expect it, in a case where my very senses reject their own evidence. Yet, mad am I not—and very surely do I not dream. But tomorrow I die, and today I would unburthen my soul. My immediate purpose is to place before the world, plainly, succinctly, and without comment, a series of mere household events. In their consequences, these events have terrified—have tortured—have destroyed me. Yet I will not attempt to expound them. To me they have presented little but horror—to many they still seem less terrible than *barroques*. Hereafter, perhaps, some intellect may be found which will reduce my phantasm to the commonplace—some intellect more calm, more logical, and far less excitable than my own, which will perceive, in the circumstances I detail with awe, nothing more than an ordinary succession of very natural causes and effects.

From my infancy, I was noted for the docility and humanity of my disposition. My tenderness of heart was even so conspicuous as to make me the jest of my companions. I was especially fond of animals, and was indulged by my parents with a great variety of pets. With these I spent most of my time, and never was so happy as when feeding and caressing them.

This peculiarity of character grew with my growth, and, in my manhood, I derived from it one of my principal sources of pleasure. To those who have cherished an affection for a faithful and sagacious dog, I need hardly be at the trouble of explaining the nature or the intensity of the gratification thus derivable. There is something in the unselfish and self-sacrificing love of a brute which goes directly to the heart of him who has had frequent occasion to test the paltry friendship and gossamer fidelity of mere man.

I married early, and was happy to find in my wife a disposition not uncongenial with my own. Observing my partiality for domestic pets, she lost no opportunity of procuring those of the most agreeable kind. We had birds, goldfish, a fine dog, rabbits, a small monkey, and a cat.

This latter was a remarkably large and beautiful animal, entirely black, and sagacious to an astonishing degree. In speaking of his intelligence, my wife, who at heart was not a little tinctured with superstition, made frequent allusion to the ancient popular notion which regarded all black cats as witches in disguise. Not that she was ever *serious* upon this point—and I mention the matter at all for no better reason than that it happens, just now, to be remembered.

Pluto—this was the cat's name—was my favorite pet and playmate. I alone fed him, and he attended me wherever I went about the house. It was even with difficulty that I could prevent him from following me through the streets.

Our friendship lasted in this manner for several years, during which my general temperament and character—through the instrumentality of the Fiend Intemperance—had (I blush to confess it) experienced a radical alteration for the worse. I grew, day by day, more moody, more irritable, more regardless of the feelings of others. I suffered myself to use intemperate language to my wife. At length, I even offered her personal violence. My pets, of course, were made to feel the change in my disposition. I not only neglected but ill-used them. For Pluto, however, I still retained sufficient regard to restrain me from maltreating him, as I made no scruple of maltreating the rabbits, the monkey, or even the dog, when by accident, or through affection, they came in my way. But my disease grew upon me—for what disease is like Alcohol!—and at length Pluto, who was now becoming old and consequently somewhat peevish, even Pluto began to experience the effects of my ill-temper.

One night, returning home much intoxicated from one of my haunts about town, I fancied that the cat avoided my presence. I seized him—when, in his fright at my violence, he inflicted a slight wound upon my hand with his teeth. The fury of a demon instantly possessed me. I knew myself no longer. My original soul seemed at once to take its flight from my body and a more than fiendish malevolence, gin-nurtured, thrilled every fiber of my frame. I took from my waistcoat pocket a pen-knife, opened it, grasped the poor beast by the throat, and deliberately cut one of its eyes from the socket! I blush, I burn, I shudder, while I pen the damnable atrocity.

When reason returned with the morning—when I had slept off the fumes of the night's debauch—I experienced a sentiment half of horror, half of remorse, for the crime of which I had been guilty. But it was, at best, a feeble and equivocal feeling, and the soul remained untouched. I again plunged into excess, and soon drowned in wine all memory of the deed.

In the meantime, the cat slowly recovered. The socket of the lost eye presented, it is true, a frightful appearance, but he no longer appeared to suffer any pain. He went about the house as usual, but, as might be expected, fled in extreme terror at my approach. I had so much of my old heart left as to be at first grieved by this evident dislike on the part of a creature which had once so loved me, but this feeling soon gave place to irritation. And then came, as if to my final and irrevocable overthrow, the spirit of perverseness.

Of this spirit, philosophy takes no account. Yet I am not more sure that my soul lives than I am that perverseness is one of the primitive impulses of the human heart—one of the indivisible primary faculties, or sentiments, which give direction to the character of man. Who has not, a hundred times, found himself committing a vile or a silly action for no other reason than because he knows he should *not*? Have we not a perpetual inclination, in the teeth of our last judgment, to violate that which is law merely because we understand it to be such?

This spirit of perverseness, I say, came to my final overthrow. It was this unfathomable longing of the soul to *vex itself*—to offer violence to its own nature, to do wrong for the wrong's sake only—that urged me to continue and finally to consummate the injury I had inflicted on the unoffending brute. One morning in cold blood, I slipped a noose about its neck and hung it to the limb of a tree—hung it with the tears streaming from my eyes and with the bitterest remorse at my heart, hung it *because* I knew that it had loved me and *because* I felt it had given me no reason of offense, hung it *because* I knew that in so doing I was committing a sin—a deadly sin that would so jeopardize my immortal soul as to place it, if such a thing were possible, even beyond the reach of the infinite mercy of the Most Merciful and Most Terrible God.

* * *

On the night of the day on which this cruel deed was done, I was aroused from sleep by the cry of fire. The curtains of my bed were in flames. The whole house was blazing. It was with great difficulty that my wife, a servant, and myself made our escape from the conflagration. The destruction was complete. My entire worldly wealth was swallowed up, and I resigned myself thenceforward to despair.

I am above the weakness of seeking to establish a sequence of cause and effect, between the disaster and the atrocity. But I am detailing a chain of facts and wish not to leave even a possible link imperfect.

On the day succeeding the fire, I visited the ruins. The walls, with one exception, had fallen in. This exception was found in a compartment wall, not very thick, which stood about the middle of the house, and against which had rested the head of my bed. The plastering had here, in great measure, resisted the action of the fire—a fact which I attributed to its having been recently spread.

About this wall a dense crowd had collected, and many persons seemed to be examining a particular portion of it with very minute and eager attention. The words "strange!" "singular!" and other similar expressions excited my curiosity. I approached and saw, as if graven in bas-relief upon the white surface, the figure of a gigantic cat. The impression was given with an accuracy truly marvelous. There was a rope about the animal's neck.

When I first beheld this apparition—for I could scarcely regard it as less—my wonder and my terror were extreme. But at length reflection came to my aid. The cat, I remember, had been hung in a garden adjacent to the house. Upon the alarm of fire, this garden had been immediately filled by the crowd—

and someone by whom the animal must have been cut from the tree and thrown through an open window into my chamber. This had probably been done with the view of arousing me from sleep. The falling of the other walls had compressed the victim of my cruelty into the substance of the freshly spread plaster, the lime of which with the flames, and the ammonia from the carcass, had then accomplished the portraiture as I saw it.

Although I thus readily accounted to my reason, if not altogether to my conscience, for the startling fact just detailed, it did not the less fail to make a deep impression upon my fancy. For months I could not rid myself of the phantasm of the cat, and during this period there came back into my spirit a half sentiment that seemed, but was not, remorse. I went so far as to regret the loss of the animal, and to look about me, among the vile haunts which I now habitually frequented, for another pet of the same species, and of somewhat similar appearance, with which to supply its place.

One night as I sat, half stupefied, in a den of more than infamy, my attention was suddenly drawn to some black object reposing upon the head of one of the immense hogsheads of gin, or of rum, which constituted the chief furniture of the apartment. I had been looking steadily at the top of this hogshead for some minutes, and what now caused me surprise was the fact that I had not sooner perceived the object thereupon. I approached it, and touched it with my hands.

It was a black cat—a very large one—fully as large as Pluto, and closely resembling him in every respect but one. Pluto had not a white hair upon any portion of his body, but this cat had a large although indefinite splotch of white covering nearly the whole region of the breast.

Upon my touching him, he immediately arose, purred loudly, rubbed against my hand, and appeared delighted with my notice. This, then, was the very creature of which I was in search. I at once offered to purchase it of the landlord, but this person made no claim to it—knew nothing of it—had never seen it before.

I continued my caresses, and when I prepared to go home the animal evinced a disposition to accompany me. I permitted it to do so, occasionally stopping and patting it as I proceeded. When it reached the house, it domesticated itself at once, and became immediately a great favorite with my wife.

For my own part, I soon found a dislike to it arising within me. This was just the reverse of what I had anticipated, but—I know not how or why it was—its evident fondness for me rather disgusted and annoyed.

By slow degrees, these feelings of disgust and annoyance rose into the bitterness of hatred. I avoided the creature, a certain sense of shame and the remembrance of my former deed of cruelty preventing me from physically abusing it. I did not, for some weeks, strike or otherwise violently ill-use it but gradually—very gradually—I came to look upon it with unutterable loathing, and to flee silently from its odious presence as from the breath of a pestilence.

What added, no doubt, to my hatred of the beast was the discovery, on the morning after I brought it home, that, like Pluto, it also had been deprived of one of its eyes. This circumstance, however, only endeared it to my wife, who, as I have already said, possessed in a high degree that humanity of feeling which had once been my distinguishing trait, and the source of many of my simplest and purest pleasures.

With my aversion to this cat, however, its partiality for myself seemed to increase. It followed my footsteps with a pertinacity which it would be difficult to make the reader comprehend. Whenever I sat, it would crouch beneath my chair or spring upon my knees, covering me with its loathsome caresses. If I arose to walk, it would get between my feet and thus nearly throw me down, or, fastening its long and sharp claws in my dress, clamber in this manner to my breast. At such times, although I longed to destroy it with a blow, I was yet withheld from so doing, partly by a memory of my former crime but chiefly—let me confess it at once—by absolute *dread* of the beast.

This dread was not exactly a dread of physical evil and yet I should be at a loss how otherwise to define it. I am almost ashamed to own—yes, even in this felon's cell, I am almost ashamed to own—that the terror and horror with which the animal inspired me had been heightened by one of the merest chimeras it would be possible to conceive.

My wife had called my attention, more than once, to the character of the mark of white hair, of which I have spoken, and which constituted the sole visible difference between the strange beast and the one I had destroyed. The reader will remember that this mark, although large, had been originally very indefinite. But by slow degrees—degrees almost imperceptible, and which for a long time my reason struggled to reject as fanciful—it had, at length, assumed the rigorous distinctness of outline. It was now the representation of an object that I shudder to name—and for this, above all, I loathed and dreaded and would have rid myself of the monster had I dared—it was now, I say, the image of a hideous, of a ghastly thing—of the gallows! Oh, mournful and terrible engine of Horror and of Crime—of Agony and of Death!

* * *

And now I was indeed wretched beyond the wretchedness of mere humanity. And a brute beast—whose fellow I had contemptuously destroyed—a brute beast to work out for *me*, a man fashioned in the image of the High God—so much of insufferable woe! Alas, neither by day nor by night knew I the blessing of rest any more! During the former, the creature left me no moment alone and in the latter I started, hourly, from dreams of unutterable fear to find the hot breath of *the thing* upon my face, and its vast weight—an incarnate Nightmare that I had no power to shake off—incumbent eternally upon my heart!

Beneath the pressure of torments such as these, the feeble remnant of the good within me succumbed. Evil thoughts became my sole intimates—the darkest and most evil of thoughts. The moodiness of my usual temper increased to hatred of all things and of all mankind while, for the sudden, frequent, and ungovernable outbursts of a fury to which I now blindly abandoned myself—my uncomplaining wife, alas, was the most usual and the most patient of sufferers.

One day she accompanied me, upon some household errand, into the cellar of the old building which our poverty compelled us to inhabit. The cat followed me down the steep stairs, and, nearly throwing me headlong, exasperated me to madness. Uplifting an axe, and forgetting in my wrath the childish dread which had hitherto stayed my hand, I aimed at the animal a blow, which, of course, would have proved instantly fatal had it descended as I wished. But this blow was arrested by the hand of my wife.

Goaded by the interference into a rage more than demoniacal, I withdrew my arm from her grasp and buried the axe in her brain.

She fell dead upon the spot, without a groan.

* * *

This hideous murder accomplished, I set myself forthwith, and with entire deliberation, to the task of concealing the body. I knew that I could not remove it from the house, either by day or by night, without the risk of being observed by the neighbors. Many projects entered my mind. At one period I thought of cutting the corpse into minute fragments and destroying them by fire. At another, I resolved to dig a grave for it in the floor of the cellar. Again, I deliberated about casting it in the well in the yard and then about packing it in a box, as if merchandise, with the usual arrangements, and so getting a porter to take it from the house. Finally I hit upon what I considered a far better expedient than any of these. I determined to wall it up in the cellar—as the monks of the Middle Ages are recorded to have walled up their victims.

For a purpose such as this, the cellar was well adapted. Its walls were loosely constructed and had lately been plastered throughout with a rough plaster, which the dampness of the atmosphere had prevented from hardening. Moreover, in one of the walls was a projection caused by a false chimney or fireplace that had been filled up and made to resemble the rest of the cellar. I made no doubt that I could readily displace the bricks, insert the corpse, and wall the whole up as before so that no eye could detect anything suspicious.

And in this calculation I was not deceived. By means of a crowbar, I easily dislodged the bricks and, having carefully deposited the body against the inner wall, I propped it in that position while with little trouble I relaid the whole structure as it originally stood.

Having procured mortar, sand, and hair, with every possible precaution I prepared a plaster which could not be distinguished from the old—and with this I very carefully went over the new brickwork. When I had finished, I felt satisfied that all was right. The wall did not present the slightest appearance of having been disturbed. The rubbish on the floor was picked up with the minutest care. I looked around triumphantly and said to myself, Here at least, then, my labor has not been in vain.

My next step was to look for the beast which had been the cause of so much wretchedness—for I had, at length, firmly resolved to put it to death. Had I been able to meet with it at that moment, there could have been no doubt of its fate—but it appeared that the crafty animal had been alarmed at the violence of my previous anger and forbore to present itself in my present mood.

It is impossible to describe or to imagine the deep, the blissful sense of relief the absence of the detested creature occasioned in my bosom. It did not make its appearance during the night—and thus for one night, at least, since its introduction into the house I soundly and tranquilly slept. Aye, *slept*, even with the burden of murder upon my soul!

The second and third day passed, and still my tormentor came not. Once again I breathed as a free man. The monster, in terror, had fled the premises forever! I should behold it no more! My happiness was supreme! The guilt of my dark deed disturbed me but little. Some few inquiries had been made, but these had been readily answered. Even a search had been instituted—but, of course, nothing was to be discovered. I looked upon my future felicity as secured.

Upon the fourth day of the assassination, a party of the police came very unexpectedly into the house and proceeded again to make rigorous investigation of the premises. Secure, however, in the inscrutability of my place of concealment, I felt no embarrassment whatever. The officers bade me accompany them in their search. They left no nook or corner unexplored. At length, for the third or fourth time, they descended into the cellar. I quivered not in a muscle. My heart beat calmly as that of one who slumbers in innocence. I walked the cellar from end to end. I folded my arms upon my bosom and roamed easily to and fro. The police were thoroughly satisfied and prepared to depart. The glee at my heart was too strong to be restrained. I burned to say if but one word by way of triumph, and to render doubly sure their assurance of my guiltlessness.

"Gentlemen," I said at last, as the party ascended the steps, "I delight to have allayed your suspicions. I wish you all health and a little more courtesy. By the by, gentlemen, this is a very well constructed house." (In the rabid desire to say something easily, I scarcely knew what I uttered at all.) "I may say an *excellently* well constructed house. These walls—are you going, gentlemen?—these walls are solidly put together." And here, through the mere frenzy of bravado, I rapped heavily with a cane, which I held in my hand, upon that very portion of the brickwork behind which stood the corpse of the wife of my bosom.

But may God shield and deliver me from the fangs of the Arch Fiend, no sooner had the reverberation of my blows into silence than I was answered by a voice from within the tomb—by a cry, at first muffled and broken, like the sobbing of a child, and then quickly swelling into one long, loud, and continuous scream, utterly anomalous and inhuman—a howl, a wailing shriek, half of horror and half of triumph, such as might have arisen only out of hell, conjointly from the throats of the damned in their agony and of the demons that exult in the damnation!

Of my own thoughts it is folly to speak. Swooning, I staggered to the opposite wall. For one instant, the party upon the stairs remained motionless through extremity of terror and of awe. In the next, a dozen stout arms were toiling at the wall. It fell bodily. The corpse, already greatly decayed and clotted with gore, stood erect before the eyes of the spectators. Upon its head, with red extended mouth and solitary eye of fire, sat the hideous beast whose craft had seduced me into murder, and whose informing voice had consigned me to the hangman! I had walled the monster up within the tomb!

A VISITOR TO MOMBASA

James Holding

Sergeant Harper of the Mombasa Police was day-dreaming about Rebecca Conway when his telephone rang. He reached a long arm for the instrument on his desk. "Yes?"

"Constable Jenkins here, sir. Waterfront Detail."

"What is it, Jenkins?"

"I've got a queer one, sir. Probably nothing in it, but I thought I ought to report it." Jenkins was new to the job and anxious to play everything safe.

"What is it?" Harper repeated.

"Man named Crosby, sir. Works near the end of the causeway, a night watchman. He claims he saw a leopard sneaking across the causeway into town last night. Or this morning, rather. Just before dawn."

"A leopard!" Harper's voice held surprise.

"Yes, sir." Jenkins waited respectfully for Harper's reaction.

It came promptly. "Fellow was drunk," Harper said.

"I thought of that, sir." Jenkins sounded worried now, but continued. "Crosby admits to a couple of pints on the job during the night. But he swears he saw a leopard. Walking across the causeway from the mainland, bold as brass. He couldn't see the cat's spots, it was too dark, but he says he could see the shape all right for just a moment, and he's sure it was a leopard."

Harper said, "We've had no sighting reports this morning from anyone. Which we surely would have by now, if a leopard's on the loose. Anyway, thanks, Jenkins. I'll look into it." He hung up.

Harper leaned back in his desk chair. He damned the sticky heat of his cramped office and the gullibility of all police recruits. A leopard in Mombasa—he snorted. Tsavo, Nairobi and Amboseli Parks weren't far away, of course, but no, the hell with it. He went back to picturing the bright Scandinavian beauty of Lieutenant Conway's wife.

Ten minutes later, his telephone rang again. The constable on switchboard duty said, "A lady calling about a leopard, sir. Insists on speaking to someone in authority."

Harper groaned. "Put her on."

The lady, a Mrs. Massingale, reported seeing a creature she was sure was a leopard at daybreak that morning.

"Where?" Harper asked.

"Right here in Mombasa, Sergeant!" Mrs. Massingale said indignantly. "The least we could expect in this godforsaken city, it seems to me, is protection against wild animals wandering freely about the streets!"

"I meant," explained Harper with exaggerated patience, "just where in Mombasa did you see this leopard?"

"On the old railway line near Mbaraki Creek. Our cottage isn't fifty feet from the line. I happened to look out a rear window this morning at daybreak and there was this black shadow slinking along the ties. I caught its silhouette quite clearly for a moment. It was a leopard."

"Thanks for reporting it, Mrs. Massingale," Harper said. "I'll look into the matter promptly."

"See that you do!" She hung up with a muted crash that made Harper grin.

Two reports. So perhaps there *was* a leopard in Mombasa, unlikely as it seemed. Harper stood up, a tall, solidly built man with a heavy black moustache and an air of general frustration which he made no attempt to conceal.

The frustration was easily explained, even understandable, in a man of his type. He had come late to police work after a long career as a white hunter in Tanganyika before *uhuru.* Now, after being mildly famous in East Africa, he found himself all at once a lowly sergeant of police, reduced to obeying the orders of Lieutenant Conway, a stuffy man, ten years his junior, who was married, damn his eyes, to the most beautiful woman in Mombasa.

Harper stepped two paces from his desk to the city map taped on his office wall. A leopard reported on the causeway just before dawn—he put a fingertip on the map at the end of the causeway. A leopard reported on the railway line near Mbaraki Creek at daybreak—he touched the spot with another fingertip, and regarded the space between his fingertips narrowly. Yes, he decided, it's quite possible.

Suddenly he felt a surge of cheerfulness. Dealing with a leopard was work he knew. Still looking at the wall map, he tried consciously to put himself inside the spotted skin and the narrow skull of a leopard, to think as the cat might think, to forecast the movements of the killer he had come to know so well on a hundred safaris.

Suppose, he mused, the leopard was an accidental

fugitive from one of the nearby game reserves. The unexpected sight of a long bridge, deserted and comfortably dark, might well have aroused enough feline curiosity in the leopard to make it venture out upon the causeway. Once there, a drift of scent across the water from dockside cattle pens, perhaps, may have drawn it on in quest of meat. Harper could picture vividly the silent cat, padding cautiously across the causeway, nostrils twitching with finicky distaste at the odors of diesel fuel and rotting refuse that vied with the cattle smell over Kilindini Harbor.

Having crossed the bridge, finding no direct route to the cattle scent that drew him, and suddenly surrounded by the strange effluvia of a large city, the leopard would rapidly become confused and frightened, Harper theorized. The beast's curiosity and hunger would be forgotten in an instinctive urge to find cover quickly in this unfamiliar terrain.

The cat, Harper felt, would therefore turn aside from the wide vulnerable expanse of Makupa Road into the comparative seclusion of the deserted railway line, stepping delicately along the ties through the industrial section of town to Mbaraki Creek, where Mrs. Massingale had caught a fleeting glimpse of him. Thence, it seemed obvious from the map, the leopard might be expected to come out on the bluffs overlooking the sea at Azania Drive, footsore now, apprehension growing as the daylight strengthened, the need for cover reaching panic proportions.

Azania Drive; Harper tired to recall the configuration of the land just there where the railway line bisected the Drive. It was a bleak and lonely stretch of the seaside road, as he remembered it, meandering along the bluffs past an ancient Arab watchtower and bearing little resemblance to the fashionable Azania Drive which also yielded a view of the sea to the Oceanic Hotel, the golf club, and scores of comfortable residences beyond. At that place on Azania Drive, above the ferry, a grove of baobab trees stood, defying the sea winds, Harper remembered.

He nodded to himself, utterly intent, thinking with a sense almost of excitement that the thick twisted foliage of those baobab trees just possibly might offer welcome sanctuary to a frightened leopard.

He turned his back to the map. His next step was clear. He should delegate Constable Gordon in the squad room to go at once and check out the baobab trees on Azania Drive for a stray leopard. Gordon would welcome the action, and he was an excellent shot, too, Harper knew. Yet, after the stimulating exercise of mentally plotting the leopard's probable whereabouts in Mombasa, Harper was reluctant to turn the hunt over to somebody else before he, himself, had even sighted the game. He needn't be in at the kill, he told himself. On safari, he had always turned the final shot over to his clients—he was used to that—but he *did* want to mark down the target with certainty before yielding the kill to another. Aside from his thus far unsuccessful campaign to make Rebecca Conway unfaithful to her pompous husband, this city leopard hunt was the most exciting thing that had happened to Harper since he joined the police force.

Yielding to temptation, he reached for his hat, took field glasses from the shelf under his wall map, and strode into the squad room. "Back in a few minutes, Gordon," he told the constable in passing. "Take over until Lieutenant Conway gets in, will you?" Conway never showed for duty until nine o'clock. Yet who could blame him, Harper thought enviously, with the voluptuous Rebecca to keep him at home until the last moment?

He felt the sweat start the moment he stepped out of headquarters into the compound. He climbed into one of the two police cars parked there, a Land Rover. As he turned out of the police compound and headed for Azania Drive, the sun had already warmed the driver's seat so that the cushions burned him, even through his trousers.

A hundred and fifty yards short of the baobab trees on Azania Drive, he stopped the Land Rover, parked it beside the road and walked slowly toward the trees. The field glasses hung on their strap about his neck. It was still only a little after eight. Traffic was very light on Azania Drive.

He waited until the road was empty both ways before he stepped from it onto the springy turf that ran like a shaggy carpet along the landward side of the road, solidly covering the acre of ground under the baobab grove. He walked carefully to within thirty yards of the trees, then stopped and brought the glasses up to his eyes and examined carefully the twisted branches and tangled foliage of the baobabs. He saw nothing that looked even remotely like a leopard.

After five minutes, he moved across the road, still well clear of the trees, and walked another fifty yards to a position from which he could comb the grove from a different angle. He swept the glasses slowly from tree to tree, conscious of growing disappointment as they failed to find what he sought.

The glasses were trained on the last of the trees—a gnarled giant closer to the road than its neighbors—when suddenly, with the sense of electrical shock that accompanies an unexpected explosion, he found himself gazing through the magnifying lenses at two merciless yellow eyes which seemed disembodied in the tree's sun-dappled shade.

He breathed an exclamation that was part admiration for the magnificent cat, whose savage stare transfixed him, part satisfaction at his own astuteness in locating the beast.

Carefully he marked the tree and the cat's position in it. Then he withdrew to his Land Rover and drove away, whistling softly to himself and thinking he should have brought a rifle with him when he left headquarters. Still, he hadn't really expected there was a chance in ten that he'd find the leopard in the grove of baobab trees, he justified himself.

All the same, the cat was there!

Harper felt like celebrating, all at once, his frustrations temporarily forgotten. He had brought off a surprising feat, really: tracking a wild leopard . . . mentally . . . through several miles of sprawling city to a specific lair. His mood was one of exhilaration.

This is what I am good at, he reflected, this is what I *was* meant to do—not piddling along at a stinking little police job in a dirty city, but working with wild animals, somehow, somewhere, in free, open country, tracking them down and killing them, or working to preserve them from extinction, no matter which, so long as the job was useful and, yes, dangerous. He'd made a horrible mistake when he gave up hunting animals for hunting men. If he could only convince Rebecca Conway to go with him, he'd leave Mombasa tomorrow for Nairobi, Uganda, Australia, India, Alaska—anywhere away from the imperious beck and call of Rebecca's impossible, intolerable husband.

He'd asked her a dozen times to leave the fool she was married to and join him in a new free life somewhere else; but Rebecca only smiled at his pleading, kissed him lightly on the check like a sister, called him an aging Lothario (at forty-one!) and quoted Shakespeare at him about preferring to bear those ills she had than fly to others that she knew not of. She was flattered by his passion for her, of course, yet she was too fond of her idle, easy life in Mombasa as Conway's wife to risk it lightly.

Harper decided to drive back to headquarters by way of the center of town. That would give him a little extra time to savor his success with the leopard; to anticipate the soon-to-come thrill of squeezing off the perfectly aimed shot that would rid Mombasa of its dangerous visitor in the baobab tree. Fifteen minutes delay in finishing off the leopard would make no difference to anyone, so far as he could see. The leopard was treed well off the road. It was still frightened, edgy, and hungrier than ever, no doubt, yet posed no threat, Harper knew, to passersby on Azania Drive unless someone approached its tree.

His memory played back to him one of the warnings he had always issued to hunters on safari: remember that a treed leopard, if hungry, frightened, or wounded, will usually attack anything that moves beneath it. So why would anyone approach that baobab tree? Harper was the only person in the city who could possibly have any interest in it.

The high crenellated battlements of Fort Jesus loomed on his left above the crimson blossoms of a flame tree as he passed the Mombasa Club. In the center of the turn-about, the bust of King George caught the morning sunlight and seemed to wink at Harper as he tooled the Land Rover around the circle and into Prince Arthur Street.

At police headquarters, he remembered to park his car in the compound off the street, even though he intended to use the Land Rover again at once, as soon as he secured a rifle from the gun case in his office. That was one of Lieutenant Conway's silly rules, if you like: that the curb before headquarters must be kept clear and free at all times, so that if the wooden building ever caught fire, there would be ample space for the fire-fighting apparatus to park there!

Thinking of Lieutenant Conway and, inevitably, of Rebecca, Harper's leopard-inspired high spirits drained rapidly away. The exhilaration of ten minutes ago had turned to creeping depression by the time he reached his office; the elation of winning a guessing game with a leopard lost its edge. If Rebecca refused him one more time, he swore to himself, he'd throw up this bloody job, anyway, and go off without her.

He unlocked his gun cabinet and took down one of his old rifles, unused since his last safari five years ago. As a special favor, Lieutenant Conway had allowed him to keep this personal weapon as an addition to the headquarter's arsenal. Harper was glad of it now.

He put ammunition into his pocket, relocked the gun cabinet, and was turning for the door when his telephone rang. Impatiently he paused by his desk, scooped up the receiver and said, "Yes?"

"Some fellow wants the lieutenant," the switchboard man said.

"Then give him the lieutenant," snapped Harper. "I'm busy."

"Lieutenant's not in yet, sir." The constable was apologetic.

Harper glanced at his watch. It was not yet nine o'clock. "Who's calling the lieutenant?"

"He won't say, sir. Says it's confidential and urgent. Native, I believe, and he speaks Swahili."

"Put him on."

The caller's voice was male, low-pitched, sounded very young. "Who is this?" it asked.

Harper said, "Sergeant Harper. Lieutenant Conway is not here. What do you want?"

"The reward, sir," the young voice whispered. "The reward offered by your lieutenant."

"What reward?"

"For arrow poison, sir. For the names of Wakamba doctors who make arrow poison against the new law."

"Oh." Harper remembered that Conway had been trying for six months to discover which of the Wakamba witch doctors were still manufacturing arrow poison, and thus contributing to massive native slaughter of the game in the reserves. The arrow poison of the Wakamba was made from tree sap; it smelled like licorice; it left a black discoloration in the wound; and it was capable of killing a bull elephant in fifteen minutes.

Harper said, "Have you earned the reward?"

"Yes, sir. I have two names for Lieutenant Conway."

"Who are they? I'll tell the lieutenant."

"No names," the young Wakamba murmured, "until the reward is given. Not until then."

Harper grinned. "Don't trust us, is that it?"

The boy was silent.

"We'll give you the reward first, in that case. All right? What's *your* name?"

"I have no name," said the young voice very formally. "I am risking death to give the lieutenant this information, sir. My own people will kill me if they learn of it."

Harper tried it another way. "Where are you calling from?"

"The Golden Key."

Harper knew the Golden Key, a disreputable bar immediately across the Nyalla Bridge. Used to be called the Phantom Inn because natives would dress up in sheets and act the ghost to startle customers. "You a houseboy there?" he asked.

"No, sir."

Harper hefted his rifle, impatient to go after his leopard. "How can we arrange to give you the reward if you won't tell us who you are?"

"Very simple, sir. I will meet the lieutenant in private. He brings me the reward. I give him the names of the poison makers."

Harper considered for a moment. "Where do you want the lieutenant to meet you?"

"Where no Wakamba can see me talking to a policeman." Simple and clear.

"When?" asked Harper.

"Today, sir, please. This morning, if possible. I need the reward very badly, sir. Otherwise, of course . . ." His voice, touched with desperation now, trailed off.

"All right, then," Harper said. "*I'll* meet you and bring the reward, since the lieutenant isn't here just yet. How much were you promised?"

"Ten pounds, sir." Eagerness now. "That will be good. Where shall I meet you?"

The Wakamba boy's simple question seemed to echo and reecho in a strange pervasive way inside Harper's head, and the idea that was born in his mind at that instant seemed to make his heart shift position in his chest. He sank into his desk chair, clutching the rifle on the desk before him with one hand.

He took a deep breath and said, "You know the old Arab watchtower, boy? Below Azania Drive near the ferry?"

"Yes, sir."

"I'll meet you there in an hour. Or Lieutenant Conway will, if he comes here soon enough. You can make it in an hour, can't you?"

"Yes. But remember, please, I dare not be seen,

sir. Azania Drive is very public. Is there no private place we can meet?"

"That's private enough." Harper was brusque. "Don't use Azania Drive to get there, come up the shore line on the beach under the bluffs. No one will see you. No one ever goes there, to the tower."

"Very well," said the soft boyish voice. "I'll be there, sir. One hour."

"Good," Harper said. His hand was sweating on the rifle stock. After he hung up, he dried his palms on the jacket of his uniform. He glanced again at his watch: 9:10. Conway was later than usual today.

He rose and put the rifle back in the wall cabinet. Then, pretending to be busy over a stack of reports, he sat quietly at his desk until he heard Lieutenant Conway's fussy voice in the squad room, greeting Constable Gordon as he passed through to his office.

Harper waited a moment or so before walking into Conway's room.

"Morning, Sergeant," Conway said briskly. "Something on your mind?"

Harper told him about the telephone call from the young Wakamba informer who wouldn't give his name. "Now you're here, sir," he finished matter-of-factly, "I expect you'll want to meet the boy and get his information yourself, since it's your pigeon, so to speak."

"Of course." Conway rubbed his hands together in a gesture of satisfaction that Harper found extremely irritating. He was exultant, his high voice almost a crow of pleasure as he went on. "So the clever lad, whoever he is, has a couple of witch doctors' names for me, does he? Quite a feather in our cap, Sergeant, if we can clear up this arrow-poison business at last, eh? Where am I supposed to meet him?"

Harper said quietly, "At the Arab watchtower

below Azania Drive. It's private enough to quiet the boy's fears of being seen, I thought, yet within easy reach for us. You know it, of course?"

"Certainly I know it. An admirable choice, Sergeant. There and back in fifteen minutes without unduly wasting the taxpayers' time, eh? There's an old track down the bluff to the tower's base as I remember it."

"Right, sir. You can park by the grove of the baobab trees on Azania Drive and go straight through under the trees to the cliff edge, where the track goes down."

"I must remember to take the boy's money. What time did you tell him you'd be there?"

"As soon as I could. He seemed anxious to get it over with. He's been at considerable risk, he claims."

"I'll leave at once." Lieutenant Conway stood up. "Take charge here, Sergeant." He strutted from the room, calling loudly to the cashier outside to give him ten pounds at once.

That was at 9:20. At 10:15 the call came.

"A motorist on Azania Drive just called in, sir," the switchboard man said. "Says he saw a fellow lying under a tree up there, covered with blood, as he was driving past. Stopped to see if he could help. Got to within fifty feet of the man under the tree and saw he was dead, so he called us."

"Dead!" Harper kept his voice level. "How could he tell from fifty feet away?"

"No face left, sir," the switchboard man said, as though he were reporting a shortage of beer in the commissary icebox. "Bundle of bloody flesh and shredded clothes, the motorist says. As though the fellow'd been mauled by a leopard, maybe." The constable cleared his throat. "Any chance, sir, it could have been the leopard the lady reported earlier?"

"Possible," Harper said. "Where'd he telephone from?"

"The nearest house. He'll stand by until one of our chaps gets there, he says."

"Fine. Hope he has enough sense to keep people out from under that tree where the dead man is. Where is it on Azania Drive?"

"Near the old Arab watchtower. There's a grove of baobab trees just there . . ."

"Right," Harper said. "I'm on my way. Better take a rifle, I guess. Give any calls for me to Constable Gordon."

Surprisingly, when he reached the baobab grove and drew up behind Conway's parked car, there was no one in view nearby save for the motorist, a man named Stacy, who had telephoned headquarters. Greeting Harper's arrival with obvious relief, he said he'd managed to send curiosity seekers—only a handful so far—quickly about their business by telling them there was a wild leopard loose in the grove.

"Good work," grunted Harper, stepping from his car. As though drawn by magnets, his eyes went to the ghastly figure lying asprawl under the nearest tree. Then, in a voice that sounded shocked even to him, he said, "From the looks of that poor chap under the tree, I'd say you were right about the leopard, Mr. Stacy."

Stacy swallowed hard. "I was sick in the ditch when I saw it," he said. "Then I ran like hell and called you."

Harper nodded and reached into the back of the Land Rover for the rifle. "So let's see what we can do about it," he said. "Get across the road, away from the trees, will you, Mr. Stacy, and handle anybody else who may stop to gawk?"

Stacy was more than glad to withdraw across the road.

Harper knew where his target was. For Stacy's benefit however, he was forced to carry on a pretended search of the baobab tree. He moved to various vantage points, left and right of the tree, the rifle held ready. At length, he suddenly raised a hand to Stacy and nodded vigorously, as though he had at last located the cat.

As indeed he had. Even without the field glasses, he had no trouble zeroing in on those blazing eyes turned unblinkingly toward him; and even without the field glasses, he could see quite plainly the streaks and spatters of blood on the savage muzzle. Lieutenant Conway's blood, he told himself with grim satisfaction.

He brought up the gun, steadied his sights on the small target and squeezed off his shot.

Instantly, a squalling cyclone of spotted hide and sheathed claws fell out of the tree, crashing through the baobab foliage. At the crack of the shot, a widow bird rose from the top of a neighboring tree and flapped slowly away, trailing its long black feathers. Harper wondered if that was sign. When the leopard struck the ground, only a few feet from its mangled victim, it was quite dead.

"You got him!" yelled Stacy from across the road, his voice thin from excitement, "Bravo!"

Harper didn't take his eyes off the leopard, holding the gun ready for a second shot, although he was quite sure the first had done its work thoroughly. He was remembering another of his white-hunter maxims: never approach downed game until you are certain it is dead.

At length he was satisfied. He motioned to Stacy to stay where he was, and stepping carefully on the rough turf, made his way to the baobab tree and the still figures under it. A glance showed him the leopard was quite dead; a head shot of which he could be proud.

He turned, then, toward Lieutenant Conway's corpse, his brain suddenly busy with a variety of thoughts. He must not forget to give the Wakamba boy at the watchtower his reward and settle the arrow-poison business, now that Conway was gone. He must inform Rebecca Conway of her husband's tragic end and console her as best he could. Would he be promoted now to lieutenant, and thus be able to offer Rebecca a continuation of the privileged life she seemed to find so enchanting in Mombasa? Given time, he was sure he could persuade her to marry him—and now, he thought, smiling a little, he had lots of time.

He was wrong. He didn't even have time to raise his eyes to the tree branch above him, or to bring up the rifle, still held loosely in his hand. In the last split second of his life, before pitiless teeth and talons tore his throat out, Harper had time for but a single flash of realization: there had been a *pair* of leopards visiting Mombasa!

MING'S BIGGEST PREY

Patricia Highsmith

Ming was resting comfortably on the foot of his mistress's bunk, when the man picked him up by the back of the neck, stuck him out on the deck and closed the cabin door. Ming's blue eyes widened in shock and brief anger, then nearly closed again because of the brilliant sunlight. It was not the first time Ming had been thrust out of the cabin rudely, and Ming realized that the man did it when his mistress, Elaine, was not looking.

The sailboat now offered no shelter from the sun, but Ming was not yet too warm. He leapt easily to the cabin roof and stepped on to the coil of rope just behind the mast. Ming liked the rope coil as a couch, because he could see everything from the height, the cup shape of the rope protected him from strong breezes, and also minimized the swaying and sudden changes of angle of the *White Lark*, since it was more or less the centre point. But just now the sail had been taken down, because Elaine and the man had eaten lunch, and often they had a siesta afterward, during which time, Ming knew, that man didn't like him in the cabin. Lunchtime was all right. In fact, Ming had just lunched on delicious grilled fish and a bit of lobster. Now, lying in a relaxed curve on the coil of rope, Ming opened his mouth in a great yawn, then with his slant eyes almost closed against the strong sunlight, gazed at the beige hills and the white and pink houses and hotels that circled the bay of Acapulco. Between the *White Lark* and the shore where people plashed inaudibly, the sun twinkled on the water's surface like thousands of tiny electric lights going on and off. A water-skier went by, skimming up white spray behind him. Such activity! Ming half dozed, feeling the heat of the sun sink into his fur. Ming was from New York, and he considered Acapulco a great improvement over his environment in the first weeks of his life. He remembered a sunless box with straw on the bottom, three or four other kittens in with him, and a window behind which giant forms paused for a few moments, tried to catch his attention by tapping, then passed on. He did not remember his mother at all. One day a young woman who smelled of something pleasant came into the place and took him away—away from the ugly, frightening smell of dogs, of medicine and parrot dung. Then they went on what Ming now knew was an aeroplane. He was quite used to aeroplanes now and rather liked them. On aeroplanes he sat on Elaine's lap, or slept on her lap, and there were always titbits to eat if he was hungry.

Elaine spent much of the day in a shop in Acapulco, where dresses and slacks and bathing suits hung on all the walls. This place smelled clean and fresh, there were flowers in pots and in boxes out front, and the floor was of cool blue and white tiles. Ming had perfect freedom to wander out into the patio behind the shop, or to sleep in his basket in a corner. There was more sunlight in front of the shop, but mischievous boys often tried to grab him if he sat in front, and Ming could never relax there.

Ming liked best lying in the sun with his mistress on one of the long canvas chairs on their terrace at home.

What Ming did not like were the people she sometimes invited to their house, people who spent the night, people by the score who stayed up very late eating and drinking, playing the gramophone or the piano—people who separated him from Elaine. People who stepped on his toes, people who sometimes picked him up from behind before he could do anything about it, so that he had to squirm and fight to get free, people who stroked him roughly, people who closed a door somewhere, locking him in. *People!* Ming detested people. In all the world, he liked only Elaine. Elaine loved him and understood him.

Especially this man called Teddie Ming detested now. Teddie was around all the time lately. Ming did not like the way Teddie looked at him, when Elaine was not watching. And sometimes Teddie, when Elaine was not near, muttered something which Ming knew was a threat. Or a command to leave the room. Ming took it calmly. Dignity was to be preserved. Besides, wasn't his mistress on his side? The man was the intruder. When Elaine was watching, the man sometimes pretended a fondness for him, but Ming always moved gracefully but unmistakably in another direction.

Ming's nap was interrupted by the sound of the cabin door opening. He heard Elaine and the man laughing and talking. The big red-orange sun was near the horizon.

"Ming!" Elaine came over to him. "Aren't you getting *cooked*, darling? I thought you were *in*!"

"So did I!" said Teddie.

Ming purred as he always did when he awakened. She picked him up gently, cradled him in her arms, and took him below into the suddenly cool shade of the cabin. She was talking to the man, and not in a gentle tone. She set Ming down in front of his dish of water, and though he was not thirsty, he drank a little to please her. Ming did feel addled by the heat, and he staggered a little.

Elaine took a wet towel and wiped Ming's face, his ears and his four paws. Then she laid him gently on the bunk that smelled of Elaine's perfume but also of the man whom Ming detested.

Now his mistress and the man were quarrelling, Ming could tell from the tone. Elaine was staying with Ming, sitting on the edge of the bunk. Ming at last heard the splash that meant Teddie had dived into the water. Ming hoped he stayed there, hoped he drowned, hoped he never came back. Elaine wet a bathtowel in the aluminum sink, wrung it out, spread it on the bunk, and lifted Ming on to it. She brought water, and now Ming was thirsty, and drank. She left him to sleep again while she washed and put away the dishes. These were comfortable sounds that Ming liked to hear.

But soon there was another *plash* and *plop*, Teddie's wet feet on the deck, and Ming was awake again.

The tone of quarrelling recommenced. Elaine went up the few steps on to the deck. Ming, tense but with his chin still resting on the moist bathtowel, kept his eyes on the cabin door. It was Teddie's feet that he heard descending. Ming lifted his head slightly, aware that there was no exit behind him, that he was trapped in the cabin. The man paused with a towel in his hands, staring at Ming.

Ming relaxed completely, as he might do preparatory to a yawn, and this caused his eyes to cross. Ming then let his tongue slide a little way out of his mouth. The man started to say something, looked as if he wanted to hurl the wadded towel at Ming, but he wavered, whatever he had been going to say never got out of his mouth, and he threw the towel in the sink, then bent to wash his face. It was not the first time Ming had let his tongue slide out at Teddie. Lots of people laughed when Ming did this, if they were people at a party, for instance, and Ming rather enjoyed that. But Ming sensed that Teddie took it as a hostile gesture of some kind, which was why Ming did it deliberately to Teddie, whereas among other people, it was often an accident when Ming's tongue slid out.

The quarrelling continued. Elaine made coffee. Ming began to feel better, and went on deck again, because the sun had now set. Elaine had started the motor, and they were gliding slowly towards the shore. Ming caught the song of birds, the odd screams, like shrill phrases, of certain birds that cried only at sunset. Ming looked forward to the adobe house on the cliff that was his and his mistress's home. He knew that the reason she did not leave him at home (where he would have been more comfortable) when she went on the boat, was because she was afraid that people might trap him, even kill him. Ming understood. People had tried to grab him from almost under Elaine's eyes. Once he had been suddenly hauled away in a cloth bag and, though fighting as hard as he could, he was not sure he would have been able to get out if Elaine had not hit the boy herself and grabbed the bag from him.

Ming had intended to jump up on the cabin roof again but, after glancing at it, he decided to save his strength, so he crouched on the warm, gently sloping deck with his feet tucked in, and gazed at the approaching shore. Now he could hear guitar music from the beach. The voices of his mistress and the man had come to a halt. For a few moments, the loudest sound was the *chug-chug-chug* of the boat's motor. Then Ming heard the man's bare feet climbing the cabin steps. Ming did not turn his head to look at him, but his ears twitched back a little, involuntarily. Ming looked at the water just the distance of a short leap in front of him and below him. Strangely, there was no sound from the man behind him. The hair on Ming's neck prickled, and Ming glanced over his right shoulder.

At that instant, the man bent forward and rushed at Ming with his arms outspread.

Ming was on his feet at once, darting straight towards the man, which was the only direction of safety on the rail-less deck, and the man swung his left arm and cuffed Ming in the chest. Ming went flying backward, claws scraping the deck, but his hind legs went over the edge. Ming clung with his front feet to the sleek wood which gave him little hold, while his hind legs worked to heave him up, worked at the side of the boat which sloped to Ming's disadvantage.

The man advanced to shove a foot against Ming's paws, but Elaine came up the cabin steps just then.

"What's happening? *Ming*!"

Ming's strong hind legs were getting him on to the deck little by little. The man had knelt as if to lend a hand. Elaine had fallen on to her knees also, and had Ming by the back of the neck now.

Ming relaxed, hunched on the deck. His tail was wet.

"He fell overboard!" Teddie said. "It's true, he's groggy. Just lurched over and fell when the boat gave a dip."

"It's the sun. Poor *Ming*!" Elaine held the cat against her breast, and carried him into the cabin. "Teddie—could you steer?"

The man came down into the cabin. Elaine had Ming on the bunk and was talking softly to him. Ming's heart was still beating fast. He was alert against the man at the wheel, even though Elaine was with him. Ming was aware that they had entered the little cove where they always went before getting off the boat.

Here were the friends and allies of Teddie, whom Ming detested by association, although these were merely Mexican boys. Two or three boys in shorts called "Señor Teddie!" and offered a hand to Elaine to climb on to the dock, took the rope attached to the front of the boat, offered to carry *"Ming!—Ming!"* Ming leapt on to the dock himself and crouched, waiting for Elaine, ready to dart away from any other hand that might reach for him. And there were several brown hands making a rush for him, so that Ming had to keep jumping aside. There were laughs, yelps, stomps of bare feet on wooden boards. But there was also the reassuring voice of Elaine warning them off. Ming knew she was busy carrying off the plastic satchels, locking the cabin door. Teddie with the aid of one of the Mexican boys was stretching the canvas over the cabin now. And Elaine's sandalled feet were beside Ming. Ming followed her as she walked away. A boy took the things Elaine was carrying, then she picked Ming up.

They got into the big car without a roof that belonged to Teddie, and drove up the winding road towards Elaine's and Ming's house. One of the boys was driving. Now the tone in which Elaine and Teddie were speaking was calmer, softer. The man laughed. Ming sat tensely on his mistress's lap. He could feel her concern for him in the way she stroked him and touched the back of his neck. The man reached out to put his fingers on Ming's back, and Ming gave a low growl that rose and fell and rumbled deep in his throat.

"Well, well," said the man, pretending to be amused, and took his hand away.

Elaine's voice had stopped in the middle of something she was saying. Ming was tired, and wanted nothing more than to take a nap on the big bed at home. The bed was covered with a red and white striped blanket of thin wool.

Hardly had Ming thought of this, when he found himself in the cool, fragrant atmosphere of his own home, being lowered gently on to the bed with the soft woollen cover. His mistress kissed his cheek, and said something with the word hungry in it. Ming understood, at any rate. He was to tell her when he was hungry.

Ming dozed, and awakened at the sound of voices on the terrace a couple of yards away, past the open glass doors. Now it was dark. Ming could see one end of the table, and could tell from the quality of the light that there were candles on the table. Concha, the servant who slept in the house, was clearing the table. Ming heard her voice, then the voices of Elaine and the man. Ming smelled cigar smoke. Ming jumped to the floor and sat for a moment looking out of the door towards the terrace. He yawned, then arched his back and stretched, and limbered up his muscles by digging his claws into the thick straw carpet. Then he slipped out to the right of the terrace and glided silently down the long stairway of broad stones to the garden below. The garden was like a jungle or a forest. Avocado trees and mango trees grew as high as the terrace itself, there were bougainvillaea against the wall, orchids in the trees, and magnolias and several camellias which Elaine had planted. Ming could hear birds twittering and stirring in their nests. Sometimes he climbed trees to get at their nests, but tonight he was not in the mood, though he was no longer tired. The voices of his mistress and the man disturbed him.

His mistress was not a friend of the man's tonight, that was plain.

Concha was probably still in the kitchen, and Ming decided to go in and ask her for something to eat. Concha liked him. One maid who had not liked him had been dismissed by Elaine. Ming thought he fancied barbecued pork. That was what his mistress and the man had eaten tonight. The breeze blew fresh from the ocean, ruffling Ming's fur slightly. Ming felt completely recovered from the awful experience of nearly falling into the sea.

Now the terrace was empty of people. Ming went left, back into the bedroom, and was at once aware of the man's presence, though there was no light on and Ming could not see him. The man was standing by the dressing table, opening a box. Again involuntarily Ming gave a low growl which rose and fell, and Ming remained frozen in the position he had been in when he first became aware of the man, his right front paw extended for the next step. Now his ears were back, he was prepared to spring in any direction, although the man had not seen him.

"*Ssss-st!* Damn you!" the man said in a whisper. He stamped his foot, not very hard, to make the cat go away.

Ming did not move at all. Ming heard the soft rattle of the white necklace which belonged to his mistress. The man put it into his pocket, then moved to Ming's right, out of the door that went into the big living-room. Ming now heard the clink of a bottle against glass, heard liquid being poured. Ming went through the same door and turned left towards the kitchen.

Here he miaowed, and was greeted by Elaine and Concha. Concha had her radio turned on to music.

"Fish?—Pork. He likes pork," Elaine said, speaking the odd form of words which she used with Concha.

Ming, without much difficulty, conveyed his preference for pork, and got it. He fell to with a good appetite. Concha was exclaiming "Ah-eee-ee!" as his mistress spoke with her, spoke at length. Then Concha bent to stroke him, and Ming put up with it, still looking down at his plate, until she left off and he could finish his meal. Then Elaine left the kitchen. Concha gave him some of the tinned milk, which he loved, in his now empty saucer, and Ming lapped this up. Then he rubbed himself against her bare leg by way of thanks and went out of the kitchen, made his way cautiously into the living-room en route to the bedroom. But now Elaine and the man were out on the terrace. Ming had just entered the bedroom, when he heard Elaine call:

"Ming? Where are you?"

Ming went to the terrace door and stopped, and sat on the threshold.

Elaine was sitting sideways at the end of the table, and the candlelight was bright on her long fair hair, on the white of her trousers. She slapped her thigh, and Ming jumped on to her lap.

The man said something in a low tone, something not nice.

Elaine replied something in the same tone. But she laughed a little.

Then the telephone rang.

Elaine put Ming down, and went into the living-room towards the telephone.

The man finished what was in his glass, muttered something at Ming, then set the glass on the table. He got up and tried to circle Ming, or to get him towards the edge of the terrace, Ming realized, and Ming also realized that the man was drunk—therefore moving slowly and a little clumsily. The terrace had a parapet about as high as the man's hips, but it was broken by grilles in three places, grilles with bars wide enough for Ming to pass through, though Ming never did, merely looked through the grilles sometimes. It was plain to Ming that the man wanted to drive him through one of the grilles, or grab him and toss him over the terrace parapet. There was nothing easier for Ming than to elude him. Then the man picked up a chair and swung it suddenly, catching Ming on the hip. That had been quick, and it hurt. Ming took the nearest exit, which was down the outside steps that led to the garden.

The man started down the steps after him. Without reflecting, Ming dashed back up the few steps he had come, keeping close to the wall which was in shadow. The man hadn't seen him, Ming knew. Ming leapt to the terrace parapet, sat down and licked a paw once to recover and collect himself. His heart beat fast as if he were in the middle of a fight. And hatred ran in his veins. Hatred burned his eyes as he crouched and listened to the man uncertainly climbing the steps below him. The man came into view.

Ming tensed himself for a jump, then jumped as hard as he could, landing with all four feet on the man's right arm near the shoulder. Ming clung to the cloth of the man's white jacket, but they were both falling. The man groaned. Ming hung on. Branches crackled. Ming could not tell up from down. Ming jumped off the man, became aware of direction and of the earth too late, and landed on his side. Almost at the same time, he heard the thud of the man hitting the ground, then of his body rolling a little way, then there was silence. Ming had to breathe fast with his mouth open until his chest stopped hurting. From the direction of the man, he could smell drink, cigar, and the sharp odour that meant fear. But the man was not moving.

Ming could now see quite well. There was even a bit of moonlight. Ming headed for the steps again, had to go a long way through the bush, over stones and sand, to where the steps began. Then he glided up and arrived once more upon the terrace.

Elaine was just coming on to the terrace.

"Teddie?" she called. Then she went back into the bedroom where she turned on a lamp. She went into the kitchen. Ming followed her. Concha had left the light on, but Concha was now in her own room, where the radio played.

Elaine opened the front door.

The man's car was still in the driveway, Ming saw. Now Ming's hip had begun to hurt, or now he had begun to notice it. It caused him to limp a little. Elaine noticed this, touched his back, and asked him what was the matter. Ming only purred.

"Teddie?—Where are you?" Elaine called.

She took a torch and shone it down into the garden, down among the great trunks of the avocado trees, among the orchids and the lavender and pink blossoms of the bougainvillaeas. Ming, safe beside her on the terrace parapet, followed the beam of the torch with his eyes and purred with content. The man was not below here, but below and to the right. Elaine went to the terrace steps and carefully, because there was no rail here, only broad steps, pointed the beam of the light downward. Ming did not bother looking. He sat on the terrace where the steps began.

"Teddie!" she said. "*Teddie!*" Then she ran down the steps.

Ming still did not follow her. He heard her draw in her breath. Then she cried:

"*Concha!*"

Elaine ran back up the steps.

Concha had come out of her room. Elaine spoke to

Concha. Then Concha became excited. Elaine went to the telephone, and spoke for a short while, then she and Concha went down the steps together. Ming settled himself with his paws tucked under him on the terrace, which was still faintly warm from the day's sun. A car arrived. Elaine came up the steps, and went and opened the front door. Ming kept out of the way on the terrace, in a shadowy corner, as three or four strange men came out on the terrace and tramped down the steps. There was a great deal of talk below, noises of feet, breaking of bushes, and then the smell of all of them mounted the steps, the smell of tobacco, sweat, and the familiar smell of blood. The man's blood. Ming was pleased, as he was pleased when he killed a bird and created this smell of blood under his own teeth. This was big prey. Ming, unnoticed by any of the others, stood up to his full height as the group passed with the corpse, and inhaled the aroma of his victory with a lifted nose.

Then suddenly the house was empty. Everyone had gone, even Concha. Ming drank a little water from his bowl in the kitchen, then went to his mistress's bed, curled against the slope of the pillows, and fell fast asleep. He was awakened by the *rr-rr-r* of an unfamiliar car. Then the front door opened, and he recognized the step of Elaine and then Concha. Ming stayed where he was. Elaine and Concha talked softly for a few minutes. Then Elaine came into the bedroom. The lamp was still on. Ming watched her slowly open the box on her dressing table, and into it she let fall the white necklace that made a little clatter. Then she closed the box. She began to unbutton her shirt, but before she had finished, she flung herself on the bed and stroked Ming's head, lifted his left paw and pressed it gently so that the claws came forth.

"Oh, Ming—Ming," she said.

Ming recognized the tones of love.

LONG LIVE THE QUEEN

Ruth Rendell

It was over in an instant. A flash of orange out of the green hedge, a streak across the road, a thud. The impact was felt as a surprisingly heavy jarring. There was no cry. Anna had braked, but too late and the car had been going fast. She pulled in to the side of the road, got out, walked back.

An effort was needed before she could look. The cat had been flung against the grass verge which separated road from narrow walkway. It was dead. She knew before she knelt down and felt its side that it was dead. A little blood came from its mouth. Its eyes were already glazing. It had been a fine cat of the kind called marmalade because the color is two-tone, the stripes like dark slices of peel among the clear orange. Paws, chest, and part of its face were white, the eyes gooseberry green.

It was an unfamiliar road, one she had only taken to avoid roadworks on the bridge. Anna thought, I was going too fast. There is no speed limit here but it's a country road with cottages and I shouldn't have been going so fast. The poor cat. Now she must go and admit what she had done, confront an angry or distressed owner, an owner who presumably lived in the house behind that hedge.

She opened the gate and went up the path. It was a cottage, but not a pretty one: of red brick with a low slate roof, bay windows downstairs with a green front door between them. In each bay window sat a cat, one black, one orange and white like the cat, which had run in front of her car. They stared at her, unblinking, inscrutable, as if they did not see her, as if she was not there. She could still see the black one when she was at the front door. When she put her finger to the bell and rang it, the cat did not move, nor even blink its eyes.

No one came to the door. She rang the bell again. It occurred to her that the owner might be in the back garden and she walked round the side of the house. It wasn't really a garden but a wilderness of long grass and tall weeds and wild trees. There was no one. She looked through a window into a kitchen where a tortoiseshell cat sat on top of the fridge in the sphinx position and on the floor, on a strip of matting, a brown tabby rolled sensuously, its striped paws stroking the air.

There were no cats outside as far as she could see, not living ones at least. In the left-hand corner, past a kind of lean-to coalshed and a clump of bushes, three small wooden crosses were just visible among the long grass. Anna had no doubt they were cat graves.

She looked in her bag and, finding a hairdresser's appointment card, wrote on the blank back of it her name, her parents' address and their phone number, and added, *Your cat ran out in front of my car. I'm sorry, I'm sure death was instantaneous.* Back at the front door, the black cat and the orange-and-white cat still staring out, she put the card through the letter box.

It was then that she looked in the window where the black cat was sitting. Inside was a small overfurnished living room which looked as if it smelt. Two cats lay on the hearthrug, two more were curled up together in an armchair. At either end of the mantelpiece sat a china cat, white and red with gilt whiskers. Anna thought there ought to have been another one between them, in the center of the shelf, because this was the only clear space in the room, every other corner and surface being crowded with objects, many of which had some association with the feline: cat ashtrays, cat vases, photographs of cats in silver frames, postcards of cats, mugs with cat faces on them, and ceramic, brass, silver, and glass kittens. Above the fireplace was a portrait of a marmalade-and-white cat done in oils and on the wall to the left hung a cat calendar.

Anna had an uneasy feeling that the cat in the portrait was the one that lay dead in the road. At any rate, it was very like. She could not leave the dead cat where it was. In the boot of her car were two plastic carrier bags, some sheets of newspaper, and a blanket she sometimes used for padding things she didn't want to strike against each other while she was driving. As wrapping for the cat's body, the plastic bags would look callous, the newspapers worse. She would sacrifice the blanket. It was a clean dark-blue blanket, single size, quite decent and decorous.

The cat's body wrapped in this blanket, she carried it up the path. The black cat had moved from the left-hand bay and had taken up a similar position in one of the upstairs windows. Anna took another look into the living room. A second examination of the portrait confirmed her guess that its subject was the one she was carrying. She backed away. The black cat stared down at her, turned its head, and yawned hugely. Of course it did not know she carried one of its companions, dead and now cold, wrapped in an old car blanket, having met a violent death. She had an uncomfortable feeling, a ridiculous feeling, that it would have behaved in precisely the same way if it had known.

She laid the cat's body on the roof of the coalshed. As she came back round the house, she saw a woman in the garden next door. This was a neat and tidy garden with flowers and a lawn. The woman was in her fifties, white-haired, slim, wearing a twin set.

"One of the cats ran out in front of my car," Anna said. "I'm afraid it's dead."

"Oh, dear."

"I've put the—body, the body on the coalshed. Do you know when they'll be back?"

"It's just her," the woman said. "It's just her on her own."

"Oh, well. I've written a note for her. With my name and address."

The woman was giving her an odd look. "You're very honest. Most would have just driven on. You don't have to report running over a cat, you know. It's not the same as a dog."

"I couldn't have just gone on."

"If I were you, I'd tear that note up. You can leave it to me, I'll tell her I saw you."

"I've already put it through the door," said Anna.

She said goodbye to the woman and got back into her car. She was on her way to her parents' house, where she would be staying for the next two weeks. Anna had a flat on the other side of the town, but she had promised to look after her parents' house while they were away on holiday, and—it now seemed a curious irony—her parents' cat.

If her journey had gone according to plan, if she had not been delayed for half an hour by the accident and the cat's death, she would have been in time to see her mother and father before they left for the airport. But when she got there, they had gone. On the hall table was a note for her in her mother's hand to say that they had had to leave, the cat had been fed, and there was a cold roast chicken in the fridge for Anna's supper. The cat would probably like some, too, to comfort it for missing them.

Anna did not think her mother's cat, a huge fluffy creature of a ghostly whitish-grey tabbyness named Griselda, was capable of missing anyone. She couldn't believe it had affections. It seemed to her without personality or charm, to lack endearing ways. To her knowledge, it had never uttered beyond giving an occasional thin squeak that signified hunger. It had never been known to rub its body against human legs, or even against the legs of the furniture. Anna knew that it was absurd to call an animal selfish—an animal naturally put its survival first, self-preservation being its prime instinct—yet she thought of Griselda as deeply, intensely, callously selfish. When it was not eating, it slept, and it slept in those most comfortable places where the people that owned it would have liked to sit but from which they could not bring themselves to dislodge it. And night it lay on their bed and, if they moved, dug its long sharp claws through the bedclothes into their legs.

Anna's mother didn't like hearing Griselda referred to as "it." She corrected Anna and stroked Griselda's head. Griselda, who purred a lot when recently fed and ensconced among cushions, always stopped purring at the touch of a human hand. This would have amused Anna if she had not seen that her mother seemed hurt by it, withdrew her hand and gave an unhappy little laugh.

When she had unpacked the case she brought with her, had prepared and eaten her meal and given Griselda a chicken leg, she began to wonder if the owner of the cat she had run over would phone. The owner might feel, as people bereaved in great or small ways sometimes did feel, that nothing could bring back the dead. Discussion was useless, and so, certainly, was recrimination. It had not in fact been her fault. She had been driving fast, but not *illegally* fast, and even if she had been driving at thirty miles an hour she doubted if she could have avoided the cat which streaked so swiftly out of the hedge.

It would be better to stop thinking about it. A night's sleep, a day at work, and the memory of it would recede. She had done all she could. She was very glad she had not just driven on as the next-door neighbor had seemed to advocate. It had been some consolation to know that the woman had many cats, not just the one, so that perhaps losing one would be less of a blow.

When she had washed the dishes and phoned her friend Kate, wondered if Richard, the man who had taken her out three times and to whom she had given this number, would phone and had decided he would not, she sat down beside Griselda—not *with* Griselda but on the same sofa as she was on—and watched television. It got to ten and she thought it unlikely the cat woman—she had begun thinking of her as that—would phone now.

There was a phone extension in her parents' room but not in the spare room where she would be sleeping. It was nearly eleven-thirty and she was getting into bed when the phone rang. The chance of its being Richard, who was capable of phoning late, especially if he thought she was alone, made her go into her parents' bedroom and answer it.

A voice that sounded strange, thin, and cracked said what sounded like "Maria Yackle."

"Yes?" Anna said.

"This is Maria Yackle. It was my cat that you killed."

Anna swallowed. "Yes. I'm glad you found my note. I'm very sorry, I'm very sorry. It was an accident. The cat ran out in front of my car."

"You were going too fast."

It was a blunt statement, harshly made. Anna could not refute it. She said, "I'm very sorry about your cat."

"They don't go out much, they're happier indoors. It was a chance in a million. I should like to see you. I think you should make amends. It wouldn't be right for you just to get away with it."

Anna was very taken aback. Up till then the woman's remarks had seemed reasonable. She didn't know what to say.

"I think you should compensate me, don't you? I loved her, I love all my cats. I expect you thought that because I had so many cats it wouldn't hurt me so much to lose one."

That was so near what Anna had thought that she felt a kind of shock, as if this Maria Yackle or whatever she was called had read her mind. "I've told you I'm sorry. I am sorry, I was very upset, I *hated* it happening. I don't know what more I can say."

"We must meet."

"What would be the use of that?" Anna knew she sounded rude, but she was shaken by the woman's tone, her blunt, direct sentences.

There was a break in the voice, something very like a sob. "It would be of use to me."

The phone went down. Anna could hardly believe it. She had heard it go down but still she said several times over, "Hallo? Hallo?" and "Are you still there?"

She went downstairs and found the telephone directory for the area and looked up Yackle. It wasn't there. She sat down and worked her way through all the Ys. There weren't many pages of Ys, apart from Youngs, but there was no one with a name beginning with Y at that address on the rustic road among the cottages.

She couldn't get to sleep. She expected the phone to ring again, Maria Yackle to ring back. After a while, she put the bedlamp on and lay there in the light. It must have been three, and still she had not slept, when Griselda came in, got on the bed, and stretched her length along Anna's legs. She put out the light, deciding not to answer the phone if it did ring, to relax, forget the run-over cat, concentrate on nice things. As she turned face-downward and stretched her body straight, she felt Griselda's claws prickle her calves. As she shrank away from contact, curled up her legs, and left Griselda a good half of the bed, a thick rough purring began.

The first thing she thought of when she woke up was how upset that poor cat woman had been. She expected her to phone back at breakfast time but nothing happened. Anna fed Griselda, left her to her house, her cat flap, her garden and wider territory, and drove to work. Richard phoned as soon as she got in. Could they meet the following evening? She agreed, obscurely wishing he had said that night, suggesting that evening herself only to be told he had to work late, had a dinner with a client.

She had been home for ten minutes when a car drew up outside. It was an old car, at least ten years old, and not only dented and scratched but with some of the worst scars painted or sprayed over in a different shade of red. Anna, who saw it arrive from a front window, watched the woman get out of it and approach the house. She was old, or at least elderly—is elderly older than old or old older than elderly?—but dressed like a teenager. Anna got a closer look at her clothes, her hair, and her face when she opened the front door.

It was a wrinkled face, the color and texture of a chicken's wattles. Small blue eyes were buried somewhere in the strawberry redness. The bright white hair next to it was as much of a contrast as snow against scarlet cloth. She wore tight jeans with socks pulled up over the bottoms of them, dirty white trainers, and a big loose sweatshirt with a cat's face on it, a painted smiling bewhiskered mask, orange and white and green-eyed.

Anna had read somewhere the comment made by a young girl on an older woman's boast that she could wear a miniskirt because she had good legs: "It's not your legs, it's your face." She thought of this as she looked at Maria Yackle, but that was the last time for a long while she thought of anything like that.

"I've come early because we shall have a lot to talk about," Maria Yackle said and walked in. She did this in such a way as to compel Anna to open the door farther and stand aside.

"This is *your* house?"

She might have meant because Anna was so young or perhaps there was some more offensive reason for asking.

"My parents.' I'm just staying here."

"Is it this room?" She was already on the threshold of Anna's mother's living room.

Anna nodded. She had been taken aback but only for a moment. It was best to get this over. But she did not care to be dictated to. "You could have let me know. I might not have been here."

There was no reply because Maria Yackle had seen Griselda.

The cat had been sitting on the back of a wing chair between the wings, an apparently uncomfortable place though a favorite, but at sight of the newcomer had stretched, got down, and was walking toward her. Maria Yackle put out her hand. It was a horrible hand, large and red with ropelike blue veins standing out above the bones, the palm calloused, the nails black and broken and the sides of the forefinger and thumb ingrained with brownish dirt. Griselda approached and put her smoky whitish muzzle and pink nose into this hand.

"I shouldn't," Anna said rather sharply, for Maria Yackle was bending over to pick the cat up. "She isn't very nice. She doesn't like people."

"She'll like me."

And the amazing thing was that Griselda did. Maria Yackle sat down and Griselda sat on her lap. Griselda the unfriendly, the cold-hearted, the cat who purred when alone and who ceased to purr when touched, the ice-eyed, the standoffish walker-by-herself, settled down on this unknown, untried lap, having first climbed up Maria Yackle's chest and onto her shoulders and rubbed her ears and plump furry cheeks against the sweatshirt with the painted cat face.

"You seem surprised."

Anna said, "You could say that."

"There's no mystery. The explanation's simple." It was a shrill, harsh voice, cracked by the onset of old age, articulate, the usage grammatical but the accent raw cockney. "You and your mum and dad, too, no doubt, you all think you smell very nice and pretty. You have your bath every morning with bath essence and scented soap. You put talcum powder on and spray stuff in your armpits, you rub cream on your bodies and squirt on perfume. Maybe you've washed your hair, too, with shampoo and conditioner and—what-do-they-call-it?—mousse. You clean your teeth and wash your mouth, put a drop more perfume behind your ears, paint your faces—well, I daresay your dad doesn't paint his face, but he shaves, doesn't he? More mousse and then aftershave.

"You put on your clothes. All of them clean, spotless. They've either just come back from the dry-cleaners or else out of the washing machine with biological soap and spring-fresh fabric softener. Oh, I know, I may not do it myself but I see it on the TV.

"It all smells very fine to you, but it doesn't to her. Oh, no. To her it's just chemicals, like gas might be to you or paraffin. A nasty strong chemical smell that puts her right off and makes her shrink up in her furry skin. What's her name?"

This question was uttered on a sharp bark. "Griselda," said Anna, and, "How did you know it's a she?"

"Face," said Maria Yackle. "Look—see her little nose. See her smiley mouth and her little nose and her fat cheeks? Tomcats got a big nose, got a long muzzle. Never mind if he's been neutered, still got a big nose."

"What did you come here to say to me?" said Anna.

Griselda had curled up on the cat woman's lap, burying her head, slightly upward turned, in the crease between stomach and thigh. "I don't go in for all that stuff, you see." The big red hand stroked Griselda's head, the stripy bit between her ears. "Cat likes the smell of me because I haven't got my clothes in soapy water every day, I have a bath once a week, always have and always shall, and I don't waste my money on odorizers and deodorizers. I wash my hands when I get up in the morning and that's enough for me."

At the mention of the weekly bath, Anna had reacted instinctively and edged her chair a little farther away. Maria Yackle saw, Anna was sure she saw, but her response to this recoil was to begin on what she had in fact come about: her compensation.

"The cat you killed, she was five years old and the queen of the cats, her name was Melusina. I always have a queen. The one before was Juliana and she lived to be twelve. I wept, I mourned her, but life has to go on. 'The queen is dead,' I said, 'long live the queen!' I never promote one, I always get a new kitten. Some cats are queens, you see, and some are not. Melusina was eight weeks old when I got her from the Animal Rescue people, and I gave them a donation of twenty pounds. The vet charged me twenty-seven pounds fifty for her injections—all my cats are immunized against feline enteritis and leptospirosis—so that makes forty-seven pounds fifty. And she had her booster at age two, which was another twenty-seven fifty. I can show you the receipted bills, I always keep everything, and that makes seventy-five pounds. Then there was my petrol getting her to the vet—we'll say a straight five pounds, though it was more—and then we come to the crunch, her food. She was a good little trencherwoman."

Anna would have been inclined to laugh at this ridiculous word, but she saw to her horror that the tears were running down Maria Yackle's cheeks. They were running unchecked out of her eyes, over the rough red wrinkled skin, and one dripped unheeded onto Griselda's silvery fur.

"Take no notice. I do cry whenever I have to talk about her. I loved that cat. She was the queen of the cats. She had her own place, her throne—she used to sit in the middle of the mantelpiece with her two china ladies-in-waiting on each side of her. You'll see one day, when you come to my house.

"But we were talking about her food. She ate a large can a day—it was too much, more than she should have had, but she loved her food, she was a good little eater. Well, cat food's gone up over the years, of course, what hasn't, and I'm paying fifty pee a can now, but I reckon it'd be fair to average it out at forty pee. She was eight weeks old when I got her, so we can't say five times three hundred and sixty-five. We'll say five times three fifty-five and that's doing you a favor. I've already worked it out at home, I'm not that much of a wizard at mental arithmetic. Five three-hundred and fifty-fives are one thousand, seven hundred and seventy five, which multiplied by forty makes seventy-one thousand pee or seven hundred and ten pounds. Add to that the seventy-five plus the vet's bill of fourteen pounds when she had a tapeworm and we get a final figure of seven hundred and ninety-nine pounds."

Anna stared at her. "You're asking me to give you nearly eight hundred pounds?"

"That's right. Of course, we'll write it down and do it properly."

"Because your cat ran under the wheels of my car?"

"You murdered her," said Maria Yackle.

"That's absurd. Of course I didn't murder her." On shaky ground, she said, "You can't murder an animal."

"You did. You said you were going too fast."

Had she? She had been, but had she said so?

Maria Yackle got up, still holding Griselda, cuddling Griselda, who nestled purring in her arms. Anna watched with distaste. You thought of cats as fastidious creatures but they were not. Only something insensitive and undiscerning would put its face against that face, nuzzle those rough grimy hands. The black fingernails brought to mind a phrase, now unpleasantly appropriate, that her grandmother had used to children with dirty hands: in mourning for the cat.

"I don't expect you to give me a check now. Is that what you thought I meant? I don't suppose you have that amount in your current account. I'll come back tomorrow or the next day."

"I'm not going to give you eight hundred pounds," said Anna.

She might as well not have spoken.

"I won't come back tomorrow, I'll come back on Wednesday." Griselda was tenderly placed on the seat of an armchair. The tears had dried on Maria's Yackle's face, leaving salt trails. She took herself out into the hall and to the front door. "You'll have thought about it by then. Anyway, I hope you'll come to the funeral. I hope there won't be any hard feelings."

That was when Anna decided Maria Yackle was mad. In one way, this was disguieting—in another, a comfort. It meant she wasn't serious about the compensation, the seven hundred and ninety-nine pounds. Sane people don't invite you to their cat's funeral. Mad people do not sue you for compensation.

"No, I shouldn't think she'd do that," said Richard when they were having dinner together. He wasn't a lawyer but had studied law. "You didn't admit you were exceeding the speed limit, did you?"

"I don't remember."

"At any rate, you didn't admit it in front of witnesses. You say she didn't threaten you?"

"Oh, no. She wasn't unpleasant. She cried, poor thing."

"Well, let's forget her, shall we, and have a nice time?"

Although no note awaited her on the doorstep, no letter came, and there were no phone calls, Anna knew the cat woman would come back on the following evening. Richard had advised her to go to the police if any threats were made. There would be no need to tell them she had been driving very fast. Anna thought the whole idea of going to the police bizarre. She rang up her friend Kate and told her all about it and Kate agreed that telling the police would be going too far.

The battered red car arrived at seven. Maria Yackle was dressed as she had been for her previous visit, but, because it was rather cold, wore a jacket made of synthetic fur as well. From its harsh, too-shiny texture there was no doubt it was synthetic, but from a distance it looked like a black cat's pelt.

She had brought an album of photographs of her cats for Anna to see. Anna looked through it—what else could she do? Some were recognizably of those she had seen through the windows. Those that were not, she supposed might be of animals now at rest under the wooden crosses in Maria Yackle's back garden. While she was looking at the pictures, Griselda came in and jumped onto the cat woman's lap.

"They're very nice, very interesting," Anna said. "I can see you're devoted to your cats."

"They're my life."

A little humoring might be in order. "When is the funeral to be?"

"I thought on Friday. Two o'clock on Friday. My sister will be there with her two. Cat's don't usually take to car travel, that's why I don't often take any of mine with me, and shutting them up in cages goes against the grain—but my sister's two Burmese love the car, they'll go and sit in the car when it's parked. My friend from the Animal Rescue will come if she can get away and I've asked our vet, but I don't hold out much hope there. He has his goat clinic on Fridays. I hope you'll come along."

"I'm afraid I'll be at work."

"It's no flowers by request. Donations to the Cat's Protection League instead. Any sum, no matter how small, gratefully received. Which brings me to money. You've got a check for me."

"No, I haven't, Mrs. Yackle.'

"Miss. And it's Yakop. J-A-K-O-B. You've got a check for me for seven hundred and ninety-nine pounds."

"I'm not giving you any money, Miss Jakob. I'm very, very sorry about your cat, about Melusina, I know how fond you were of her, but giving you compensation is out of the question. I'm sorry."

The tears had come once more into Maria Jakob's eyes, had spilled over. Her face contorted with misery. It was the mention of the wretched thing's name, Anna thought. That was the trigger that started the weeping. A tear splashed onto one of the coarse red hands. Griselda opened her eyes and licked up the tear.

Maria Jakob pushed her other hand across her eyes. She blinked. "We'll have to think of something else then," she said.

"I beg your pardon?" Anna wondered if she had really heard. Things couldn't be solved so simply.

"We shall have to think of something else. A way for you to make up to me for murder."

"Look, I will give a donation to the Cats' Protection League. I'm quite prepared to give them—say, twenty pounds." Richard would be furious, but perhaps she wouldn't tell Richard. "I'll give it to you, shall I, and then you can pass it on to them?"

"I certainly hope you will. Especially if you can't come to the funeral."

That was the end of it, then. Anna felt a great sense of relief. It was only now that it was over that she realized quite how it had got to her. It had actually kept her from sleeping properly. She phoned Kate and told her about the funeral and the goat clinic, and Kate laughed and said Poor old thing. Anna slept so well that night that she didn't notice the arrival of Griselda who, when she woke, was asleep on the pillow next to her face but out of touching distance.

Richard phoned and she told him about it, omitting the part about her offer of a donation. He told her that being firm, sticking to one's guns in situations of this kind, always paid off. In the evening, she wrote a check for twenty pounds but, instead of the Cats' Protection League, made it out to Maria Jakob. If the cat woman quietly held onto it, no harm would be done. Anna went down the road to post her letter, for she had written a letter to accompany the check, in which she reiterated her sorrow about the death of the cat and added that if there was anything she could do Miss Jakob had only to let her know. Richard would have been furious.

Unlike the Jakob cats, Griselda spent a good deal of time out of doors. She was often out all evening and did not reappear until the small hours, so that it was not until the next day, not until the next evening, that Anna began to be alarmed at her absence. As far as she knew, Griselda had never been away so long before. For herself, she was unconcerned—she had never liked the cat, did not particularly like any cats, and found this one obnoxiously self-centered and cold. It was for her mother, who unaccountably loved the creature, that she was worried. She walked up and down the street calling Griselda, though the cat had never been known to come when it was called.

It did not come now. Anna walked up and down the next street, calling, and around the block and farther afield. She half expected to find Griselda's body, guessing that it might have met the same fate as Melusina. Hadn't she read somewhere that nearly forty thousand cats are killed on British roads annually?

On Saturday morning, she wrote one of those melancholy lost-cat notices and attached it to a lamp standard, wishing she had a photograph. But her mother had taken no photographs of Griselda.

Richard took her to a friend's party and afterward, when they were driving home, he said, "You know what's happened, don't you? It's been killed by that old mad woman. An eye for an eye, a cat for a cat."

"Oh, no, she wouldn't do that. She loves cats."

"Murderers love people. They just don't love the people they murder."

"I'm sure you're wrong," said Anna, but she remembered how Maria Jakob had said that if the money was not forthcoming, she must think of something else—a way to make up to her for Melusina's death. And she had not meant a donation to the Cats' Protection League.

"What shall I do?"

"I don't see that you can do anything. It's most unlikely you could prove it, she'll have seen to that. You can look at this way—she's had her pound of flesh."

"Fifteen pounds of flesh," said Anna. Griselda had been a large, heavy cat.

"Okay, fifteen pounds. She's had that, she's had her revenge. It hasn't actually caused you any grief—you'll just have to make up some story for your mother."

Anna's mother was upset, but nowhere near as upset as Maria Jakob had been over the death of Melusina. To avoid too much fuss, Anna had gone further than she intended, told her mother that she had seen Griselda's corpse and talked to the offending motorist, who had been very distressed.

A month or so later, Anna's mother got a kitten, a grey tabby tomkitten, who was very affectionate from the start, sat on her lap, purred loudly when stroked, and snuggled up in her arms, though Anna was sure her mother had not stopped having baths or using perfume. So much for the Jakob theories.

Nearly a year had gone by before she again drove down the road where Maria Jakob's house was. She had not intended to go that way. Directions had been given her to a smallholding where they sold early strawberries on a roadside stall but she must have missed her way, taken a wrong turning, and come out here.

If Maria Jakob's car had been parked in the front, she would not have stopped. There was no garage for it to be in and it was not outside, therefore the cat woman must be out. Anna thought of the funeral she had not been to—she had often thought about it, the strange people and strange cats who had attended it.

In each of the bay windows sat a cat, a tortoiseshell and a brown tabby. The black cat was eyeing her from upstairs. Anna didn't go to the front door but round the back. There, among the long grass, as she had expected, were four graves instead of three, four wooden crosses, and on the fourth was printed in black gloss paint: MELUSINA, THE QUEEN OF THE CATS. MURDERED IN HER SIXTH YEAR. RIP.

That "murdered" did not please Anna. It brought back all the resentment at the unjust accusations of eleven months before. She felt much older, she felt wiser. One thing was certain, ethics or no ethics, if she ever ran over a cat again she'd drive on—the last thing she'd do was go and confess.

She came round the side of the house and looked in at the bay window. If the tortoiseshell had still been on the windowsill, she probably would not have looked in, but the tortoiseshell had removed itself to the hearthrug.

A white cat and the marmalade-and-white lay curled up side by side in an armchair. The portrait of Melusina hung above the fireplace and this year's cat calendar was up on the left-hand wall. Light gleamed on the china cats' gilt whiskers—and between them, in the empty space that was no longer vacant, sat Griselda.

Griselda was sitting in the queen's place in the middle of the mantelpiece. She sat in the sphinx position with her eyes closed. Anna tapped on the glass and Griselda opened her eyes, stared with cold indifference, and closed them again.

The queen is dead, long live the queen!